D0987620

LOOK TO THE LADY

LOOK TO THE LADY

Margery Allingham

FELONY & MAYHEM PRESS • NEW YORK

LOOK TO THE LADY

A Felony & Mayhem mystery

PRINTING HISTORY
First UK edition (Jarrolds): 1931
First US edition (Doubleday Crime Club,
as the *Gyrth Chalice Mystery*): 1931
Felony & Mayhem edition: 2006

ISBN: 1-978-933397-57-3

Manufactured in the United States of America

To Orlando

The icon above says you're holding a copy of a book in the Felony & Mayhem "Vintage" category. These books were originally published prior to about 1965, and feature the kind of twisty, ingenious puzzles beloved by fans of Agatha Christie and John Dickson Carr. If you enjoy this book, you may well like other "Vintage" titles from Felony & Mayhem Press, including:

For more about these books, and other Felony & Mayhem titles, or to place an order, please visit our website at

www.FelonyAndMayhem.com

or contact us at

Felony and Mayhem Press
156 Waverly Place
New York, NY 10014

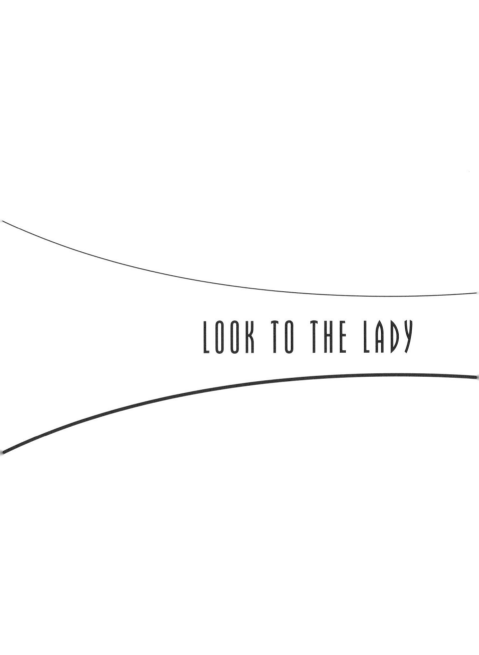

LOOK TO THE LADY

CHAPTER ONE

"Reward for Finder?"

"IF YOU'LL ACCEPT this, sir," said the policeman, pressing a shilling into the down-and-out's hand, "you'll have visible means of support and I shan't have to take you along. But," he added with a delightful hint of embarrassment, "I'll have to ask you to move on; the Inspector is due round any minute."

Percival St John Wykes Gyrth, only son of Colonel Sir Percival Christian St John Gyrth, Bt, of the Tower, Sanctuary, Suffolk, reddened painfully, thrust the coin into his trouser pocket, and smiled at his benefactor.

"Thank you, Baker," he said. "This is extraordinarily kind of you. I shan't forget it."

"That's all right, sir." The man's embarrassment increased. "You gave me five pounds the night you was married." He opened his mouth as though to continue, but thought the better of it, and the young man's next remark indicated clearly that he was in no mood for reminiscences.

"I say, where the devil can I sit where I shan't be moved on?"

The policeman glanced nervously up South Molton Street, whence even now the dapper form of the Inspector was slowly approaching.

"Ebury Square—just off Southampton Row," he murmured hastily. "You'll be as safe as houses there. Good night, sir."

The final words were a dismissal; the Inspector was almost upon them. Val Gyrth pulled his battered hat over his eyes, and hunching his shoulders, shuffled off towards Oxford Street. His "visible means of support" flopped solitarily in the one safe pocket of his suit, a suit which had once come reverently from the hands of the tailor whose shop he was passing. He crossed into Oxford Street and turned up towards the Circus.

It was a little after midnight and the wide road was almost deserted. There were a few returning revellers, a sprinkling of taxicabs, and an occasional late bus.

Val Gyrth chose the inside of the pavement, keeping as much in the shadow as possible. The summer smell of the city, warm and slightly scented like a chemist's shop, came familiarly to his nostrils and in spite of his weariness there was an impatience in his step. He was bitterly angry with himself. The situation was impossible, quixotic, and ridiculous. Old Baker had given him a shilling to save him from arrest as a vagrant on his own doorstep. It was unthinkable.

He had not eaten since the night before, but he passed the coffee-stall outside the French hat shop in the Circus without a thought. He had ceased to feel hungry at about four o'clock that afternoon and had been surprised and thankful at the respite. The swimming sensation which had taken the place of it seemed eminently preferable.

The pavement was hot to that part of his foot which touched it through the hole in an expensive shoe, and he was beginning to limp when he turned down by Mudie's old building and found himself after another five minutes' plodding in a dishevelled little square whose paved centre was intersected by two rows of dirty plane trees, beneath which, amid the litter of a summer's day, were several dilapidated wooden benches. There were one or two unsavoury-looking bundles dotted here and there, but there were two seats unoccupied. Val Gyrth chose the one under a street lamp and most aloof from its fellows; he sank down, realizing for the first time the full sum of his weariness.

A shiver ran through the dusty leaves above his head, and as he glanced about him he became obsessed with a curious feeling of apprehension which could not be explained by the sudden chill of the night. A car passed through the square, and from far off beyond the Strand came the mournful bellow of a tug on the river. None of the bundles huddled on the other seats stirred, but it seemed to the boy, one of the least imaginative of an unimaginative race, that something enormous and of great importance was about to happen, or was, indeed, in the very act of happening all round him; a sensation perhaps explainable by partial starvation and a potential thunderstorm.

He took off his hat and passed his fingers through his very fair hair, the increasing length of which was a continual source of annoyance to him. He was a thick-set, powerful youngster in his early twenties, with a heavy but by no means unhandsome face and an habitual expression of dogged obstinacy; a pure Anglo-Saxon type, chiefly remarkable at the moment for a certain unnatural gauntness which accentuated the thickness of his bones.

He sighed, turned up his coat collar, and was about to lift his feet out of the miscellaneous collection of paper bags, orange skins, and cigarette cartons on to the bench, when he paused and sat up stiffly, staring down at the ground in front of him. He was conscious of a sudden wave of heat passing over him, of an odd shock that made his heart jump unpleasantly.

He was looking at his own name, written on a battered envelope lying face upwards among the other litter.

He picked it up and was astonished to see that his hand was shaking. The name was unmistakable. "P. St J. W. Gyrth, Esq." written clearly in a hand he did not know.

He turned the envelope over. It was an expensive one, and empty, having been torn open across the top apparently by an impatient hand. He sat staring at it for some moments, and a feeling of unreality took possession of him. The address, "Kemp's, 32a Wembley Road, Clerkenwell, EC 1", was completely unfamiliar.

He stared at it as though he expected the words to change before his eyes, but they remained clear and unmistakable: "P. St J. W. Gyrth, Esq."

At first it did not occur to him to doubt that the name was his own, or that the envelope had been originally intended for him. Gyrth is an unusual name, and the odd collection of initials combined with it made it impossible for him to think that in this case it could belong to anyone else.

He studied the handwriting thoughtfully, trying to place it. His mind had accepted the astounding coincidence which had brought him to this particular seat in this particular square and led him to pick up the one envelope which bore his name. He hunted among the rubbish at his feet in a futile attempt to find the contents of the envelope, but an exhaustive search convinced him that the paper in his hand was all that was of interest to him there.

The hand puzzled him. It was distinctive, square, with heavy downstrokes and sharp Greek E's; individual handwriting, not easily to be forgotten. He turned his attention to the postmark, and the bewildered expression upon his young face became one of blank astonishment. It was dated the fifteenth of June. To-day was the nineteenth. Then the letter was therefore only four days old.

It was over a week since he had possessed any address. Yet he was convinced, and the fact was somehow slightly uncanny and unnerving, that someone had written to him, and someone else had received the letter, the envelope of which had been thrown away to be found by himself.

Not the least remarkable thing about a coincidence is that once it has happened, one names it, accepts it, and leaves it at that.

Gyrth sat on the dusty seat beneath the street lamp and looked at the envelope. The rustling in the leaves above his head had grown fiercer, and an uncertain wind ricocheted down the square; in a few minutes it would rain.

Once again he was conscious of that strange sensation of being just on the outside of some drama enacted quite near to him. He had felt it before to-night. Several times in the past few days this same uneasy feeling had swept over him in the most crowded streets at the height of noon, or at night in the dark alleyways of the city where he had tried to sleep. Experienced criminals recognize this sensation as the instinctive knowledge that one is being "tailed", but young Gyrth was no criminal, nor was he particularly experienced in anything save the more unfortunate aspects of matrimony.

He looked again at the address on the tantalizing envelope: "32a Wembley Rd, Clerkenwell." This was not far from where he now sat, he reflected, and the impulse to go there to find out for himself if he were not the only P. St J. W. Gyrth in the world, or, if he was, to discover who was impersonating him, was very strong.

His was a conservative nature, however, and perhaps if the experience had happened to him in ordinary circumstances he would have shrugged his shoulders and taken no further active interest in the matter. But at the moment he was down-and-out. A man who is literally destitute is like a straw in the wind; any tiny current is sufficient to set him drifting in a new direction. His time and energies are of no value to him; anything is worth while. Impelled by curiosity, therefore, he set off across the square, the storm blowing up behind him.

He did not know what he expected to find, but the envelope fascinated him. He gave up conjecturing and hurried.

Clerkenwell in the early hours of the morning is one of the most unsavoury neighbourhoods in the whole of East Central London, which is saying a great deal, and the young man's ragged and dishevelled appearance was probably the only one which would not have attracted the attention of those few inhabitants who were still abroad.

At length he discovered a pair of policemen, of whom he inquired the way, gripping their colleague's shilling defiantly as he did so. They directed him with the unhurried omniscience of their kind, and he eventually found himself crossing a dirty ill-lit thoroughfare intersected with tramlines and flanked by the lowest of all lodging-houses, and shabby dusty little shops where everything seemed to be second-hand.

Number 32a turned out to be one of the few establishments still open.

It was an eating-house, unsavoury even for the neighbourhood, and one stepped down off the pavement a good eighteen inches to reach the level of the ground floor. Even Val Gyrth, now the least cautious of men, hesitated before entering.

The half-glass door of the shop was pasted over with cheap advertisements for boot polish and a brand of caramel, and the light from within struggled uncertainly through the dirty oiled paper.

Gyrth glanced at the envelope once more and decided that there was no doubt at all that this was his destination. The number, 32a, was printed on a white enamelled plaque above the door, and the name "Kemp's" was written across the shop front in foot-high letters.

Once again the full sense of the absurdity of his quest

came over him, and he hesitated, but again he reflected that he had nothing to lose and his curiosity to appease. He turned the door-handle and stepped down into the room.

The fetid atmosphere within was so full of steam that for a moment he could not see at all where he was. He stood still for some seconds trying to penetrate the haze, and at last made out a long dingy room flanked with high, greasy pew seats, which appeared to be empty.

At the far end of the aisle between the tables there was a counter and a cooking-stove from which the atmosphere obtained most of its quality. Towards this gastronomic altar the young man advanced, the envelope clutched tightly in his coat pocket.

There was no one in sight, so he tapped the counter irresolutely. Almost immediately a door to the right of the stove was jerked open and there appeared a mountain of a man with the largest and most lugubrious face he had ever seen. A small tablecloth had been tied across the newcomer's stomach by way of an apron, and his great muscular arms were bare to the elbow. For the rest, his head was bald, and the bone of his nose had sustained an irreparable injury.

He regarded the young man with mournful eyes.

"This is a nice time to think about getting a bit of food," he observed more in sorrow than in anger, thereby revealing a sepulchral voice. "Everything's off but sausage and mash. I'm 'aving the last bit o' stoo meself."

Gyrth was comforted by his melancholy affability. It was some time since an eating-house keeper had treated him with even ordinary humanity. He took the envelope out of his pocket and spread it out on the counter before the man.

"Look here," he said. "Do you know anything about this?"

Not a muscle of the lugubrious face stirred. The mountainous stranger eyed the envelope for some time as if he had never seen such a thing before and was not certain if it were worth consideration. Then, turning suddenly, he looked the boy straight in the eyes and made what was in the circumstances a most extraordinary observation.

"I see," he said clearly, and with a slightly unnecessary deliberation, "*you take the long road.*"

Gyrth stared at him. He felt that some reply was expected, that the words had some significance which was lost upon him. He laughed awkwardly.

"I don't quite follow you," he said. "I suppose I am tramping, if that's what you mean? But I came to inquire about this envelope. Have you seen it before?"

The big man ventured as near a smile as Gyrth felt his features would permit.

"Suppose I 'ave?" he said cautiously. "Wot then?"

"Only that it happens to be addressed to me, and I'm anxious to know who opened it," said Gyrth shortly. "Can you tell me who collected it?"

"Is that your name?" The big man placed a heavy forefinger upon the inscription. "I suppose you couldn't prove it, could yer?"

Gyrth grew red and uncomfortable. "I can't get anyone to identify me, if that's what you mean, and I haven't got a visiting-card. But," he added, "if you care to take my tailor's word for it there's the tab inside my coat here."

He unbuttoned the threadbare garment and turned down the edge of the inside breast pocket, displaying a tailor's label with his name and the date written in ink across it. In his eagerness he did not realize the incongruity of the situation.

The sad man read the label and then surveyed his visitor critically.

"I suppose it *was* made for yer?" he said.

Gyrth buttoned up his coat. "I've got thinner," he said shortly.

"Awright. No offence," said the other. "I believe yer—some wouldn't. Name o' Lugg meself. Pleased to meet yer, I'm sure. I got another letter for you, by the way."

He turned round ponderously, and after searching among the cups and plates upon the dresser behind him, he returned bearing a similar envelope to the one which Gyrth had put down upon the counter. It was unopened.

The young man took it with a sense of complete bewilderment. He was about to tear the seal when the gentleman who had just introduced himself with such light-hearted friendliness tapped him on the shoulder.

"Suppose you go and sit down," he observed. "I'll bring yer a spot o' coffee and a couple o' Zepps in a smoke screen. I always get peckish about this time o' night meself."

"I've only got a shilling—" Gyrth began awkwardly.

Mr Lugg raised his eyebrows.

"A bob?" he said. "Where d'you think you're dining? The Cheshire Cheese? You sit down, my lad. I'll do you proud for a tanner. Then you'll 'ave yer 'visible means' and tuppence to spare for emergencies."

Gyrth did as he was told. He edged on to one of the greasy benches and sat down before a table neatly covered with a clean newspaper bill. He tore at the thick envelope with clumsy fingers. The smell of the place had reawakened his hunger, and his head was aching violently.

Three objects fell out upon the table; two pound notes and an engraved correspondence card. He stared at the card in stupefaction:

Mr Albert Campion
At Home

—and underneath, in the now familiar square handwriting:

Any evening after twelve.
Improving Conversation.
Beer, Light Wines, and Little Pink Cakes.
Do come.
The address was engraved:

17, Bottle Street, W1
(Entrance on left by Police Station).

Scribbled on the back were the words; "Please forgive crude temporary loan. Come along as soon as you can. It's urgent. Take care. A.C."

Val Gyrth turned the card over and over.

The whole episode was becoming fantastic. There was a faintly nonsensical, Alice-through-the-Looking-Glass air about it all, and it did just cross his mind that he might have been involved in a street accident and the adventure be the result of a merciful anaesthetic.

He was still examining the extraordinary message when the gloomy but also slightly fantastic Mr Lugg appeared with what was evidently his personal idea of a banquet. Gyrth ate what was set before him with a growing sense of gratitude and reality. When he had finished he looked up at the man who was still standing beside him.

"I say," he said, "have you ever heard of a Mr Albert Campion?"

The man's small eyes regarded him solemnly. "Sounds familiar," he said. "I can't say as I place 'im, though." There was a stubborn blankness in his face which told the boy that further questioning would be useless. Once again Gyrth took up the card and the two bank-notes.

"How do you know," he said suddenly, "that I am the man to receive this letter?"

Mr Lugg looked over his shoulder at the second envelope.

"That's yer name, ain't it?" he said. "It's the name inside yer suit, any'ow. You showed me."

"Yes, I know," said Val patiently. "But how do you know that I am the Percival St John Wykes Gyrth—?"

"Gawd! It don't stand for all that, do it?" said Mr Lugg, impressed. "That answers yer own question, my lad. There ain't two mothers 'oo'd saddle a brat with that lot. That's your invitation ticket all right. Don't you worry. I should 'op it—it's gettin' late."

Gyrth considered the card again. It was mad, of course. And yet he had come so far that it seemed illogical not to go on. As though to clinch the matter with himself he paid for his food out of his new-found wealth, and after tipping his host prodigally he bade the man good-night and walked out of the deserted eating-house.

It was not until he was outside the door and standing on the pavement that the problem of transportation occurred to him. It was a good three miles across the city to Piccadilly, and although his hunger was sated he was still excessively tired. To make the situation more uncomfortable it was very late and the rain had come in a sullen downpour.

While he stood hesitating, the sound of wheels came softly behind him.

"Taxi, sir?"

Gyrth turned thankfully, gave the man the address on the card, and climbed into the warm leather depths of the cab.

As he sank back among the cushions the old feeling of well-being stole over him. The cab was speeding over the glistening roads along which he had trudged so wearily less than an hour before. For some minutes he reflected upon the extraordinary invitation he had accepted so unquestioningly. The ridiculous card read like a hoax, of course, but two pounds are not a joke to a starving man, and since he had nothing to lose he saw no reason why he should not investigate it. Besides, he was curious.

He took the card out of his pocket and bent forward to read it by the light from the meter lamp. He could just make out the scribbled message: "Come along as soon as you can. It's urgent. Take care."

The last two words puzzled him. In the circumstances they seemed so ridiculous that he almost laughed.

It was at that precise moment that the cab turned to the right in Gray's Inn Road and he caught a glimpse of a quiet tree-lined Bloomsbury square. Then, and not until then, did it dawn upon him with a sudden throb and quickening of his pulse that the chance of picking up a taxi accidentally at three o'clock in the morning in Wembley Road, Clerkenwell was one in a million, and secondly, that the likelihood of any ordinary cabman mistaking him in his present costume for a potential fare was nothing short of an absurdity. He bent forward and ran his hand along the doors. There were no handles. The windows too appeared to be locked.

Considerably startled, but almost ashamed of himself for suspecting a danger for which he was hardly eligible, he rapped vigorously on the window behind the driver.

Even as Gyrth watched him, the man bent over his wheel and trod heavily on the accelerator.

CHAPTER TWO

Little Pink Cakes

VAL SAT FORWARD in the half-darkness and peered out. The old cab was, he guessed, travelling all out at about thirty-five miles an hour. The streets were rain-swept and deserted and he recognized that he was being carried directly out of his way.

On the face of it he was being kidnapped, but this idea was so ridiculous in his present condition that he was loth to accept it. Deciding that the driver must be drunk or deaf, he thundered again on the glass and tried shouting down the speaking tube.

"I want Bottle Street—off Piccadilly."

This time he had no doubt that his driver heard him, for the man jerked his head in a negative fashion and the cab rocked and swayed dangerously. Val Gyrth had to accept the situation, absurd though it might be. He was a prisoner being borne precipitately to an unknown destination.

During the past eighteen months he had discovered himself in many unpleasant predicaments, but never one that called for such immediate action. At any other time he might have hesitated until it was too late, but to-night the cumulative effects of starvation and weariness had produced in him a dull recklessness, and the mood which had permitted him to follow such a fantastic will-o'-the-wisp as his name on a discarded envelope, and later to accept the hardly conventional invitation of the mysterious Mr Campion, was still upon him. Moreover, the kindly ministrations of Mr Lugg had revived his strength and with it his temper.

At that moment, hunched up inside the cab, he was a dangerous person. His hands were knotted together, and the muscles of his jaw contracted.

The moment the idea came into his head he put it into execution.

He bent down and removed the heavy shoe with the thin sole, from which the lace had long since disappeared. With this formidable weapon tightly gripped in his hand, he crouched in the body of the cab, holding himself steady by the flower bracket above the spare seats. He was still prodigiously strong, and put all he knew into the blow. His arm crashed down like a machine hammer, smashing through the plate glass and down on to the driver's skull.

Instantly Gyrth dropped on to the mat, curling himself up, his arms covering his head. The driver's thick cap had protected him considerably, but the attack was so sudden that he lost control of his wheel. The cab skidded violently across the greasy road, mounted the pavement and smashed sickeningly into a stone balustrade.

The impact was terrific: the car bounded off the stonework, swayed for an instant and finally crashed over on to its side.

Gyrth was hurled into the worn hood of the cab, which tore beneath his weight. He was conscious of warm blood trickling down his face from a cut across his forehead, and one of his shoulders was wrenched, but he had been prepared for the trouble and was not seriously injured. He was still angry, still savage. He fought his way out through the torn fabric on to the pavement, and turned for an instant to survey the scene.

His captor lay hidden beneath the mass of wreckage and made no sound. But the street was no longer deserted. Windows were opening and from both ends of the road came the sound of voices and hurrying footsteps.

Gyrth was in no mood to stop to answer questions. He wiped the blood from his face with his coat-sleeve and was relieved to find that the damage was less messy than he had feared. He slipped on the shoe, which he still gripped, and vanished like a shadow up a side street.

He finished the rest of his journey on foot.

He went to the address in Bottle Street largely out of curiosity, but principally, perhaps, because he had nowhere else to go. He chose the narrow dark ways, cutting through the older part of Holborn and the redolent alleys of Soho.

Now, for the first time for days, he realized that he was free from that curious feeling of oppression which had vaguely puzzled him. There was no one in the street behind him as he turned from dark corner to lighted thoroughfare and came at last to the cul-de-sac off Piccadilly which is Bottle Street.

The single blue lamp of the Police Station was hardly inviting, but the door of Number Seventeen, immediately upon the left, stood ajar. He pushed it open gingerly.

He was well-nigh exhausted, however, and his shreds of caution had vanished. Consoling himself with the thought that nothing could be worse than his present predicament, he climbed painfully up the wooden steps. After the first landing there was a light and the stairs were carpeted, and he came at last to a full stop before a handsome linenfold oak door. A small brass plate bore the simple legend, *"Mr Albert Campion. The Goods Dept."*

There was also a very fine florentine knocker, which, however, he did not have occasion to use, for the door opened and an entirely unexpected figure appeared in the opening.

A tall thin young man with a pale inoffensive face, and vague eyes behind enormous horn-rimmed spectacles smiled out at him with engaging friendliness. He was carefully, not to say fastidiously, dressed in evening clothes, but the correctness of his appearance was somewhat marred by the fact that in his hand he held a string to which was attached a child's balloon of a particularly vituperant pink.

He seemed to become aware of this incongruous attachment as soon as he saw his visitor, for he made several unsuccessful attempts to hide it behind his back. He held out his hand.

"Doctor Livingstone, I presume?" he said in a well-bred, slightly high-pitched voice.

Considerably startled, Gyrth put out his hand. "I don't know who you are," he began, "but I'm Val Gyrth and I'm looking for a man who calls himself Albert Campion."

"That's all right," said the stranger releasing the balloon, which floated up to the ceiling, with the air of one giving up a tiresome problem. "None genuine without my face on the wrapper. This is me—my door—my balloon. Please come in and have a drink. You're rather late—I was afraid you weren't coming," he went on, escorting his visitor across a narrow hall into a small but exceedingly comfortable sitting-room, furnished and decorated in a curious and original fashion. There were several odd trophies on the walls, and above the mantelpiece, between a Rosenberg drypoint and what looked like a page from an original 'Dance of Death', was a particularly curious group composed of a knuckle-duster surmounted by a Scotland Yard Rogues' Gallery portrait of a well-known character, neatly framed and affectionately autographed. A large key of a singular pattern completed the tableau.

Val Gyrth sank down into the easy chair his host set for him. This peculiar end to his night's adventure, which in itself had been astonishing enough, had left him momentarily stupefied. He accepted the brandy-and-soda which the pale young man thrust into his hands and began to sip it without question.

It was at this point that Mr Campion appeared to notice the cut on his visitor's forehead. His concern was immediate.

"So you had a spot of trouble getting here?" he said. "I do hope they didn't play rough."

Val put down his glass, and sitting forward in his chair looked up into his host's face.

"Look here," he said, "I haven't the least idea who you are, and this night's business seems like a fairy tale. I find an envelope addressed to me, open, in the middle of Ebury Square. Out of crazy curiosity I follow it up. At Kemp's eatinghouse in Clerkenwell I find a letter waiting for me from you, with two pounds in it and an extraordinary invitation card. I get in a taxi to come here and the man tries to shanghai me. I scramble out of that mess with considerable damage to myself, and more to the driver, and when I get here I find you apparently quite *au fait* with my affairs and fooling about with a balloon. I may be mad—I don't know."

Mr Campion looked hurt. "I'm sorry about the balloon," he said. "I'd just come back from a gala at the Athenaeum, when Lugg phoned to say you were coming. He's out to-night, so I had to let you in myself. I don't see that you can grumble about that. The taxi sounds bad. That's why you were late, I suppose?"

"That's all right," said Val, who was still ruffled. "But it must be obvious to you that I want an explanation, and you know very well that you owe me one."

It was then that Mr Campion stepped sideways so that the light from the reading-lamp on the table behind him shone directly upon his visitor's face. Then he cleared his throat and spoke with a curious deliberation quite different from his previous manner.

"I see you take the long road, Mr. Gyrth," he said quietly.

Val raised his eyes questioningly to his host's face. It was the second time that night that the simple remark had been made to him, and each time there had been this same curious underlying question in the words.

He stared at his host blankly, but the pale young man's slightly vacuous face wore no expression whatsoever, and his eyes were obscured behind the heavy spectacles. He did not stir, but stood there clearly waiting a reply, and in that instant the younger man caught a glimpse of waters running too deep for him to fathom.

CHAPTER THREE

The Fairy Tale

VAL GYRTH ROSE to his feet.

"The man at Kemp's said that to me," he said. "I don't know what it means—since it's obvious that it must mean something. What do you expect me to say?"

Mr Campion's manner changed instantly. He became affable and charming. "Do sit down," he said. "I owe you an apology. Only, you see, I'm not the only person who's interested in you—I shall have to explain my interest, by the way. But if my rival firm got hold of you first—"

"Well?" said Val.

"Well," said Mr Campion, "you might have understood about the Long Road. However, now that we can talk, suppose I unbosom myself—unless you'd like to try a blob of iodine on that scalp of yours?"

Val hesitated, and his host took his arm. "A spot of warm water and some nice lint out of my Militia Red Cross Outfit will settle that for you," he said. "No one can be really absorbed by a good story if he's got gore trickling into his eyes. Come on."

After ten minutes' first-aid in the bathroom they returned once more to the study, and Mr. Campion refilled his guest's glass. "In the first place," he said, "I think you ought to see this page out of last week's *Society Illustrated.* It concerns you in a way."

He walked across the room, and unlocking a drawer in a Queen Anne bureau, returned almost immediately with a copy of the well-known weekly. He brushed over the pages and folded the magazine at a large full-page portrait of a rather foolish-looking woman of fifty odd, clad in a modern adaptation of a medieval gown, and holding in her clasped hand a chalice of arresting design. A clever photographer had succeeded in directing the eye of the beholder away from the imperfections of the sitter by focusing his attention upon the astoundingly beautiful object she held.

About eighteen inches high, it was massive in design, and consisted of a polished gold cup upon a jewelled pedestal. Beneath the portrait there were a few lines of letterpress.

"A *Lovely Priestess,*" ran the headline, and underneath:

"*Lady Pethwick, who before her marriage to the late Sir Lionel Pethwick was, of course, Miss Diana Gyrth, is the sister of Col. Sir Percival Gyrth, Bt, owner of the historic 'Tower' at Sanctuary in Suffolk, and keeper of the ageless Gyrth Chalice. Lady Pethwick is here seen with the precious relic, which is said to date from before the Conquest. She is also the proud possessor of the honorary title of 'Maid of the Cuppe'. The Gyrths hold the custody of the Chalice as a sacred family charge. This is the first time it has ever been photographed. Our readers may remember that it is of the Gyrth Tower that the famous story of the Secret Room is told.*"

Val Gyrth took the paper with casual curiosity, but the moment he caught sight of the photograph he sprang to his feet and stood towering in Mr Campion's small room, his face crimson and his intensely blue eyes narrowed and appalled. As he tried to read the inscription his hand shook so violently that he was forced to set the paper on the table and decipher it from there. When he had finished he straightened himself and faced his host. A new dignity seemed to have enveloped him in spite of his ragged clothes and generally unkempt appearance.

"Of course," he said gravely, "I quite understand. You're doing this for my father. I ought to go home."

Mr Campion regarded his visitor with mild surprise.

"I'm glad you feel like that," he said. "But I'm not assisting your father, and I had no idea you'd feel so strongly about this piece of bad taste."

Val snorted. "Bad taste?" he said. "Of course, you're a stranger, and you'll appreciate how difficult it is for me to explain how we"—he hesitated—"regard the Chalice." He lowered his voice upon the last word instinctively.

Mr Campion coughed. "Look here," he said at last, "if you could unbend a little towards me I think I could interest you extremely. For Heaven's sake sit down and be a bit human."

The young man smiled and dropped back into his chair, and just for a moment his youth was apparent in his face.

"Sorry," he said, "but I don't know who you are. Forgive me for harping on this," he added awkwardly, "but it does make it difficult, you know. You see, we never mention the Chalice at home. It's one of these tremendously important things one never talks about. The photograph knocked me off my balance. My father must be crazy, or—" He sat up, a sudden gleam of apprehension coming into his eyes. "Is he all right?"

The pale young man nodded. "Perfectly, I believe," he said. "That photograph was evidently taken and given to the Press without his knowledge. I expect there's been some trouble about it."

"I bet there has." Val spoke grimly. "Of course, you would hardly understand, but this is sacrilege." A flush spread over his face which Mr Campion realized was shame.

Gyrth sat huddled in his chair, the open paper on his knee. Mr Campion sighed, and perching himself upon the edge of the table began to speak.

"Look here," he said, "I'm going to give you a lesson in economics, and then I'm going to tell you a fairy tale. All I ask you to do is to listen to me. I think it will be worth your while."

Val nodded. "I don't know who you are," he said, "but fire away."

Mr Campion grinned. "Hear my piece, and you shall have my birth certificate afterwards if you want it. Sit back, and I'll go into details."

Val leant back in his chair obediently and Mr Campion bent forward, a slightly more intelligent expression than usual upon his affable, ineffectual face.

"I don't know if you're one of these merchants who study psychology and economics and whatnot," he began, "but if you are you must have noticed that there comes a point when, if you're only wealthy enough, nothing else matters except what you happen to want at the moment. I mean you're above trifles like law and order and who's going to win the Boat Race." He hesitated. Val seemed to understand. Mr Campion continued.

"Well," he said, "about fifty years ago half a dozen of the wealthiest men in the world—two Britons, an American, two Spaniards, and a Frenchman—made this interesting discovery with regard to the collection of *objets d'art*. They each had different hobbies, fortunately, and they all had the divine mania."

Once again he paused. "This is where the lesson ends and the fairy story begins. Once upon a time six gentlemen found that they could buy almost anything they wanted for their various collections, of which they were very fond. Then one of them, who was a greedy fellow, started wanting things that couldn't be bought, things so valuable that eminent philanthropists had given them to museums. Also national relics of great historical value. Do you follow me?"

Gyrth nodded. "I don't see where it's leading," he said, "but I'm listening."

"The first man," continued Mr Campion, "whom we will call Ethel because that was obviously not his name, said to himself: 'Ethel, you would like that portrait of Marie Antoinette which is in the Louvre, but it is not for sale, and if you tried to buy it very likely there would be a war, and you would not be so rich as you are now. There is only one way, therefore, of getting this beautiful picture.' So he said to his servant George, who was a genius but a bad lot, I regret to say: 'What do you think, George?' And George thought it could be stolen if sufficient money was forthcoming, as he knew just the man who was famous for his clever thieving. And that," went on Mr Campion, his slightly absurd voice rising in his enthusiasm, "is how it all began."

Gyrth sat up. "You don't expect me to take this seriously, do you?" he said.

"Listen," said his host sharply, "that's all I'm asking you. When Ethel had got the picture, and the police of four countries were looking everywhere for it except in Ethel's private collection at his country house, where they didn't go because he was an Important Person, Evelyn, a friend of his who was as wealthy as he was, and a keen collector of ceramics, came to Ethel's house, and Ethel could not resist the temptation of showing him the picture. Well, Evelyn was more than impressed. 'How did you get it?' he said. 'If you can get your picture of Marie Antoinette, why should I not obtain the Ming vase which is in the British Museum, because I am as rich as you?'

"'Well,' said Ethel, 'as you are a friend of mine and will not blackmail me, because you are too honourable for that, I will introduce you to my valet George, who might arrange it for you.' And he did. And George did arrange it, only this time he went to another thief who was at the top of his class for stealing vases. Then Evelyn was very pleased and could not help telling his friend Cecil, who was a king in a small way and a collector of jewels in a large way. And of course, in the end they went to George and the thing happened all over again.

"After fifty years," said Campion slowly, "quite a lot of people who were very rich had employed George and George's successor, with the result that there is to-day quite a number of wealthy Ethels and Cecils and Evelyns. They are hardly a society, but perhaps they could be called a ring—the most powerful and the most wealthy ring in the world. You see, they are hardly criminals," he went on, "in the accepted sense. It is George, and George's friends, who meet the trouble when there is any, and they also pocket all the money.

"Besides, they never touch anything that can be bought in the open market. They are untouchable, the Ethels and the Cecils, because (a) they are very important people, and (b) nobody but George and George's successor ever knows where the treasures go. That is the strength of the whole thing. Now do you see what I mean?"

As his voice died away the silence in the little room became oppressive. In spite of the lightness of his words he had managed to convey a sense of reality into his story. Gyrth stared at him.

"Is this true?" he said. "It's extraordinary if it is. Almost as extraordinary as the rest of the things that have happened to me to-night. But I don't see how it concerns me."

"I'm coming to that," said Mr Campion patiently. "But first of all I want you to get it into your head that my little fairy story has one thing only to mitigate its obvious absurdity—it happens to be perfectly true. Didn't the 'Mona Lisa' disappear on one occasion, turning up after a bit in most fishy circumstances? If you think back, several priceless, unpurchasable treasures have vanished from time to time; all things, you will observe, without any marketable value on account of their fame."

"I suppose some of the original members of—of this 'ring' died?" said Gyrth, carried away in spite of himself by the piquancy of the story.

"Ah," said Mr Campion, "I was coming to that too. During the last fifty years the percentage of millionaires has gone up considerably. This little circle of wealthy collectors has grown. Just after the War the membership numbered about twenty, men of all races and colours, and the organization which had been so successful for a small number got a bit swamped. It was at this point that one of the members, an organizing genius, a man whose name is famous over three continents, by the way, took the thing in hand and set down four or five main maxims: pulled the thing together, and put it on a business basis, in fact. So that the Society, or whatever you like to call it—it has no name that I know of—is now practically omnipotent in its own sphere."

He paused, allowing his words to sink in, and rising to his feet paced slowly up and down the room.

"I don't know the names of half the members," he said. "I can't tell you the names of those I do know. But when I say that neither Scotland Yard, the Central Office, nor the Sûreté will admit a fact that is continually cropping up under their noses, you'll probably see that Ethel and his friends are pretty important people. Why, if the thing was exposed there'd be a scandal which would upset at least a couple of thrones and jeopardize the governments of four or five powers."

Gyrth set his glass down on a small book-table beside him. "It's a hell of a tale," he said, "but I think I believe you."

The pale young man shot him a grateful smile. "I'm so

glad," he said. "It makes the rest of our conversation possible."

Val frowned. "I don't see *how* they did it," he said, ignoring Campion's last remark. "The George in your fairy story: how did he set about it?"

Campion shrugged his shoulders. "That was easy enough," he said. "It was so simple. That's where the original gentleman's gentleman was so clever. That's what's made the business what it is to-day. He simply set himself up as a 'fence', and let it be known in the right quarter he would pay a fabulous sum for the article indicated. I dare say it sounds rather like a 'Pre-Raffleite' Brotherhood to you," he added cheerfully. "But you must take Uncle Albert's word for it. They pay their money and they take their choice."

Gyrth sighed. "It's extraordinary," he said. "But where do I come in? I'm not a famous crook," he added, laughing. "I'm afraid I couldn't pinch anything for you."

Mr Campion shook his head. "You've got me all wrong," he said. "I do *not* belong to the firm. Don't you see why I've got you here?"

Val looked at him blankly for a moment, and then a wave of understanding passed over his face and he looked at Campion with eyes that were frankly horrified.

"Good heavens!" he said, "the Chalice!"

Mr Campion slipped off the table. "Yes," he said gravely, "it's the chalice."

"But that's impossible!" A moment's reflexion had convinced Val of the absurdity of any such suggestion. "I won't discuss it," he went on. "Hang it all! You're a stranger. You don't know—you can't know the absurdity of a story like this."

"My dear chump," said Campion patiently, "you can't protect anything unless you accept the reality of its danger. I've spent the last two weeks trying to find you because I happen to know for a fact that unless you do something the Gyrth

Chalice will be in the private collection of a particularly illustrious Mohammedan within six months from to-day."

For a moment the boy was speechless. Then he laughed. "My dear sir," he said, "you're mad."

Mr Campion was hurt. "Have it your own way," he said. "But who do you suppose went to the length of trying to kidnap you in a taxi? Why do you imagine there are at least four gentlemen at present watching my front door? You'll probably see them if you care to look."

The young man was still incredulous, but considerably startled. All the vagueness had for a moment vanished from his host's manner. Mr Campion was alert, eager, almost intelligent.

Val shook his head.

"You're not serious," he said.

Campion took off his spectacles and looked his visitor straight in the eyes.

"Now, listen, Val Gyrth," he said. "You've got to believe me. I'm not nearly so ignorant of the position that the Gyrth Chalice holds in your family, *and in the country,* as you imagine. By warning you I am placing myself at direct variance with one of the most powerful organizations in the world. By offering you my assistance I am endangering my life." He paused, but went on again immediately after.

"Would you like me to tell you of the ceremony connected with the Chalice? Of the visits of the King's Chamberlain every ten years which have taken place regularly ever since the Restoration? Or of the deed by which your entire family possessions are forfeit to the Crown should the Chalice be lost? There's a great deal more I could tell you. According to your family custom you come of age on your twenty-fifth birthday, when there is a ceremony in the East Wing of the Tower. You'll have to go to Sanctuary for that."

Val took a deep breath. The last barriers of his prejudice

were down. There was something in his host's sudden change from the inane to the fervent which was extraordinarily convincing.

Mr Campion, who was pacing rapidly up and down the room, now turned.

"However you look at it, I think you and your family are in for a pretty parroty time. That's why I looked you up. 'Ethel' and his friends are after the Chalice. And they'll get it unless we do something."

Val was silent for some minutes, surveying his host with critical eyes. His colour had heightened, and the heavy muscles at the side of his jaw beneath his stubbly beard were knotted.

"The swine!" he said suddenly. "Of course, if this comes off it'll mean the end of us. As you know so much you must realize that this relic is the reason for our existence. We're one of the oldest families in England. Yet we take no part in politics or anything else much, simply devoting ourselves to the preservation of the Chalice."

He stopped dead and glanced at his host, a sudden suggestion of suspicion in his eye.

"Why are you interesting yourself in this affair?" he demanded.

Mr Campion hesitated. "It's rather difficult to explain," he said. "I am—or rather I was—a sort of universal uncle, a policeman's friend, and master-crook's factotum. What it really boiled down to, I suppose, is that I used to undertake other people's adventures for them at a small fee. If necessary I can give you references from Scotland Yard, unofficial, of course, or from almost any other authority you might care to mention. But last year my precious uncle, His Grace the Bishop of Devizes, the only one of the family who's ever appreciated me, by the way, died and left me the savings of an episcopal lifetime. Having become a capitalist, I couldn't very well go on with my fourpence-an-hour business, so that I've been forced to look for suitable causes to which I could donate a small portion of my brains and beauty. That's one reason.

"Secondly, if you'll respect my confidence, I have a slightly personal interest in the matter. I've been practically chucked out by my family. In fact most of it is under the impression that I went to the Colonies ten years ago…"

Gyrth stopped him. "When you took off your spectacles a moment ago," he said, "you reminded me of…"

Mr Campion's pale face flushed. "Shall we leave it at that?" he suggested.

A wave of understanding passed over the boy's face. He poured himself out another drink.

"I hope you don't mind," he said, "but you've treated me to a series of shocks and opened a bit of a chasm beneath my feet. You're a bit hard to swallow, you know, especially after the way you hooked me in here. How did you do it?"

"Conjuring," said Mr Campion simply and unsatisfactorily. "It's all done with mirrors. As a matter of fact," he went on, becoming suddenly grave, "I've been looking for you for a fortnight. And when I spotted you I couldn't approach you, because 'George's' friends were interested in you as well, and I didn't want to put my head in a hornet's nest. You see, they know me rather better than I know them."

"I was followed?" said Val. "What on earth for?"

"Well, they wanted to get hold of you, and so did I," said Mr Campion. "If a friend of mine had tapped you on the shoulder and led you into a pub, one of 'George's' friends would have come too. You had to come to me of your own volition, or apparently so. That explains why my people had to drop a score of envelopes under your nose before you'd rise to the bait. Lugg's been spending his evenings at Kemp's for the last fortnight. He's my man, by the way.

"You see," he added apologetically, "I had to get you to go

down to Clerkenwell first just to make sure they hadn't already approached you. I fancy they wanted to see you in slightly more desperate straits before they came forward with their proposition." He paused and looked at his visitor "Do you follow me?" he said.

"I'm trying to," said Gyrth valiantly. "But I don't see why they should want to get hold of me. Here am I, completely penniless, I'm no use to anyone. I can't even get a job."

"That," said the pale young man gravely, "is where we come to a personal and difficult matter. You are—estranged from your father?"

Val nodded, and the obstinate lines round his mouth hardened. "That's true," he said.

Mr Campion bent forward to attend to the fire. "My dear young sir," he said, "as I told you, the practice of these collectors is to employ the most suitable agent for the job on hand. And although it might be perfectly obvious to anyone who knew you that the chance of buying your services was about as likely as my taking up barbola work, the dark horse who's taken on this job obviously hasn't realized this. Some people think a starving man will sell anything."

Val exploded wrathfully. The young man waited until the paroxysm was over and then spoke mildly.

"Quite," he said. "Still, that explains it, doesn't it?"

Val nodded. "And the 'long road'?" he said.

"A form of salutation between 'George's' friends."

Val sighed. "It's incredible," he said. "I'll put myself in your hands if I may. What are we going to do? Call in the police?"

Campion dropped into a chair beside his kinsman. "I wish we could," he said. "But you see our difficulty there. If we call in the police when nothing has been stolen they won't be very sympathetic, and they won't hang about indefinitely. Once the treasure has been stolen it will pass almost immediately into the hands of people who are untouchable. It wouldn't be fair do's for the policemen. I have worked for Scotland Yard in my time. One of my best friends is a big Yard man. He'll do all he can to help us, but you see the difficulties of the situation."

Val passed a hand over his bandaged forehead. "What happens next?" he said.

Mr Campion reflected. "You have to patch things up with your father," he said quietly. "I suppose you've realized that?"

The boy smiled faintly. "It's funny how a single piece of information can make the thing that was worth starving for this morning seem small," he said. "I knew I should have to go down to Sanctuary in July. I'm twenty-five on the second. But I meant to come away again. I don't know how we're going to put this to Father. And yet," he added, a sudden blank expression coming into his face, "if this is true, what can we do? We can't fight a ring like this for ever. It's incredible; they're too strong."

"There," said Mr Campion, "is the point which resolves the whole question into a neat 'what should A do?' problem. We've got just one chance, old bird, otherwise the project would not be worth fighting and we should not have met. The rules of this acquisitive society of friends are few, but they are strict. Roughly, what they amount to is this: all members' commissions—they have to be for things definitely unpurchasable, of course—are treated with equal deference, the best agent is chosen for the job, unlimited money is supplied, and there the work of 'George' and 'Ethel' ends until the treasure is obtained." He paused and looked steadily at the young man before him. "However—and this is our one loophole—should the expert whom they have chosen meet his death in the execution of his duty—I mean, should the owner of the treasure in question kill him to save it—then they leave well alone and look out for someone else's family album."

"If he's caught—?" began Val dubiously.

Mr Campion shrugged his shoulders. "If he's caught he takes the consequences. Who on earth would believe him if he squealed? No, in that case the society lets him take his punishment and employs someone else. That's quite understandable. It's only if their own personal employee gets put out that they get cold feet. Not that the men they employ mind bloodshed," he added hastily. "The small fry—burglars, thugs, and homely little forgers—may die like flies. 'George' and 'Ethel' don't have anything to do with that. It's if their own agent gets knocked on the head that they consider that the matter is at an end, so to speak." He was silent.

"Who is the agent employed to get the Chalice?" said Gyrth abruptly.

Mr Campion's pale eyes behind his heavy spectacles grew troubled. "That's the difficulty," he said. "I don't know. So you see what a mess we're in."

Gyrth rose to his feet and stood looking at Campion in slow horror.

"What you are saying is, in effect, then," he said, "if we want to protect the one thing that's really precious to me and my family, the one thing that must come before everything else with me, we must find out the man employed by this society, and murder him?"

Mr Campion surveyed his visitor with the utmost gravity. "Shall we say 'dispose of him'?" he suggested gently.

CHAPTER FOUR

Brush with the County

"THE LAST TIME I come past 'ere," said Mr Lugg sepulchrally, from the back of the car, "it was in a police van. I remember the time because I was in for three months hard. The joke was on the Beak, though. I was the wrong man as it 'appened, and that alibi was worth something, I can tell yer."

Campion, at the wheel, spoke without turning. "I wish you'd shut up, Lugg," he said. "We may be going to a house where they have real servants. You'll have to behave."

"Servants?" said Mr Lugg indignantly. "I'm the gent's gent of this outfit, let me tell yer, and I'm not taking any lip. Mr Gyrth knows 'oo I am. I told 'im I'd been a cut-throat when I shaved 'im this morning."

Val, seated beside Campion in the front, chuckled. "Lugg and Branch, my pater's old butler, ought to get on very well together," he said. "Branch had a wild youth, I believe, although of course his family have looked after us for years."

"'Is other name ain't Roger, by any chanst?" Mr Lugg's

voice betrayed a mild interest. "A little thin bloke with a 'ooked nose—talked with a 'orrible provincial accent?"

"That's right." Val turned round in his seat, amused surprise on his face. "Do you know him?"

Lugg sniffed and nodded. "The Prince of Parkhurst, we used to call 'im, I remember," he said, and dismissed the subject of conversation.

Val turned to Campion. "You are a fantastic pair," he said.

"Not at all," said the pale young man at the wheel. "Since we learned to speak French we can take our place in any company without embarrassment. They ought to quote Lugg's testimonial. I know he wrote 'em."

Val laughed, and the talk languished for a minute or so. They were speeding down the main Colchester road, some thirty-six hours after Gyrth had stumbled into Mr Campion's flat off Piccadilly. Reluctantly he had allowed himself to be equipped and valeted by his host and the invaluable Lugg, and he looked a very different person from the footsore and unkempt figure he had then appeared. After his first interview with Campion he had put himself unreservedly into that extraordinary young man's hands.

Their departure from London had not been without its thrills. He had been smuggled out of the flat down a service lift into an exclusive restaurant facing into Regent Street, and thence had been spirited away in the Bentley at a reckless speed. He could not doubt that, unless his host proved to be a particularly convincing lunatic, there was genuine danger to be faced.

Mr Campion's mild voice cut in upon his thoughts.

"Without appearing unduly curious," he ventured, "I should like to know if you anticipate any serious difficulty in getting all friendly with your parent. It seems to me an important point just now."

The boy shook his head. "I don't think so," he said. "It has really been my own pigheadedness that has kept me from going back ever since—" He broke off, seeming unwilling to finish the sentence.

Mr Campion opened his mouth, doubtless to make some tactful reply, when he was forestalled by the irrepressible Lugg.

"If it's anything about a woman, you can tell 'im. 'E's been disappointed 'imself," he observed lugubriously.

Mr Campion sat immovable, his face a complete blank. They were passing through one of the many small country towns on the road, and he swung the car to the side before an elaborately restored old Tudor inn.

"The inner Campion protests," he said. "We must eat. You go and lose yourself, Lugg."

"All right," said Mr Lugg. He was very much aware of his *gaffe*, and had therefore adopted a certain defiance. "Whilst you're messing about with 'the Motorist's Lunch'—seven and a kick and coffee extra—I'll go and get something to eat in the bar. It's mugs like you wot changes 'The Blue Boar' into 'Ye Olde Stuck Pigge for Dainty Teas'."

He lumbered out of the car, opening the door for Campion but not troubling to stand and hold it. His employer looked after him with contempt.

"Buffoon," he said. "That's the trouble with Lugg. He's always got the courage of his previous convictions. He used to be quite one of the most promising burglars, you know. We'll go in and see what the good brewery firm has to offer."

Val followed the slender, slightly ineffectual figure down the two steps into the cool brick-floored dining-room, which a well-meaning if not particularly erudite management had rendered a little more Jacobean than the Jacobeans. The heavily carved oak beams which supported the ceiling had been varnished to an ebony blackness and the open fireplace at the end of the room was a mass of rusty spits and dogs, in a profusion which would have astonished their original owners.

"That spot looks good for browsing," said Mr Campion, indicating a table in an alcove some distance from the other patrons.

As Val seated himself he glanced round him a little apprehensively. He was not anxious to encounter any old acquaintances. Mr Campion looked about also, though for a different reason. But the few people who were still lunching were for the most part cheerful, bovine persons more interested in *The East Anglian* and their food than in their neighbours.

Mr Campion frowned. "If only I knew," he said, "who they'll choose to do their dirty work."

Val bent forward. "Any fishy character in the vicinity ought to come in for a certain amount of suspicion," he murmured. "The natives don't get much beyond poaching."

The pale young man at his side did not smile. "I know," he said. "That makes it worse. I flatter myself that our grasping friends will do me the honour of picking on a stranger to do their homework for them. I'm afraid it may even be amateur talent, and that's usually illogical, so you never know where you are. I say, Val," he went on, dropping his voice, "to put a personal question, is your Aunt Diana—er—Caesar's wife, what? I mean you don't think they could approach her with flattery and guile?"

Val frowned." My Aunt Diana," he said softly, "treats herself like a sort of vestal virgin. She's lived at the Cup House—that's on the estate, you know—ever since Uncle Lionel died, and since Father was a widower she rather took it upon herself to boss the show a bit. Penny has a dreadful time with her, I believe."

"Penny?" inquired Mr Campion.

"My sister Penelope," Val explained. "One of the best."

Mr Campion made a mental note of it. "To return to your

aunt," he said, "I'm sorry to keep harping on this but is she—er—batty?"

Val grinned. "Not certifiable," he said. "But she's a silly, slightly conceited woman who imagines she's got a heart; and she's made copy out of that 'Maid of the Cup' business. Until her time that part of the ceremonial had been allowed to die down a bit. She looked it up in the records and insisted on her rights. She's a strong-minded person, and Father puts up with her, I think, to keep her quiet."

Mr Campion looked dubious. "This 'Maid of the Cup' palaver," he said. "What is it exactly? I've never heard of it."

The young man reflected. "Oh, it's quite simple," he said at last. "Apparently in medieval times, when the menfolk were away fighting, the eldest daughter of the house was supposed to remain unmarried and to shut herself up in the Cup House and attend to the relic. Naturally this practice fell into abeyance when times got more peaceful, and that part of the affair had been obsolete until Aunt Diana hunted it all up as soon as she became a widow. She set herself up with the title complete. Father was annoyed, of course, but you can't stop a woman like that."

"No-o," said Mr Campion. "Any other peculiarities?"

"Well, she's bitten by the quasi-mystical cum 'noo-art' bug, or used to be before I went away," Val went on casually. "Wears funny clothes and wanders about at night communing with the stars and disturbing the game. Quite harmless, but rather silly. I should think that if anyone put a fishy suggestion up to her she'd scream the place down and leave it at that."

A decrepit waiter brought them the inevitable cold roast beef and pickles of the late luncher, and shuffled away again.

Val seemed inclined to make further confidences. "I don't expect trouble with Father," he said. "You know why I walked out, don't you?"

Mr Campion looked even more vague than usual. "No," he said. "You got into a row at Cambridge, didn't you?"

"I got married at Cambridge," said Val bitterly. "The usual tale, you know. She was awfully attractive—a Varsity hanger-on. There's a good lot of 'em, I suppose. I 'phoned the news to Dad. He got angry and halved my allowance, so—" he shrugged his shoulders, "she went off—back to Cambridge."

He paused a little, and added awkwardly: "You don't mind my telling you all this, do you? But now you're in it I feel I ought to tell you everything. Well, I came back to Sanctuary, and Hepplewhite, Dad's solicitor, was fixing up the necessary legal separation guff when I had a letter from her. She was ill, and in an awful state in London. Dad was bitter, but I went up and looked after her by selling up my flat and one thing and another, until she died. There was a filthy row at the time and I never went back. Hepplewhite tried to get hold of me several times for the old boy, but I wouldn't see him. Rather a hopeless sort of tale, I'm afraid, but you can see how it happened. Women always seem to muck things up," he added a trifle self-consciously.

Mr Campion considered. "Oh, I don't know," he said, and then was silent.

They had been so engrossed in their conversation that they had not noticed a certain commotion at the far end of the room as a woman entered and saluted one or two acquaintances as she passed to her table. It was only when her high strident voice had drowned the subdued conversation in the room that the young men in the secluded corner observed her.

She was of a type not uncommon among the "landed gentry," but mercifully rare elsewhere. Superbly self-possessed, she was slightly masculine in appearance, with square flat shoulders and narrow hips. Her hair was cut short under her mannish felt, her suit was perfectly tailored and the collar of her blouse fitted tightly at her throat.

She managed to enter the room noisily and sat down so that her face was towards them. It was a handsome face, but one to which the epithet of "beautiful" would have seemed absurd. She was pale, with a strong prominent nose and hard closely-set blue-grey eyes. She hurled a miscellaneous collection of gloves, scarves, and papers into the chair in front of her and called loudly to the waiter.

It was evident that she was a personage, and that vague sense of uneasiness which invariably steals upon a room full of people when a celebrity is present was apparent in the stolid dining-room. Val averted his face hastily.

"Oh, Lord!" he said.

Mr Campion raised his eyebrows. "Who is the rude lady?" he inquired casually.

Val lowered his voice. "Mrs Dick Shannon," he muttered. "Surely you've heard of her? She's got a racing stable on Heronhoe Heath. One of these damn women-with-a-personality. She knows me, too. Could you wriggle in front of me, old man? She's got an eye like a hawk."

Mr Campion did his best, but as they rose to go, their path to the door led them directly past her table. His protégé was quick, but he was not quick enough.

"Val Gyrth!" The name was bellowed through the room until Mrs Dick Shannon's victim felt as though the entire township must have heard it. The woman caught the boy's coatsleeve and jerked him backward with a wrist like flexed steel.

"So you're back, eh? I didn't know you'd made friends with your father again." This piece of intimate information was also shouted. "When did this happen?" She ignored Mr Campion with the studied rudeness which is the hall-mark of her type. He hovered for some moments ineffectually, and then drifted out into the corridor to settle the score.

Left unprotected, Val faced his captor and strove to make his excuses. He was quite aware that every ear in the room was strained to catch his reply. Gyrth was a name to conjure with in that part of the country.

Mrs Dick seemed both aware and contemptuous of her audience. "I've just come down from the Tower," she said. "I'm trying to make your father sell me two yearlings. What does he want with race-horses? I told him he hadn't got the sense to train properly; and that man he's got is a fool. I saw your aunt, too," she went on, not waiting for any comment from him. "She gets sillier every day."

Val gulped and murmured a few incoherent words of farewell. Mrs Dick gripped his hand and shook it vigorously.

"Well, good-bye. I shall see you again. You can tell your father I'm going to have those yearlings if I have to steal them. He's not capable of training 'em."

The boy smiled politely and a little nervously, and turned away.

"I heard your wife was dead—so sorry," bawled Mrs Dick for the world to hear. Val fled.

His forehead was glistening with sweat when he came up with Campion on the broad doorstep of the inn.

"Let's get away from here," he said. "I loathe that woman."

"'I did but see her passing by.' The rest of the song does not apply," said Mr Campion. "That's her car, I suppose." He indicated a superb red and white Frazer Nash. "Hallo, here comes Lugg, looking like a man with a mission."

At that moment Mr Lugg appeared from the doorway of the four-ale bar. His lugubrious face was almost animated.

"'Op in," he said huskily as he came up with them. "I got something to tell yer. While you've bin playing the gent, I've bin noticin'."

It was not until they were once more packed into the Bentley that he unburdened himself. As they shot out of the town he leant forward from the back seat and breathed heavily into Mr Campion's ear.

"'Oo d'yer think I saw in the bar?" he mumbled.

"Some low friend of yours, no doubt," said his master, skilfully avoiding a trade van which cut in front of an approaching lorry.

"I should say!" said Lugg heavily. "It was little Natty Johnson, one of the filthiest, dirtiest, lousiest little race-gang toughs I've ever taken off me 'at to."

Mr Campion pricked up his ears. "The Cleaver Gang?" he said. "Was he with anyone?"

"That's what I'm coming to," said Lugg reproachfully. "You're always 'urrying on, you are. 'E was talking to a funny chap with a beard. An arty bloke. I tell yer wot—'e reminded me of that Bloomsbury lot 'oo came to the flat and sat on the floor and sent me out for kippers and Chianti. They were talkin' nineteen to the dozen, sittin' up by theirselves in the window. I 'ad a bit o' wool in one ear or I'd 'ave 'eard all they was saying.

"'Owever, that's not the reely interestin' part. Where we come in is this. The artist chap, and some more like 'im, is staying at the Tower, Sanctuary. I know, because the barman told me when I was laughin' at 'em. Friends of Lady Pethwick's, they are, 'e said, as if that explained 'em."

Mr Campion's pale eyes flickered behind his spectacles.

"That's interesting," he said. "And this man—"

"Yes," cut in Mr. Lugg, "'e was talkin' confidential with Natty Johnson. I know first-class dicks 'oo'd arrest 'im fer that."

CHAPTER FIVE

Penny: For Your Thoughts

THE VILLAGE OF SANCTUARY lay in that part of Suffolk which the railway has ignored and the motorists have not yet discovered. Moreover, the steep-sided valley of which it consisted, with the squat Norman church on one eminence and the Tower on the other, did not lie on the direct route to anywhere, so that no one turned down the narrow cherry-lined lane which was its southern approach unless they had actual business in the village. The place itself was one of those staggering pieces of beauty that made Morland paint in spite of all the noggins of rum in the world.

A little stream ran across the road dividing the two hills; while the cottages, the majority pure Elizabethan, sprawled up each side of the road like sheep asleep in a meadow. It is true that the smithy kept a petrol store housed in a decrepit engine boiler obtained from Heaven knows what dumping ground, but even that had a rustic quality. It was a fairy-tale village peopled by yokels who, if they did not wear the traditional white smocks so beloved of film producers, at least climbed the rough steps to the church on a Sunday morning in top hats of unquestionable antiquity.

The Three Drummers stood crazily with its left side a good two feet lower down the northern hill than its right side. It was of brown unrestored oak and yellow plaster, with latticed windows and a red tiled roof. It had three entrances, the main one to the corridor on the level of the road, the bar parlour up four steps upon the left, and the four-ale down two steps on the right.

It was at about five o'clock, when the whole village was basking in a quiet yellow light, that the Bentley drew up outside the Three Drummers and deposited Val Gyrth and Campion at the centre door. Lugg took the car across the road to the smithy "garage", and the two young men stepped into the cool, sweet-smelling passage. Val had turned up his coat collar.

"I don't want to be spotted just yet," he murmured, "and I'd like a chat with Penny before I see the Governor. If I can get hold of Mrs Bullock, she'll fix everything."

He tiptoed down the passage and put his head round the door of the kitchen at the far end.

"Bully!" he called softly.

There was a smothered scream and a clatter of pans on a stone floor. The next moment the good lady of the house appeared, a big florid woman in a gaily patterned cotton dress and a large blue apron. Her sleeves were rolled above her plump elbows and her brown hair was flying. She was radiant. She caught the boy by the arm and quite obviously only just prevented herself from embracing him vigorously.

"You've made it up," she said. "I knew you would—your birthday coming and all."

She had a deep resonant voice with very little trace of accent in spite of her excitement.

"Won't you come into the bar and show yourself?—sir," she added as an afterthought.

Val shook his head. "I say, Bully," he said, "things aren't quite settled yet. Could you give my friend Mr Campion here a room and find us somewhere we can talk? I'd like a note taken up to Penny if possible. How is everyone at the Tower? Do you know?"

Mrs Bullock, who had sensed the urgency of his request, was wise enough to ask no questions. She had been the faithful friend and confidante of the children at the Tower ever since her early days as cook at that establishment, and their affairs were as always one of her chief concerns.

She led her visitors upstairs to a magnificent old bedroom with a small sitting-room leading out of it.

"You write your note, sir, and I'll bring you up something," she said, throwing open the window to let in the scented evening air. "You were asking about the folk, Mr Val. Your father's well, but worried looking. And Penny—she's lovely. Oh, I can see your mother in her—same eyes, same walk, same everything."

"And Aunt?" said Val curiously.

Mrs Bullock snorted. "You'll hear about your aunt soon enough," she said. "Having herself photographed with the Thing." She dropped her eyes on the last word as though she experienced some embarrassment in referring to the Chalice.

"I've heard about that," said Val quietly. "Otherwise—she's all right?"

"Right enough, save that she fills the whole place with a pack of crazy no-goods—strutting about in funny clothes like actors and actresses. Your Ma'll turn in her grave, if she hasn't done that already."

"The artists?" Val suggested.

"Artists? They ain't artists," said Mrs Bullock explosively. "I know artists. I've 'ad 'em staying here. Quiet tidy little fellows—fussy about their victuals. I don't know what your aunt's got hold of—Bolsheviks, I shouldn't wonder. You'll find paper and pen over there, Mr Val." And with a rustle of skirts she bustled out of the room.

Vat sat down at the square table in the centre of the smaller room and scribbled a few words.

"*Dear Penny,*" he wrote, "*I am up here at 'The Drummers.' Can you come down for a minute? Love, Val.*"

He folded the paper, thrust it in an envelope and went to the top of the oak cupboard staircase. Mrs Bullock's tousled head appeared round the door at the foot.

"Throw it down," she whispered, "and I'll send young George around with it."

Vat went back to Campion. "I say," he said, "what about Lugg? He won't talk, will he?"

Mr. Campion seemed amused. "Not on your life," he said. "Lugg's down in the four-ale with his ears flapping, drinking in local wit and beer."

Val crossed to the window and looked out over the inn garden, a mass of tangled rambler roses and vivid delphiniums stretching down amid high old red walls to the tiny stream which trickled through the village.

"It seems impossible," he said slowly. "Up in your flat the story sounded incredible enough, but down here with everything exactly as it always was, so quiet and peaceful and miles away from anywhere, it's just absurd. By jove, I'm glad to get back."

Mr Campion did not speak, and at that moment the door opened and Mrs Bullock returned with a tray on which were two tankards, bread and butter, and a great plate of water-cress.

"It's home-brew," she said confidentially. "I only keep it for ourselves. The stuff the company sends down isn't what it used to be. You can taste the Government's hand in it, I say. I'll send Miss Penny up the moment she comes."

She laid a fat red hand on Val's shoulder as she passed him, an ineffably caressing gesture, and went out, closing the door behind her.

"Here's to the fatted calf," said Mr Campion, lifting his tankard. "There's something so Olde English about you, Val, that I expect a chorus of rustic maidens with garlands and a neat portable maypole to arrive any moment. Stap me, Sir Percy! Another noggin!"

Val suddenly turned upon his companion, a shadow of suspicion in his eyes. "Look here, Campion," he said, "this isn't some silly theatrical stunt to get me back into the bosom of the family, is it? You're not employed by Hepplewhite, are you?"

Mr Campion looked hurt. "Oh, no," he said. "I'm my own master now. No more selling my soul to commerce—not while Uncle's money lasts, anyhow. I'm one of these capitalistic toots. Only one in five has it."

Val grinned. "Sorry," he said. "But thinking it over in cold blood, I suppose you know that the Chalice is in the Cup House chapel, and that is burglar-proof. No ordinary thief could possibly touch it."

"No ordinary thief would want to," said Mr Campion pointedly. "You seem to have forgotten your fun in the taxi-cab. I suppose you know you bashed that chap up pretty permanently, and he didn't even mention to the hospital authorities that he had a fare on board? If someone doesn't try to murder one of us every two days you seem to think there's nothing up. Drink up your beer like a good boy, and old Uncle Al will find a nice crook for you to beat up. All I'm worrying about is if they've already got busy while we're hanging about. I say, I wish your sister would come. The Tower isn't far away, is it?"

"It's just up at the top of the hill," said Val. "You can't see it because of the trees. Hold on a moment—I think this is she."

There was a chatter of feminine voices on the staircase. Campion walked over to the bedroom.

"I'll stay here till the touching reunion is over," he said.

"Don't be a fool," said Val testily. He got no further, for the door opened, and not one but two young women came in, with Mrs Bullock hovering in the background.

At first glance it was easy to pick out Val's sister. Penelope Gyrth was tall like her brother, with the same clear-cut features, the same very blue eyes. Her hair, which was even more yellow than Val's, was bound round her ears in long thick braids. She was hatless, and her white frock was sprinkled with a scarlet pattern. She grinned at her brother, revealing suddenly how extremely young she was.

"Hallo, old dear," she said, and crossing the room slipped her arm through his.

A more unemotional greeting it would have been difficult to imagine, but her delight was obvious. It radiated from her eyes and from her smile.

Val kissed her, and then looked inquiringly at her companion. Penny explained.

"This is Beth," she said. "We were coming down to the post office when young George met us with your note, so I brought her along. Beth, this is my brother, and Val, this is Beth Cairey. Oh, of course, you haven't heard about the Caireys, have you?"

The girl who now came forward was very different from her companion. She was *petite* and vivacious, with jet-black hair sleeked down from a centre parting to a knot at the nape of her neck. Her brown eyes were round and full of laughter, and there was about her an air of suppressed delight that was well-nigh irresistible. She was a few years older than the youthful Penny, who looked scarcely out of her teens.

Mr Campion was introduced, and there was a momentary awkward pause. A quick comprehending glance passed between him and the elder girl, a silent flicker of recognition, but neither spoke. Penny sensed the general embarrassment and came to the rescue, chattering on breathlessly with youthful exuberance.

"I forgot you didn't know Beth," she said. "She came just after you left. She and her people have taken Tye Hall. They're American, you know. It's glorious having neighbours again—or it would be if Aunt Di hadn't behaved so disgustingly. My dear, if Beth and I hadn't conducted ourselves like respectable human beings there'd be a feud."

Beth laughed. "Lady Pethwick doesn't like strangers," she said, revealing a soft unexpectedly deep voice with just a trace of a wholly delightful New England accent.

Penny was plainly ill at ease. It was evident that she was trying to behave as she fancied her brother would prefer, deliberately forcing herself to take his unexpected return as a matter of course.

Campion watched her curiously, his pale eyes alight with interest behind his huge spectacles. In spite of her gaiety and the brilliance of her complexion there were distinct traces of strain in the faint lines about her eyes and in the nervous twisting of her hands.

Val understood his sister's restraint and was grateful for it. He turned to Beth and stood smiling down at her.

"Aunt Di has always been rather difficult," he said. "I hope Father has made up for any stupidity on her part."

The two girls exchanged glances.

"Father," said Penny, "is sulky about something. You know what a narrow-minded old darling he is. I believe he's grousing about the Professor—that's Beth's father—letting the Gypsies camp in Fox Hollow. It's rather near the wood, you know. It would be just like him to get broody about it in secret and feel injured without attempting to explain."

Beth chuckled. "The Gypsies are Mother's fault," she

said. "She thinks they're so picturesque. But four of her leg-horns vanished this morning, so I shouldn't wonder if your Dad's grievance would be sent about its business fairly soon."

Val glanced from one to the other of the two girls.

"Look here," he said after a pause, "is everything all right?"

His sister blushed scarlet, the colour mounting up her throat and disappearing into the roots of her hair. Beth looked uncomfortable. Penny hesitated.

"Val, you're extraordinary," she said. "You seem to smell things out like an old pointer. It doesn't matter talking in front of Beth, because she's been the only person that I could talk to down here and she knows everything. There's something awfully queer going on at home."

Mr Campion had effaced himself. He sat at the table now with an expression of complete inanity on his pale face. Val was visibly startled. This confirmation of his fears was entirely unexpected.

"What's up?" he demanded.

Penny's next remark was hardly reassuring.

"Well, it's the Chalice," she said. There was reluctance in her tone as though she were loth to name the relic. "Of course, I may be just ultra-sensitive, and I don't know why I'm bothering you with all this the moment you arrive, but I've been awfully worried about it. You remember the Cup House chapel has been a sacred place ever since we were kids—I mean it's not a place where we'd take strangers except on the fixed day, is it? Well, just lately Aunt Diana seems to have gone completely mad. She was always indiscreet on the subject, of course, but now—well—" she took a deep breath and regarded her brother almost fearfully—"she was photographed with it. I suppose that's what's brought you home. Father nearly had apoplexy, but she just bullied him."

As Val did not respond, she continued.

"That's not the worst, though. When she was in London last she developed a whole crowd of the most revolting people—a sort of semi-artistic new religion group. They've turned her into a kind of High Priestess and they go about chanting and doing funny exercises in sandals and long white nightgowns. Men, too. It's disgusting. She lets them in to see the Chalice. And one man's making a perfectly filthy drawing of her holding it."

Val was visibly shocked. "And Father?" he said.

Penny shrugged her shoulders. "You can't get anything out of Father," she said. "Since you went he's sort of curled up in his shell and he's more morose than ever. There's something worrying him. He has most of his meals in his room. We hardly ever see him. And, Val"—she lowered her voice—"there was a light in the East Wing last night."

The boy raised his eyebrows in silent question, and she nodded.

Val picked up his coat.

"Look here," he said, "I'll come back with you if you can smuggle me into the house without encountering the visitors." He turned to Campion. "You'll be all right here, won't you?" he said. "I'll come down and fetch you in the morning. We'd better stick to our original arrangement."

Mr Campion nodded vigorously.

"I must get Lugg into training for polite society," he said cheerfully.

He saw Penny throw a glance of by no means unfriendly curiosity in his direction as he waved the three a farewell from the top of the stairs.

Left to himself he closed the door carefully, and sitting down at the table, he removed his spectacles and extracted two very significant objects from his suitcase, a small but wicked-looking rubber truncheon and an extremely serviceable Colt revolver. From his hip-pocket he produced an exactly similar gun, save in the single remarkable fact that it was constructed to project nothing more dangerous than water. He considered the two weapons gravely.

Finally he sighed and put the toy in the case: the revolver he slipped into his hip pocket.

CHAPTER SIX

The Storm Breaks

"'E RE, WOT D'YOU THINK you're doing?"

Mr Lugg's scandalized face appeared round the corner of the door.

"Mind your own business," said Campion without looking up. "And, by the way, call me 'sir'."

"You've bin knighted, I suppose?" observed Mr Lugg, oozing into the room and shutting the door behind him. "I'm glad that chap's gone. I'm sick o' nobs. As soon as I caught a bosso of 'im and 'is 'arem going up that street I come up to see what the 'ell you was up to—sir."

Mr Campion resumed his spectacles. "You're a disgrace," he said. "You've got to make the 'valet' grade somehow before to-morrow morning. I don't know if you realize it, but you're a social handicap."

"Now then, no 'idin' be'ind 'igh school talk," said Mr Lugg, putting a heavy hand on the table. "Show us what you've got in yer pocket."

Mr Campion felt in his hip-pocket and produced the revolver obediently.

"I thought so." Mr Lugg examined the Colt carefully and handed it back to his master with evident contempt. "You know we're up against something. You're as jumpy as a cat. Well, I'm prepared too, in me own way." He thrust his hand in his own pocket and drew out a life-preserver with a well-worn handle. "You don't catch me carryin' a gun. I'm not goin' to swing for any challenge cup that ever was—but then I'm not one of the gentry. And I don't know wot you think you're up to, swankin' about the cash your uncle left you. I know it paid your tailor's bill, but only up to nineteen twenty-eight, remember. You'll land us both in regular jobs workin' for a livin' if you're so soft-'earted that you take on dangerous berths for charity."

He was silent for a moment, and then he bent forward. His entire manner had changed and there was unusual seriousness in his little black eyes.

"Sir," he said, with deep earnestness, "let's 'op it."

"My dear fellow," said Mr Campion with affable idiocy, "I have buttered my bun and now I must lie on it. And you, my beautiful, will stand meekly by. It is difficult, I admit. Gyrth's a delightful chap, but he doesn't know what we're up against yet. After all, you can't expect him to grasp the significance of the *Société Anonyme* all at once. You're sure that was Natty Johnson?"

"Wot d'you take me for—a private dick?" said Mr Lugg with contempt. "Of course I saw 'im. As little and as ugly as life. I don't like it."

He glanced about him almost nervously and came a step nearer. "There's something unnatural about this business," he breathed. "I was listenin' down in the bar just now and an old bloke come out with a 'orrible yarn. D'you know they've got a blinkin' two-'eaded monster up at that place?"

"Where?" said Mr Campion, considerably taken aback.

"Up at the Tower—where we've got to do the pretty. I'm not going to be mixed with the supernatural, I warn yer."

Campion regarded his faithful servitor with interest. "I like your 'fanny'," he said. "But they've been pulling your leg."

"All right, clever," said Mr Lugg, nettled. "But it's a fac', as it 'appens. They've got a secret room in the east wing containin' some filfy family secret. There's a winder but there's no door, and when the son o' the house is twenty-five 'is father takes 'im in and shows 'im the 'orror, and 'e's never the same again. Like the king that ate the winkles. That's why they leave comin' of age till the boy is old enough to stand the shock." He paused dramatically, and added by way of confirmation: "The bloke 'oo was telling me was a bit tight, and the others was tryin' to shut 'im up. You could see it was the truth—they was so scared. It's bound to be a monster—somethin' you 'ave to feed with a pump."

"Lugg, sit down."

The words were rapped out in a way quite foreign to Mr Campion's usual manner. Considerably surprised, the big man obeyed him.

"Now, look here," said his employer, grimly, "you've got to forget that, Lugg. Since you know so much you may as well hear the truth. The Gyrths are a family who were going strong about the time that yours were leaping about from twig to twig. And there is, in the east wing of the Tower, I believe, a room which has no visible entrance. The story about the son of the house being initiated into the secret on his twenty-fifth birthday is all quite sound. It's a semireligious ceremony of the family. But get this into your head. It's nothing to do with us. Whatever the Gyrths' secret is, it's no one's affair but their own, and if you so much as refer to it, even to one of the lowest of the servants, you'll have made an irreparable bloomer, and I won't have you within ten miles of me again."

"Right you are, Guv'nor. Right you are." Mr Lugg was apologetic and a little nervous. "I'm glad you told me, though," he added. "It fair put the wind up me. There's one or two things, though, that ain't nice 'ere. F'rinstance, when I was comin' acrost out of the garage, a woman put 'er 'ead out the door o' that one-eyed shop next door. She didn't arf give me a turn; she was bald—not just a bit gone on top, yer know, but quite 'airless. I asked about 'er, and they come out with a yarn about witchcraft and 'aunting and cursin' like a set o' 'eathens. There's too much 'ankypanky about this place. I don't believe in it, but I don't like it. They got a 'aunted wood 'ere, and a set o' gippos livin' in a 'ollow. Let's go 'ome."

Mr Campion regarded his aide owlishly.

"Well, you have been having fun in your quiet way," he said. "You're sure your loquacious friend wasn't a Cook's Guide selling you Rural England by any chance? How much beer did it take you to collect that lot?"

"You'll see when I put in my bill for expenses," said Mr Lugg unabashed. "What do we do to-night? 'Ave a mike round or stay 'ere?"

"We keep well out of sight," said Mr Campion. "I've bought you a book of *Etiquette for Upper Servants.* It wouldn't hurt you to study it. You stay up here and do your homework."

"Sauce!" grumbled Mr Lugg. "I'll go and unpack yer bag. Oh, well, a quiet beginning usually means a quick finish. I'll 'ave a monument put up to you at the 'ead of the grave. A life-size image of yerself dressed as an angel—'orn-rimmed spectacles done in gold."

He lumbered off. Mr Campion stood at the window and looked over the shadowy garden, still scented in the dusk. There was nothing more lovely, nothing more redolent of peace and kindliness. Far out across the farther fields a nightingale had begun to sing, mimicking all the bird chatter of the sunshine. From the bar beneath his feet scraps of the strident

Suffolk dialect floated up to him, mingled with occasional gusts of husky laughter.

Yet Mr Campion was not soothed. His pale eyes were troubled behind his spectacles, and once or twice he shivered. He felt himself hampered at every step. Forces were moving which he had no power to stay, forces all the more terrible because they were unknown to him, enemies which he could not recognize.

The picture of Val and the two girls standing smiling in the bright old-fashioned room sickened him. There was, as Lugg said, something unnatural about the whole business, something more than ordinary danger and the three young people had been so very young, so very ignorant and charming. His mind wandered to the secret room, but he put the subject from him testily. It could not have any significance in the present business or he would surely have been told.

Presently he closed the window and crossed to the table, where the best dinner that Mrs Bullock could conjure was set waiting for him. He ate absently, pausing every now and then to listen intently to the gentle noises of the countryside.

But it was not until early the following morning, as he lay upon a home-cured feather bed beneath an old crocheted quilt of weird and wonderful design, that the storm broke.

He was awakened by a furious tattoo on his door and raised himself upon his elbow to find Mrs Bullock, pink and horror-stricken.

"Oh, sir," she said, "as Mr Val's friend, I think you ought to go up to the Tower at once. It's Lady Pethwick, sir, Mr Val's aunt. They brought her in this morning, sir—stone dead."

CHAPTER SEVEN

Death in the House

THE TOWER AT SANCTUARY managed to be beautiful in spite of itself. It stood at the top of the hill almost hidden in great clumps of oak and cedar trees with half a mile of park surrounding it in all directions. It was a mass of survivals, consisting of excellent examples of almost every period in English architecture.

Its centre was Tudor with a Georgian front; the west wing was Queen Anne; but the oldest part, and by far the most important, was the east wing, from which the house got its name. This was a great pile of old Saxon stone and Roman brick, circular in shape, rising up to a turreted tower a good sixty feet above the rest of the building. The enormously thick walls were decorated with a much later stone tracery near the top, and were studded with little windows, behind one of which, it was whispered, lay the room to which there was no door.

In spite of the odd conglomeration of periods, there was something peculiarly attractive and even majestic in the old pile. To start with, its size was prodigious, even for a country mansion. Every age had enlarged it.

The slight signs of neglect which a sudden rise in the cost of labour combined with a strangling land tax had induced upon the lawns and gardens had succeeded only in mellowing and softening the pretentiousness of the estate, and in the haze of the morning it looked kindly and inviting in spite of the fact that the doctor's venerable motor-car stood outside the square doorway and the blinds were drawn in all the front windows.

Val and Penny were standing by the window in a big shabby room at the back of the west wing. It had been their nursery when they were children, and had been regarded by them ever since as their own special domain. There were still old toys in the wide cupboards behind the yellow-white panelling, and the plain heavy furniture was battered and homely.

The view from the window, half obscured by the leaves of an enormous oak, led the eye down the steep green hill-side to where a white road meandered away and lost itself among the fields which stretched as far as the horizon.

The scene was incredibly lovely, but the young people were not particularly impressed. Penny was very pale. She seemed to have grown several years older since the night before. Her plain white frock enhanced the pallor of her face, and her eyes seemed to have become wider and more deep in colour. Val, too, was considerably shaken.

"Look here," he said, "I've sent word down for Campion to come up as we arranged before. It was just Aunt's heart, of course, but it's awkward happening like this. I thought she was disgustingly full of beans at dinner last night." He pulled himself up. "I know I ought not to talk about her like this," he said apologetically, "still, it's silly to pretend that we liked her."

He was silent for a moment, and then went on gloomily, "The village will be seething with it, of course. Being picked up in the Pharisees' Clearing like that. What on earth did she want to go wandering about at night for?"

Penny shuddered and suddenly covered her face with her hands.

"Oh, Val," she said "did you see her? I was the first to go down into the hall this morning when Will and his son brought her in on a hurdle. That look on her face—I shall never forget it. She saw something dreadful, Val. She died of fright."

The boy put his arm round her and shook her almost roughly.

"Don't think of it," he said. "She'd got a bad heart and she died, that's all. It's nothing to do with—with the other thing."

But there was no conviction in his tone and the girl was not comforted, realizing that he spoke as much to reassure himself as to soothe her.

Their nerves were so taut that a tap on the door made them both start violently. It opened immediately to admit old Doctor Cobden, the man who had brought them both into the world, and whose word had been the ultimate court of appeal ever since they could remember.

He was a large, benign old gentleman with closely cropped white hair and immense white eyebrows and he was dressed in an unconventional rough tweed suit fitting snugly to his rotund form.

He advanced across the room, hand outstretched, exuding a faint aroma of iodoform as he came.

"Val, my boy, I'm glad to see you," he said. "You couldn't have come back at a better time. Your father and the estate have needed you very much lately, but never so much as now." He turned to Penny and patted her hand gently as it lay in his own. "Pull yourself together, my dear," he said. "It's been a shock, I know, but there's nothing to be afraid of. I'm glad I found you two alone. I wanted to have a chat. Your father, good man, is not much assistance in an emergency."

He spoke briskly and with a forthrightness that they had learned to respect. Val shot him a glance under his eyelashes.

"There'll have to be an inquest, I suppose, sir?" he said.

Doctor Cobden took out a pair of pince-nez and rubbed them contemplatively with an immense white handkerchief.

"Why no, Val. I don't think that'll be necessary, as it happens," he said. "I'm the coroner of this district, don't you know. And whereas I should perhaps have felt it was my duty to inquire into your aunt's death if I hadn't been in attendance on her quite so often lately, I really don't see any need to go into it all again." He paused and regarded them solemnly. "There was always a danger, of course. Any severe shock might have aggravated this aortic regurgitation, don't you know, but she was a nervy creature, poor soul, and I never saw any reason to frighten her."

"But, Doctor, something did frighten her. Her face—" Penny could not restrain the outburst. The old man's mottled face took on a slightly deeper tone of red.

"My dear," he said, "death is often ugly. I'm sorry you should have had to see your aunt. Of course," he went on hastily as he saw the doubt in their eyes, "she must have *had* a shock, don't you know. Probably saw an owl or trod on a rabbit. I warned her against this stupid wandering about at night. Your aunt was a very peculiar woman."

He coughed. "Sometimes," he added, "I thought her a very silly woman. All this semi-mystical nonsense was very dangerous in her condition. And that's where I come to the business I wanted to discuss with you. I don't want your father bothered. I've persuaded him to take things easily. It's been a great shock to him. He's in his own rooms and I don't want him disturbed. Now, Val, I want all this crowd of your aunt's friends out of the house before to-morrow." He paused, and his little bright eyes met the boy's inquiringly. "I don't know how many there are," he said, "or who they are. Some—ah—some

Bohemian set, I understand. They've been getting on your father's nerves. I don't know what your aunt was doing filling the place with dozens of strangers."

Penny looked a little surprised.

"There's only seven visitors, and they're at the Cup House now," she said. "We don't see much of them. Aunt used to keep them to herself."

"Oh, I see," the doctor looked considerably relieved. "I understood from your father that there was an army of lunatics encamped somewhere. Oh, well, it won't be so difficult. I don't suppose they'll want to stay, don't you know."

The old man had brightened visibly. Clearly a weight was off his mind. "There's just one other thing," he went on rather more slowly than usual, evidently choosing his words with deliberation. "With regard to the funeral, I should—ah—get it over quietly, don't you know. As little fuss as possible. I don't think there's any necessity to fill the house with visitors. No last looks or any morbid rubbish of that sort. I'm sorry to speak frankly," he went on, directing his remarks to Val, "but it's your father we've got to think of. It's getting near your twenty-fifth birthday, you know, my boy, and that is a very trying time for both you and your father." He paused to let his words sink in, and then added practically: "There's no near relative that you'll offend, is there?"

Penny considered. "There's Uncle Lionel's brothers," she said dubiously.

"Oh, no need to worry about them. Write to them and leave it at that." The doctor dismissed the family of the late Sir Lionel Pethwick with a wave of his hand.

Penny laid her hand upon his arm affectionately.

"You dear," she said. "You're trying to hush it all up for us."

"My dear child!" The old man appeared scandalized. "I've never heard such nonsense. There's nothing to hush up.

A perfectly normal death. I'm merely considering your father, as I keep on telling you. You young people are too eager to listen to the superstitious chatter of the country folk. There's no such thing as a look of horror on a dead face. It's death itself that is horrifying. A case of sudden end like this is always shocking. I'll make you up a sedative, Penny. One of the men can come down for it. Take it three times a day, and go to bed early.

"I'll speak to Robertson too, Val, as I go through Sudbury. You can leave everything to him. I should fix the funeral for Wednesday. Without appearing callous, the sooner you get these things over the better. You're modern young people. I'm sure you'll understand me. Now I'll go," he added, turning briskly towards the door. "Don't trouble to come down with me. I want to have a word with Branch on my way out. I believe that old rascal is more capable than the whole lot of you. Good-bye. I shall drop in to-morrow. Good-bye, Penny, my dear."

He closed the door firmly behind him and they heard him padding off down the parquetted corridor. Penny turned to her brother, her eyes wide and scared.

"Val, he suspects something." she said. "All this quiet funeral business—it's so unlike him. Don't you remember, Mother used to say that he was as proud at a funeral as if he felt he was directly responsible for the whole thing? He doesn't like the look of it. Poor Aunt Di, she was a thorn in the flesh, but I never dreamed it would all end so quickly and horribly as this. I'd give anything to be able to hear her explain her psychic reaction to sunset over Monaco again."

Val was troubled. "Do you mean you think it wasn't heart failure?" he said.

"Oh, nonsense," said Penny. "Of course it was. But I think the doctor feels, as I did, that she must have seen something terrible. There *is* something terrible down in Pharisees'

Clearing. There's something round here that we don't understand—I've known it for a long time. I—"

A gentle knocking silenced her, and they both turned to see a pale ineffectual face half-hidden by enormous glasses, peering in at them from the doorway.

"Enter Suspicious Character," said Mr Campion, introducing the rest of himself into the room. "By the way, I met an irate old gentleman downstairs who told me there was a goods train at 6.15 from Hadleigh. I hope that wasn't your father, chicks." He paused, and added awkwardly, "I heard a rumour in the village that something rather terrible had happened."

Val stepped forward to meet him. "Look here, Campion," he said, "it's all infernally mysterious and it is terrible. Aunt Di was brought in by two yokels. They found her in a clearing in the woods quite near here. She was dead, and they insist that she had an expression of absolute horror on her face, but of course we know that's impossible. That was the doctor you saw just now. He's giving a certificate, but I can't help feeling he wouldn't be so sanguine if he didn't know the family so well. Father has shut himself up in the library and the doc says we're to clear Aunt's crowd out as soon as we can."

He paused for breath.

"An expression of horror?" said Mr Campion. "This is where we get out of our depth. I'm terribly sorry this has happened, Gyrth. How do you stand with your father?"

"Oh, that's all right." The boy spoke hastily. "I ought to have come home before. I had my own affairs too much on the brain. I think the old boy was worrying about me. Anyhow, he's very grateful to you. He wanted to send for you last night. I had to hint who you were—you don't mind that, do you? He seems to understand the situation perfectly. Frankly, I was amazed by his readiness to accept the whole story."

Campion did not answer, but smiled affably at the boy. Val seemed relieved.

"Now I'd better go round and politely turf out that Bohemian crowd," he said. "I don't suppose you want to interview them, Campion?"

The young man with the pleasant vacuous face shook his head.

"No," he said, "I think it would be better if we did not become acquainted, as it were. There's only one thing. Branch, I suppose, will superintend the luggage?"

"Why, yes, I suppose so." Val was almost impatient.

"Good," said Campion. "See that he does. By the way, he and Lugg were having an Old Boys' Reunion in the hall when I came up." He turned to the girl. "I say, while your brother's speeding the parting guests, I wonder if I could ask you to take me down to the clearing where they found Lady Pethwick?"

She shot him a glance of surprise, but his expression was mild and foolish as ever. "Of course I will," she said.

"Perhaps we could go by some back way that may exist?" Mr Campion persisted. "I don't want my bad taste to be apparent."

Val glanced at his sister and hesitated. "We don't know the exact spot," he said awkwardly.

"Naturally," said Campion, and followed his guide out of the room.

They went down a shallow Elizabethan staircase, along a wide stone-flagged passage, and came out of a side door into a flower garden. As Mr Campion stepped out blinking into the sunshine, the girl laid a hand upon his arm.

"Look," she said, "you can see the Cup House from here."

Her companion followed the direction of her eyes and saw a curious rectangular building which had been completely hidden from the front of the house by the enormous eastern wing.

It was situated in a little courtyard of its own, and consisted of what appeared to be two storeys built of flint cobbles reinforced with oak, the lower floor being clearly the Chapel of the Cup, while the upper section had several windows indicating a suite of rooms.

Mr Campion regarded the structure, the sun glinting on his spectacles.

"Your aunt's artistic friends are upstairs, I suppose?" he said.

"Oh, yes," said Penny hastily. "The chapel is always kept locked."

Mr Campion hesitated. "There's no doubt," he ventured, "that the relic is safe at the moment?"

The girl stared at him in astonishment. "Of course it is," she said. "I'm afraid all this talk of painting my aunt with the Chalice has given you a wrong impression. There were always two of the servants there at the time—Branch and someone else—and the relic was returned to its place and the doors locked after each sitting. There are three rooms up there over the chapel," she went on, "the Maid of the Cup's private apartments in the old days. Aunt had the big room as a sort of studio, but the two small ones are the bedrooms of the two men who have charge of this garden and the chapel building. There's an outside staircase to the first storey."

"Oh," said Mr Campion.

They walked down the broad grass path towards a small gate at the end of the garden. For some time there was silence, and then the girl spoke abruptly.

"Mr Campion," she said, "I made Val tell me about everything last night—I mean about the danger to the Chalice. You'll have to let me help. You'll find me quite as useful as he. For one thing," she added, dropping her voice, "I haven't got the shadow of The Room hanging over me. Besides," she went on with a wry little smile, "I'm the Maid of the Cup now, you know. I've got a right to come into this and you can count on me."

Mr Campion's reply was unexpected. "I shall hold you to that," he said. "Now I think we'd better hurry."

They went through the garden gate and across the broad meadow on the other side. Here it was semi-parkland with a great bank of trees upon their left, and presently they entered a small iron gate in the hedge surrounding the wood and struck a footpath leading down into the heart of the greenery.

"Pharisees' Clearing," said Penny, "is just through here. It's really a strip of grass which separates our wood from the other coppice which is the Tye Hall property where Beth lives."

"Ah," said Mr Campion. "And where is Fox Hollow?"

She shot him a quick glance. "You remembered that? It's higher up on the other side of their woodlands. Dad really had cause for a grievance, you see, only Professor Cairey himself doesn't shoot, so you can't expect him to understand. And anyhow, he only wants asking. Dad's so silly that way."

"Professor?" said Campion thoughtfully. "What does he profess?"

"Archaeology," said Penny promptly. "But you don't think—?"

"My dear girl," said Mr Campion, "I can't see the wood for trees. 'And in the night imagining some fear, how easy doeth a bush appear a bear.' You see," he added with sudden seriousness, "if your aunt met her death by someone's design, I'm not only out of my depth, but I might just as well left my waterwings at home." He paused and looked about him. "I suppose this is a happy hunting ground for poachers?"

Penny shook her head. "I don't think there's a man, woman or child in the whole of Sanctuary who'd come within a mile of Pharisees' Clearing after dark," she said. She hesitated for some seconds as if debating whether to go on. "I get on very well with the country folk," she added suddenly, "and naturally I hear a good deal of local chatter. They believe that this wood and the clearing are haunted—not by a ghost, but by something much worse than that. No one's ever seen it that I know of, but you know what country people are."

"I thought the breed had died out," said her companion. "Gone are the dimpled milkmaids and the ancient gaffers of my youth. You can't even see them on the pictures."

Penny smiled faintly. "We're very much behind the times here," she said. "We've even got a local witch—poor old Mrs Munsey. She lives with her son in a little henhouse of a place some distance away from the village. They're both half-wits, you know, really, poor things. But there's a world of prejudice against them, and they're both so bad-tempered you can't do anything for them. Sammy Munsey is the village idiot, I suppose, but the old woman is a venomous old party. And that's why—" she hesitated, "you'll probably think I'm a fool for mentioning this, but she put a curse on Aunt Di at the last full moon, and it was full moon again last night."

She reddened and glanced furtively at her companion, whose pleasant vacant face conveyed nothing but polite interest. She looked absurdly modern in her smart white crêpe de Chine jumper suit, her bare brown arms hanging limply at her sides, and it was certainly odd to hear her speak of such an archaic practice as witchcraft as though she half believed in it.

"Now I've said it, it sounds stupid," she remarked. "After all, it may not even be true. It's only gossip."

Campion regarded her quizzically. "Did Mrs Munsey ever curse anybody with such startling success before?" he said. "How did she build up her business, so to speak?"

The girl shrugged her shoulders. "I don't really know," she said, "except that there's a list of witches burnt in 1624 still in the Lady Chapel of the church—this village managed to escape Cromwell, you know—and every other name on the sheet is Munsey. It's partly that, and then—the poor old creature is perfectly bald. In the winter it's all right, she wears a bonnet of sorts, but in hot weather she goes about uncovered. Aunt Di was always trying to be kind to her, but she had an officious way and she annoyed the old biddy somehow. Do you think I'm mad?"

"My dear young lady," said her companion judicially, "there are lots of rum professions. There's nothing unusual about witchcraft. I used to be a bit of a wizard myself, and I once tried to change a particularly loathsome old gentleman into a seal on a voyage to Oslo. Certainly the vulgar creature fell overboard, and they only succeeded in hauling up a small walrus, but I was never sure whether I had done it or not. They had the same moustaches, but that was all. I've often wondered if I was successful. I went in for wireless accessories after that."

Penny regarded him with astonishment, but he seemed to be perfectly serious. They were half-way through the wood by this time. The place was a fairyland of cool green arcades with moss underfoot, and a tiny stream meandering along among the tree roots.

She pointed to a patch of sunlight at the far end of the path. "That's the entrance to Pharisees' Clearing," she said. "Pharisee means 'fairy', you know."

Mr Campion nodded. "Be careful how you talk about fairies in a wood," he said. "They're apt to think it disrespectful."

They walked on, and came at last to the edge of the clearing. It was a tiny valley, walled in by high trees on each side, and possessing, even at that hour of the morning, a slightly sinister aspect.

The grey-green grass was sparse, and there were large stones scattered about; a bare unlovely place, all the more uninviting after the beauty of the wood.

The girl paused and shivered. "It was here," she said quietly. "As far as I could gather from Will Tiffin, Aunt was lying quite close to this gateway—staring up with that awful look on her face."

Campion did not move, but stood regarding the scene, his pale face even more vacuous than usual. The girl took a deep breath.

"Mr Campion," she said, "I've got to tell you something. I've kept quiet about it so far, but I think if I don't tell someone I shall go mad."

She was speaking impulsively, the quick colour rising in her cheeks.

"Will Tiffin told me early this morning, and I made him swear not to breathe it to another soul. When he found her she was lying here on her back, not twisted or dishevelled as she would have been if she had lain where she had fallen, but stiff and straight, with her hands folded and her eyes closed. Don't you see—" her voice quivered and sank to a whisper—"Will said it looked as if she had been laid out as a corpse."

CHAPTER EIGHT

The Professional Touch

"You'D BE DOING ME a service, Mr Lugg, if you'd refrain from referring to me as No 705. Sir Percival did my father the honour of forgetting my little lapse twenty-five years ago."

Mr Branch, a small dignified person in black tie and jacket, paused and regarded his shady old friend with something like appeal in his eyes.

"No good thinkin' o' that," he added, dropping his official voice and speaking with his natural Suffolk inflection.

Mr Lugg, himself resplendent in black cloth, sniffed contemptuously. "'Ave it yer own way," he said. "Anyway, you nipped that lot out o' the satchel as if you still knew a thing or two."

He jerked his head towards a pile of water-colours and pencil sketches lying face downwards upon a bureau top. The two men were in one of the smaller bedrooms in the front of the mansion, at present in disuse.

The little man fidgeted nervously.

"I shan't be happy till they're out of the house," he said. "It's not my regular job to do the packing. The housekeeper would smell a rat immediately if any fuss was made."

"There won't be no fuss. 'Ow many more times 'ave I got to tell yer?" Mr Lugg was irritated. "Mr Gyrth and my young bloke said they'd take full responsibility. Livin' down 'ere on the fat of the land 'as made you flabby, my son."

Mr Branch glanced under his eyelashes at the big man opposite him.

"Your Mr Campion," he said. "I shouldn't be at all surprised if 'is real name didn't begin with a K. And figuring it all out, 'is Christian name ought to be Rudolph."

Mr Lugg's large mouth fell open. "'Ow d'yer make that out?" he demanded.

His friend wagged his head knowingly. "A confidential family servant in a big 'ouse gets to know things by a sort of instinct," he observed. "Family likenesses—family manners—little tricks of 'abit, and so on."

Unwillingly, Mr Lugg was impressed. "Lumme!" he said. "'Ow did you get a line on 'is nibs?"

"About an hour ago," said Branch precisely, "I went into Mr Campion's bedroom to see if the maids had done their work. Quite by chance," he went on studiously, "I caught sight of 'is pyjamas. Light purple stripe—silk—come from Dodds. That didn't tell me much. But then I noticed a bit of flannel, sewed in by the firm, across the shoulder-blades. Now that's a silly idea, a woman's idea. Also I fancy I could lay me finger on the only woman 'oo could ever make Dodds do it. Then, a thing like that comes from 'abit—lifelong 'abit. It wouldn't be a wife. It'd 'ave to be a mother to fix it on a chap so's it 'ud last 'im all 'is life. I started thinkin' and remembered where I'd seen it before. Then of course I knew. The gilded bit of aristocracy 'oo comes down 'ere sometimes is just the chap to 'ave a little brother like your young bloke."

He paused and Mr Lugg was mortified.

"Branch," he said, "who d'you make me out to be—Doctor Watson?"

It was evident that the butler did not follow him, and Lugg laughed. "You're smart, but you've got no education," he said complacently. "What's the point of all this knowledge of yours? What d'you use it for—graft?"

Branch was shocked, and said so. Afterwards he deigned to explain. "In the days when 'er Ladyship was alive and we used to entertain," he said, "it was as well to keep an eye on who was in the 'ouse. Oh, I was very useful to 'er Ladyship. She quite come to depend on me. First morning at breakfast when they come in, she'd raise 'er eyebrows at me, ever so faint, if there was any doubt, and if I knoo they was O.K., I'd nod."

"Yes?" said Lugg, fascinated by this sidelight into High Life. "And if you wasn't satisfied?"

"Then I'd ignore 'er," said Branch majestically.

Mr Lugg whistled. "'Ard lines on a bloke with ragged pants," he observed.

"Oh no, you don't foller me." Branch was vehement. "Why, there's one pair of underpants that's been into this 'ouse reg'lar for the last fourteen years. Darned by the Duchess 'erself, bless 'er! I can tell it anywhere—it's a funny cross-stitch what she learnt in France in the 'fifties. You see it on all 'er family's washin'. It's as good as a crest." He shook his head. "No, this 'ere knowledge of mine comes by instinc'. I can't explain it."

"Well, since you're so clever, what about this lot that's just off?" said Lugg, anxious to see if the remarkable attribute could be turned to practical account. "Anything nobby in the way of darns there?"

Branch was contemptuous.

"Fakes!" he said. "Low fakes, that's what they were. Nice

new outfits bought for the occasion. 'Something to show the servants,' " he mimicked in a horribly refined voice. "Not every pair of legs that's covered by Burlington Arcade first kicked up in Berkeley Square, you can take it from me."

Mr Lugg, piqued by this exhibition of talent, was stung to retort.

"Well, anyway, 'ere's your watch back," he said, handing over a large gold turnip, and gathering up a sheaf of drawings he strode out of the room.

He padded softly down the corridor and tapped upon a door on his left. Penny's voice bade him enter, and he went in to find himself in a small sitting-room elaborately decorated in the dusty crimson and gold of the later Georges.

Mr Campion and the daughter of the house were standing beside the window, well hidden from the outside by heavy damask curtains. The young man, who had turned round as Lugg entered, raised his eyebrows inquiringly.

"I've got the doings, sir," Lugg murmured huskily, the faded splendours of the old mansion combined with Penelope's beauty producing a certain respect in his tone. "Just like what you thought."

"Good," said Mr Campion. "Hold hard for a moment, Lugg. I'm watching our young host and your friend Branch, who I see has just come out to him, packing the intelligentsia into a couple of cars."

"Ho." Mr Lugg advanced on tiptoe and stood breathing heavily over his master's shoulder. They could just see a group of weirdly dressed people surrounding a venerable Daimler and a still more ancient Panhard, both belonging to the house, which were stationed outside the front door.

Lugg nudged his master. "That's the chap I saw with Natty," he rumbled. "That seedy looking bloke with the ginger beard. It was 'is traps that this lot come out of." He tapped the pile of papers in his hand.

"Do you recognize any of the others?" Mr Campion spoke softly.

Mr Lugg was silent for some moments. Then he sniffed regretfully.

"Can't say I do," he said. "They look genuine to me. They've got that 'Gawd-made-us-and-this-is-'ow-'e-likes us' look."

Penny touched Mr Campion's arm.

"Albert," she said, "do you recognize that man with the ginger beard?"

Mr Campion turned away from the window and advanced towards the table in the centre of the room.

"Rather," he said. "An old employee of mine. That's why I'm so glad he didn't see me. His trade name before he took up art and grew a beard was Arthur Earle. He's a jeweller's copyist, and one of the best on the shady side of the line." He turned to Penny and grinned. "When Lady Ermyntrude gives her dancing partner the old Earl's jewelled toodleoo clock to keep the wolf from the door, the old Earl is awakened every morning by a careful copy of our Arthur's making. Likewise Lady Maud's ruby dog collar and the necklace Sir George gave little Eva on her twenty-first. They're all copies of the originals made by our Arthur. Arthur, in fact, is one of the lads who make Society what it is to-day." He took the pile of papers from Lugg. "This, I fancy, is some of his handiwork. Now we'll see."

There had been a sound of wheels in the drive, and Val came in almost immediately afterwards.

"Well, they've gone," he said. "Hullo, what have you got there?"

Mr Campion was busy spreading out the drawings. "A spot of Noo-Art," he said. "When they discover they've lost this lot they'll realize we're not completely in the dark, but we can't help that."

The brother and sister bent forward eagerly. There were about a dozen drawings in all, each purporting to be a portrait of Lady Pethwick. In each drawing the Chalice figured. In fact the Chalice was the only subject which the artist had attempted to treat with any realism, whilst the drawings of the lady were ultra-modern, to say the best of them.

Mr Campion chuckled. "There's not much about the treasure that our friend missed," he said. "It's a miracle your aunt didn't spot what he was up to. Look, here's the Chalice from the right side, from the left, from the top—see, he's even jotted down the measurements here. And I should fancy he had a pretty good idea of the weight. That's what I call thoroughness."

Val looked at him questioningly. "I don't quite see the idea," he said.

"My dear old bird," said Mr Campion, "our Arthur was a conscientious workman in spite of his murky reputation. He must have been a bit of an actor, too, by the way, to deceive your aunt like that. These are plans"—he waved his hand to the drawings on the table—"working diagrams, in fact. I should say that, given the materials, our Arthur could turn you out a very good copy of the Chalice from these."

"But if they could make a copy that would deceive us, why not let his Mohammedan client have it?" said Val testily.

Mr Campion was shocked. "My dear fellow, have you no respect for a collector's feelings?" he said. "Arthur couldn't make anything that would deceive an expert."

"So they were going to exchange it?" It was Penny who spoke, her eyes blazing with anger and her cheeks flushed. "To give them plenty of time to get the real thing out of the country before we spotted anything. Pigs! Oh, the insufferable farmyard pigs! Pigs in the French sense! Why don't we wire down to the station and get the man arrested?"

"I shouldn't do that," said Mr Campion. "We've spiked his

guns pretty effectively anyhow. And after all, I don't see what we could charge him with. He might retort that we'd pinched his drawings, which would be awkward. Lugg's record would come out and we'd all be in the soup. Besides," he went on gravely, "Arthur is very small fry—just about as small as Natty Johnson, in fact. That's what's worrying me," he added with unusual violence. "The place is swarming with minnows, but there's not a trout in the stream. And the big man is the only one who's any good to us at all. I wish I knew what your aunt saw last night."

He gathered up the drawings and tore them neatly across and across. "Now you can go and play bonfires, Lugg," he said, handing him the pieces.

It was growing dark in the room, and at any moment the dinner gong might sound.

The little party was disturbed by the sudden entrance of Branch, who came in without ceremony, his usual composure completely gone.

"Mr Val, sir," he burst out, "would you step across the passage? There's a stranger peering in through the chapel window."

With a smothered exclamation Val started after the butler into the spare bedroom on the opposite side of the corridor, followed by the entire company. The window afforded a perfect view of the Cup House.

"There!" said Branch, pointing down towards the old flint building. It was almost dusk, but the watchers could easily make out the figure of a man balanced upon a pile of loose stones peering in through one of the narrow lattice windows of the chapel. He was hidden by a yew hedge from the lower windows of the house, and apparently thought himself completely secluded. He had a torch in his hand with which he was trying to penetrate the darkness inside the building.

As they watched him, fascinated, the hastily improvised

pedestal on which the intruder stood collapsed beneath his weight, and he stumbled to the ground with a rattle of stones. He picked himself up hastily and shot a single startled glance up at the house.

Even at that distance the features were dimly visible, revealing a handsome little man of sixty odd, with a sharp white vandyke beard and a long nose.

The next moment he was off, streaking through the flower garden like a shadow.

Penny gasped, and she and the butler exchanged glances. When at last she spoke, her voice trembled violently.

"Why, Branch," she said, "that—that looked very like Professor Gardner Cairey."

Branch coughed. "Begging your pardon, miss," he said, "that *was* him."

CHAPTER NINE

The Indelicate Creature

IF THE EXTREME unpopularity of Lady Pethwick produced in her immediate household an emotion more akin to quiet shock than overwhelming grief at her death, the village of Sanctuary seethed with excitement at the news of it, and the most extravagant gossip was rife.

Mr Campion wandered about the vicinity in a quiet, ineffectual fashion, his eyes vague and foolish behind his spectacles, but his ears alert. He learnt within a very short space of time, and on very good authority in every case, that Lady Pethwick had been *(a)* murdered by Gypsies; *(b)* confronted by the Devil, who had thereupon spirited her away at the direct instigation of Mrs Munsey; and *(c)* according to the more prosaic wiseacres, had died in the normal way from drink, drugs, or sheer bad temper.

Even the rational Mrs Bullock held no belief in the doctor's verdict.

On the afternoon of the funeral he absented himself, and spent that day and part of the night pursuing and finally interviewing his old friends Jacob Benwell and his mother, Mrs Sarah, mère and compère of the Benwell Gypsy tribe, who had seen fit for obvious reasons to remove from Fox Hollow on the morning on which Lady Pethwick was found in Pharisees' Clearing.

It was early afternoon of the following day, after a luncheon at which Sir Percival did not appear, that Mr Campion was standing at the nursery window regarding the flower garden attentively when Lugg came to him, an expression of mild outrage upon his ponderous face.

"A party 'as just come visitin'," he remarked. "Tourists on 'orseback. Day after the funeral—get me? Not quite the article, I thought."

This announcement was followed almost immediately by the entrance of Penny. Her eyes were dark and angry.

"Albert," she said, "have you ever heard such cheek? Mrs Dick Shannon has just arrived with two complete strangers. She has the nerve to say that she has come to pay a call of condolence, and incidentally, if you please, to show her two beastly friends the Chalice. We open the chapel to visitors on Thursdays as a rule—it's part of Royal Charter—but this is a bit stiff, isn't it?"

She paused for breath.

"Mrs Dick Shannon?" said Mr Campion. "Ah, yes, I remember. The megaphonic marvel. Where is she now? I suppose your father is doing the honours?"

"Father can't stand her," said Penny. "She's trying to make him sell her some horses—that's the real reason why she's come. Look here, you'd better come downstairs and support us. Father likes you. If you could get rid of them he might offer you my hand in marriage or put you up for his club. Anyway, come on."

She went out of the room and Campion followed. Almost immediately Mrs Dick's penetrating voice met them from the hall below.

"Well, of course, drink's better than lunacy in a family, as I told the mother."

The phrase met them as they descended the stairs.

Penny snorted. "I bet she's talking about one of our relatives," she whispered. "It's her idea of making conversation."

Mrs Dick, backed by her two friends, who to do them justice looked considerably embarrassed, was standing with her feet planted far apart in the centre of the huge lounge-hall. All three were in riding kit, Mrs Dick looking particularly smart in a black habit.

Once again Mr Campion was conscious of the faint atmosphere of importance which her dashing personality seemed to exude.

Colonel Sir Percival Gyrth, supported by his son, stood listening to the lady. He was a sturdy old man of the true Brass Hat species, but there was about him a suggestion that some private worry had undermined his normal good-tempered simple character. At the moment he was quite obviously annoyed. His plump hands were folded behind his back, and his eyes, blue and twinkling like his children's, had a distinctly unfriendly gleam. He was a by no means unhandsome man, with curling iron-grey hair, and a heavy-featured clean-shaven face. He glanced up hopefully as Campion entered.

"Ah," he said, "let me present you. Mrs Shannon, this is a young friend of Val's. Mr Campion—Mr Albert Campion."

Mrs Dick's cold glance wandered leisurely over the young man before her. Had she spoken, her contempt could not have been more apparent. Finally she honoured him with a slight but frigid bow. Then she turned to her companions.

"Major King and Mr Horace Putnam," she said, and then quite patently dismissed all of them as negligible.

Major King proved to be a large, florid and unhappy-looking person, slightly horsey in appearance and clearly not at his ease. Mr Putnam, on the other hand, was a small man with little bright eyes and a shrewd, wrinkled face. He too was clearly a stranger to his surroundings, but was not letting the fact worry him.

"Well?" Mrs Dick whipped the company together with the single word. "Now, Penny Gyrth, if you'll take us over the museum, we'll go. I'm afraid the horses may be getting bored. You still maintain your complete unreasonableness about those two yearlings, Colonel?"

It said a great deal for Sir Percival's upbringing that his tone when he replied was as charming as ever.

"My dear lady, I don't want to sell. And just at the moment," he added simply, "I'm afraid I don't feel much like business of any sort."

"Oh, of course. Poor Diana." Mrs. Dick was not in the least abashed. "I always think it best to face things," she went on, bellowing the words like a bad loudspeaker. "Mawkishness never did anyone any good. The only wonder to my mind is that it didn't happen years ago. Cobden's such an old fool. I wouldn't let him vet me for chilblains."

By this time the entire Gyrth family were smarting. Only their inborn politeness saved Mrs Dick and her protégés from an untimely and undignified exit. Mr Campion stood by smiling foolishly as though the lady had irresistible charm for him.

Mrs Dick moved towards the door. "Come on," she said. "I'm not very interested in these things myself, but Mr Putnam is amused by all this ancient rubbish."

Penny hung back. "The Chalice is veiled," she said. "It always is, for ten days after a—" The word "death" died on her lips as Mrs Dick interrupted her.

"Then unveil it, my dear," she said. "Now come along, all of you—we can't keep the horses waiting. How you've let this place go down since your wife's time, Colonel! Poor Helen, she always believed in making a good show."

Impelled by the very force of her vigorous personality,

the little company followed her. At least three of the party were bristling at her outrageous monologue, but she was superbly oblivious of any effect she might create. It was this quality which had earned her the unique position in the county which she undoubtedly occupied. Everybody knew her, nobody liked her, and most people were a little afraid of her. Her astounding success with any species of horseflesh earned her a grudging admiration. Nobody snubbed her because the tongue capable of it had not yet been born. Her rudeness and studied discourtesy were a byword for some fifty square miles, yet she came and went where she pleased because the only way of stopping her would have been to hurl her bodily from one's front door, no mean feat in itself, and this method had not yet occurred to the conservative minds of her principal victims.

Outside on the gravel path there was still a very marked reluctance on the part of the members of the household to continue towards the Cup House, but at last the Colonel, realizing that there was no help for it, decided to get the matter over as soon as possible. Branch was dispatched for the keys and the little procession wandered round the east wing, through a small gate at the side, and came out into the flower garden. Mrs Dick still held forth, maintaining a running commentary calculated to jade the strongest of nerves.

"A very poor show of roses, Colonel. But then roses are like horses, you know. If you don't understand 'em, better leave 'em alone."

She stood aside as Branch advanced to unlock the heavy oak and iron door of the chapel. The lock was ancient and prodigiously stiff, so that the little butler experienced considerable difficulty in inserting the great key, and there was a momentary pause as he struggled to turn it.

Before Val could step forward to assist the old man, Mrs Dick had intervened. She thrust Branch out of her way like a cobweb, and with a single twist of her fingers shot the catch back. Major King laughed nervously.

"You're strong in the wrist," he observed.

She shot him a single withering glance. "You can't be flabby in my profession," she said.

The unpleasant Mr Putnam laughed. "That's one for you, Major," he said. "I was watching Mrs Shannon dealing with Bitter Aloes this morning. That mare will beat you," he added, turning to the lady. "She's got a devil in her. I thought she was going to kill you. A bad woman and a vicious mare, they're both incorrigible. Lose 'em or shoot 'em, it's the only way."

He turned to the rest of the party, who were unimpressed.

"There was Bitter Aloes rearing up, pawing with her front feet like a prizefighter," he said, "and Mrs Shannon hanging on to the halter rope, laying about with a whip like a ringmaster. She got the brute down in the end. I never saw such a sight."

It was with this conversation that the unwelcome visitors came into the ancient and sacred Chapel of the Cup.

It was a low room whose slightly vaulted ceiling was supported by immensely thick brick and stone columns, and was lit only by narrow, diamond-paned windows set at irregular intervals in the walls, so that the light was always dim even on the brightest day. The floor was paved with flat tombstones on which were several very fine brasses. It was entirely unfurnished save for a small stone altar at the far end of the chamber, the slab of which was covered with a crimson cloth held in place by two heavy brass candlesticks.

Let into the wall, directly above the centre of the altar, was a stout iron grille over a cavity in the actual stone, which was rather ingeniously lit by a slanting shaft open to the air many feet above, and sealed by a thick sheet of glass inserted at some later period than the building of the chapel.

At the moment the interior of the orifice was filled by a pyramid of embroidered black velvet.

Colonel Gyrth explained.

"Immediately a death occurs in the family," he murmured, "the Chalice is veiled. This covering was put on here three days ago. It is the custom," he added, "not to disturb it for at least ten days." He hesitated pointedly.

Mrs Dick stood her ground. "I suppose the grille opens with another key," she said. "What a business you make of it! Is there a burglar alarm concealed in the roof?"

Quite patently it had dawned upon the Colonel that the only way to get rid of his unwelcome visitors was to show them the Chalice and have done with it. He was a peace-loving man, and realizing that Mrs Dick would not shy at a scene, he had no option but to comply with her wishes. He took the smaller key which Branch handed him, and bending across the altar carefully unlocked the grille, which swung open like a door. With reverent hands he lifted the black covering.

Mr Campion, whose imagination ran always to the comic, was reminded irresistibly of a conjuring trick. A moment later his mental metaphor was unexpectedly made absolute.

There was a smothered exclamation from the Colonel and a little scream from Penny. The removal of the black cloth had revealed nothing more than a couple of bricks taken from the loose pedestal of one of the columns.

Of the Chalice there was no sign whatever.

Mrs Dick was the only person who did not realize immediately that some calamity had occurred.

"Not my idea of humour." Her stentorian voice reverberated through the cool, dark chapel. "Sheer bad taste."

But Val stared at Mr Campion, and his father stared at Branch, and there was nothing but complete stupefaction and horror written on all their faces.

It was Colonel Gyrth who pulled himself together and provided the second shock within five minutes.

"Of course," he said, "I had quite forgotten. I'm afraid you'll be disappointed to-day, Mr Putnam. The Chalice is being cleaned. Some other time."

With remarkable composure he smiled and turned away, murmuring to Val as he passed him: "For God's sake get these people out of the house, my boy, and then come into the library, all of you."

CHAPTER TEN

Two Angry Ladies

COLONEL SIR PERCIVAL GYRTH walked up and down the hearthrug in his library, while his two children, with Mr Campion and Branch, stood looking at him rather helplessly.

"Thank God that woman's gone." The old man passed his hand across his forehead. "I don't know if my explanation satisfied her. I hope so, or we'll have the whole country buzzing with it within twenty-four hours."

Val stared at his father. "Then it really has gone?"

"Of course it has." There was no misunderstanding the consternation in the Colonel's voice. "Vanished into thin air. I veiled it myself on Sunday evening, just after you said that busybody Cairey was fooling about in the courtyard. It was perfectly safe then. I brought the keys back and put them in my desk. Branch, you and I, I suppose, are the only people who knew where they were kept."

Branch's expression was pathetic, and his employer reassured him. "Don't worry, man. I'm not accusing anybody. It's ridiculous. The thing can't have gone."

For a moment no one spoke. The suddenness of the loss seemed to have stunned them.

"Hadn't I better send someone for the police, sir? Or perhaps you'd rather I phoned?" It was Branch who made the suggestion.

Sir Percival hesitated. "I don't think so, thank you, Branch," he said. "Anyway, not yet. You see," he went on, turning to the others, "to make a loss like this public entails very serious consequences. We are really the guardians of the Chalice for the Crown. I want the chapel locked as usual, Branch, and no mention of the loss to be made known to the staff, as yet."

"But what shall we do?" said Val breathlessly. "We can't sit down and wait for it to reappear."

His father looked at him curiously. "Perhaps not, my boy," he said. "But there's one point which must have occurred to all of you. The Chalice is both large and heavy, and no stranger has left the house since I locked it up myself. No one except ourselves could possibly have had access to it, and we are all very particularly concerned in keeping it here."

"According to that argument," said Val bluntly, "it can't have gone. And if so, where is it? Can't you send for the Chief Constable? He used to be a friend of yours."

His father hesitated. "I could, of course," he said, "though I don't see what he could do except spread the alarm and question all the servants—search the house, probably, and make a lot of fuss. No, we must find this thing ourselves."

There was an astonishing air of finality in his tone which was not lost upon the others.

"I'm not calling in the police," he said, "not yet, at any rate. And I must particularly ask you not to mention this loss to anyone. I'm convinced," he went on as they gasped at him, "that the relic is still in the house. Now I should like to be left alone."

They went out, all of them, except Val, who lingered, and when the door had closed behind the others he went over to the old man, who had seated himself at his desk.

"Look here, Dad," he said, "if you've hidden the Cup for some reason or other, for Heaven's sake let me in on it. I'm all on edge about this business, and frankly I feel I've got a right to know."

"For Heaven's sake, boy, don't be a fool." The older man's voice was almost unrecognizable, and the face he lifted towards his son was grey and haggard. "This is one of the most serious, most terrifying things I have ever experienced in my whole lifetime," he went on, his voice indubitably sincere. "All the more so because, as it happens, we are so situated that at the moment it is impossible for me to call in the police."

He looked the boy steadily in the eyes. "You come of age in a week. If your birthday were to-day perhaps I should find this easier to explain."

Early the following morning Mr Campion walked down the broad staircase, through the lounge-hall, and out into the sunlight. There seemed no reason for him to be particularly cheerful. So far his activities at Sanctuary seemed to have met with anything rather than conspicuous success. Lady Pethwick had died mysteriously within eight hours of his arrival, and now the main object of his visit had disappeared from almost directly beneath his nose.

Yet he sat down on one of the ornamental stone seats which flanked the porch and beamed upon a smiling world.

Presently, as his ears detected the sound for which he was listening, he began to stroll in a leisurely fashion down the drive. He was still sauntering along the middle of the broad path when the squawk of a motor-horn several times repeated made him turn to find Penny, in her little red two-seater sports car, looking at him reprovingly. She had had to stop to avoid running him over. He smiled at her foolishly from behind his spectacles.

"Where are you going to, my pretty maid?" he said. "Would you like to give a poor traveller a lift?"

The girl did not look particularly pleased at the suggestion.

"As a matter of fact," she said, "I'm running up to Town to see my dressmaker. I'll give you a lift to the village if you like."

"I'm going to London too," said Mr Campion, climbing in. "It's a long way from here, isn't it?" he went on with apparent imbecility. "I knew I'd never walk it."

Penny stared at him, her cheeks flushing. "Surely you can't go off and leave the Tower unprotected," she said, and there was a note of amusement in her voice.

"Never laugh at a great man," said Mr Campion. "Remember what happened to the vulgar little girls who threw stones at Elisha. I can imagine few worse deaths than being eaten by a bear," he added conversationally.

The girl was silent for a moment. She was clearly considerably put out by the young man's unexpected appearance.

"Look here," she said at last, "I'm taking Beth with me, if you really want to know. I'm meeting her at the end of the lane."

Mr Campion beamed. "That's all right," he said. "I shan't mind being squashed. Don't let me force myself on you," he went on. "I shouldn't dream of doing that, but I've got to get to London somehow, and Lugg told me I couldn't use the Bentley."

The girl looked at him incredulously. "What is that man Lugg?" she said.

Her companion adjusted his spectacles. "It depends how you mean," he said. "A species, definitely human, I should say, oh yes, without a doubt. Status—none. Past—filthy. Occupation— my valet."

Penny laughed. "I wondered if he were your keeper," she suggested.

"Tut, tut," said Mr Campion, mildly offended. "I hope I'm going to enjoy my trip. I don't want to be 'got at' in a parroty fashion all the way up. Ah, there's your little friend waiting for us. Would you like me to sit in the dickey?"

"No!" said Penny, so vehemently that he almost jumped. She bit her lip as though annoyed with herself and added more quietly, "Sit where you are. Beth can squeeze in."

She brought the car to a standstill against the side of the road where Beth Cairey, smart and coolly attractive in navy and white, stood waiting. She seemed surprised to see Mr Campion and her greeting was subdued.

"This appalling creature has insisted on our giving him a lift," said Penny. "I do hope you won't be squashed in front here."

Mr Campion made way for her between himself and the driver.

"I couldn't very well refuse him," Penny added apologetically to Beth. "We shall have to put up with him."

Mr Campion continued to look ineffably pleased with himself. "What a good job there's no more for the Skylark, isn't it?" he remarked as he shut the door on the tightly packed little party. "I love riding in other people's motorcars. Such a saving of petrol, for one thing."

"Silly and rather vulgar," said Penny, and Mr Campion was silent.

"I suppose I can eat my sandwiches and drink my ginger beer so long as I don't throw the bottle on the road?" he said meekly after they had progressed a couple of miles without speaking. "I've got a few oranges I could pass round too if you like."

Penny did not deign to reply, although Beth looked upon him more kindly. Unabashed, Mr Campion continued.

"I've got a rattle to swing in the big towns," he said. "And a couple of funny noses for you two to wear. If we had some balloons we could tie them on the bonnet."

Penny laughed grudgingly. "Albert, you're an idiot," she said. "What do you think you're doing here, anyhow? Where are you going to in London?"

"To buy a ribbon for my straw hat," said Mr Campion promptly. "The thing I've got now my Aunt knitted. It's not quite the article, as Lugg would say."

Penny slowed down. "You're just being offensive," she said. "I've a good mind to make you get out and walk."

Mr Campion looked apprehensive. "You'd regret it all your life," he said warningly. "The best part of my performance is to come. Wait till you've heard me recite—wait till I've done my clog dance—wait till the clouds roll by."

"I should turn him out," said Beth stolidly. "We've come a long way, it would do him good to walk back."

They were, it happened, in one of the narrow cross-country lanes through which Penny was threading in her descent upon the main Colchester motor-way, some distance from a house of any kind, and the road was deserted.

"Don't turn me out," pleaded Mr Campion. "I knew a man once who turned such a respectable person out of his car after giving him a lift for a long way just like you and for the same reason, all because he'd taken a sudden dislike to him. And when he got home he found that his suitcase, which had been in the back of the car, was missing. Suppose that happened to you? You wouldn't like that, would you?"

Penny stopped the car, engine and all. Both girls were scarlet, but it was Penny who tried to rescue what was obviously an awkward situation.

"How silly of me," she said. "You'll have to get out and start her up. The self-starter isn't functioning."

Mr Campion moved obediently to get out, and in doing so contrived to kneel up on the seat and grasp one end of the large suitcase which protruded from the open dickey. His next movement was so swift that neither of the two girls realized what was happening until he had leapt clear of the car and stood beaming in the road, the suitcase in his arms. In fact Penny had already trodden on the self-starter and the car was in motion before she was conscious of her loss.

Mr Campion put the suitcase on the bank and sat down on it. Penny stopped the car, and she and Beth descended and came down the road towards him. She was white with anger, and there was a gleam of defiance in Beth's brown eyes that was positively dangerous.

"Mr Campion," said Penny, "will you please put that case back in the car at once? Naturally, I can't offer you a lift any farther, and if ever you have the impudence to appear at the Tower again I'll have you thrown out."

Mr Campion looked dejected, but he still retained his seat. "Don't be unreasonable," he begged. "You're making me go all melodramatic and slightly silly."

The two girls stared at him fascinated. He was juggling with a revolver which he had taken from his hip-pocket.

Penny was now thoroughly alarmed. "What do you think you're doing?" she demanded. "You can't behave like this. Another car may come along at any moment. Then where will you be?"

"Then where will *you* be?" said Mr Campion pointedly.

With his free hand he slipped open the catches of the suitcase. There was a smothered scream from Beth.

"Please—please leave it alone," she whispered.

Mr Campion shook his head. "Sorry," he said. "Dooty is dooty, miss. Hullo! Is that a car?"

The inexperienced ladies were deceived by the old trick. They turned eagerly, and in the momentary respite Mr Campion whipped open the suitcase and exposed a large bundle wrapped lightly in a travelling rug.

Beth would have sprung at him, but Penny restrained her. "It's no good," she said, "we're sunk."

And they stood sullenly in the road with pink cheeks and bright eyes regarding him steadily as he unwrapped and produced to their gaze the eighteen inches of shining glory that was called the Gyrth Chalice.

CHAPTER ELEVEN

Mr Campion Subscribes

FOR SOME MOMENTS Mr Campion stood at the side of the glittering flint road with the bank of green behind him, and the shadows of the beech leaves making a pattern on his face and clothes. The Chalice lay in his arms, dazzling in the sunshine.

Penny and Beth stood looking at him. They were both crimson, both furious, and a little afraid. Penny was fully aware of the enormity of the situation. It was Campion who spoke first.

"As amateurs," he said judicially, "you two only serve to show what a lot of undiscovered talent there is knocking about."

He re-wrapped the Chalice and put it back into the suitcase.

All this time there was an ominous silence from Penny, and glancing at her he was afraid for one horrible moment that she was on the verge of tears.

"Look here," he said, smiling at her from behind his spectacles, "I know you think I've butted into this rather unwarrantably, but consider my position. In this affair I occupy the same sort of role as the Genie of the Lamp. Wherever the Chalice is I am liable to turn up at any moment."

Penny's expression did not change for some seconds, and then, to his relief, a faint smile appeared at the corners of her mouth.

"How on earth did you know?" she said.

Mr Campion sighed with relief.

"The process of elimination," said he oracularly as he picked up the suitcase and trudged back to the car with it, "combined with a modicum of common sense, will always assist us to arrive at the correct conclusion with the maximum of possible accuracy and the minimum of hard labour. Which being translated means: I guessed it." He lifted the case into the dickey once more, and held the door open for Penny and her companion.

She hung back. "That's not fair," she said. "Suppose you explain?"

Mr Campion shrugged his shoulders. "Well, it wasn't very difficult, was it?" he said. "In the first place it was obvious that the chapel had not been burgled. Ergo, someone had opened the door with the key. Ergo, it must have been you, because the only other two people who could possibly have known where it was were your father and Branch, and they, if I may say so, are both a bit conservative on the subject of the Chalice."

Penny bit her lip and climbed into the driving seat. "Anyway," she said, "I'm the 'Maid of the Cup'."

"Quite," said Mr Campion. "Hence your very natural feeling of responsibility." He hesitated and looked at her owlishly. "I bet I could tell you what you were going to do with it."

"Well?" She looked at him defiantly.

Mr Campion laid his hand on that part of the suitcase

which projected from the dickey. "You were going to put this in Chancery Lane Safe Deposit," he said.

Penny gasped at him, and there was a little smothered squeak from Beth. Mr Campion went on.

"You had relied on the ten days' veiling of the Chalice to keep its loss a secret, and I have no doubt you intended to confess the whole matter to Val and your father before they had any real cause for worry. Unfortunately, Mrs Shannon upset the apple-cart and you had to get busy right away. And that's why I was waiting for you this morning. Now shall we go on?"

Penny sat staring at him in bewilderment. "It's not fair of you to look so idiotic," she said involuntarily. "People get led astray. I suppose you won't even be particularly bucked to know that you've guessed right?"

The young man with the simple face and gentle ineffectual manner looked uncomfortable.

"All this praise makes me unhappy," he said. "I must admit I wasn't sure until I was in the car this morning that you had the treasure in the suitcase. It was only when you were so anxious for me not to sit beside it that I knew that the rat I saw floating in the air was a *bona fide* rose to nip in the bud."

Penny drew a deep breath. "Well," she said, "I suppose we turn back."

Mr Campion laid a hand on the driving wheel.

"Please," he said pleadingly, with something faintly reminiscent of seriousness on his face, "please listen to me for a little longer. You two have got to be friends with me. We're all in the soup together. Consider the facts. Here we are, sitting in the middle of a public highway with a highly incriminating piece of antiquity in the back of the car. That's bad to start with. Then—and this is much more worthy of note—if I was bright enough to spot what you were up to, what about our nosy friends who are out for crime anyhow?"

"You mean you think they might actually come down on us on the way?" said Penny apprehensively. This aspect of the case had clearly never occurred to her. "And yet," she added, a flash of suspicion showing in her blue eyes, "it's perfectly ridiculous. How is any outside person to know that the Chalice isn't still in the Cup House? Only Father, Val, Branch, you and I know it's gone."

"You forget," said Mr Campion gently. "You had visitors yesterday, and the unpleasant Mr Putnam, who is making use of your retiring little friend Mrs Shannon, had a face vaguely familiar to me."

Penny's eyes flickered. "That revolting little man?" she said. "Is he the—the big fellow you were talking about? You know, when you said the stream was full of minnows and there were no big fish about."

Mr Campion regarded her gravely. "I'm afraid not," he said. "But he's certainly in the dab class. I fancy his real name is Matthew Sanderson. That's why I kept so quiet; I was afraid he might spot me. I don't think he did, but he certainly noticed that the Chalice had disappeared. Hang it all, he couldn't very well miss it. Anyhow, if he is the man I think he is, then I'm open to bet that he's not twenty miles away from here now."

Penny looked at him helplessly. "I've been a fool," she said. "We'll go back at once."

Campion hesitated. "Wait a minute," he said, and glanced at Beth. "I don't know if we ought to drag Miss Cairey into all this—"

An expression of determination appeared upon the elder girl's face, and her lips were set in a firm hard line.

"I'm in this with Penny," she said.

To her surprise he nodded gravely. "I told Val you'd be game," he said. "He should be waiting for us at a little pub called 'The Case is Altered' just outside Coggeshall."

"Val?" Penny was startled. "What does he know about it?"

"Just about as much as I do," said Mr Campion, considering. "While you were shouting your travelling arrangements over the phone in the hall last night, he and I were discussing fat stock prices and whatnot in the smoking-room. I told him what I thought, and I persuaded him to let you carry on the good work and smuggle the thing out of the house for us."

"Then you think it's a good idea—the safe deposit?" said Beth anxiously. "I told Penny I was sure that was the only certain way of keeping it safe."

Mr Campion did not answer her immediately. He had resumed his place in the car and sat regarding the dashboard thoughtfully as though he were making up his mind how much to say.

"Well, hardly, to begin with," he ventured finally. "Although perhaps it may come to that in the end. In the meantime I wondered if we couldn't beat our friend Arthur Earle at his own game. There's an old firm in the city—or rather the last remaining member of an old firm—who'd turn us out a first-rate copy of the Chalice, and somehow I'd rather be playing hide-and-seek with that than with the real one. I fancy we shall have to show a bait, you see, to catch the big fish."

"Just one thing," said Penny. "What about Father? Does he know anything? I seem to have made a pretty prize fool of myself."

Mr Campion looked if possible more vague than ever. "Your father, I regret to say," he murmured, and Penny was convinced that he was lying, "I thought it best to keep in the dark. You left your own excuses. Val no doubt left mine and his own. But," he went on gravely, "that is hardly the most important point to be considered at the moment. What we have to arrange now is the safe conveyance of the Chalice to London."

Penny swung the car up the narrow white road.

"I don't know if I'm going to agree with all this," she said warningly, "but I'd like to see Val. Of course, you're not really serious about this attack on the road, are you?"

Mr Campion regarded her solemnly. "The chivalry of the road," he said, "is not what it was when I used to drive my four-in-hand to Richmond, don't you know. Natty Johnson is no Duval, but he might make a very fine Abbershaw, and old Putnam Sanderson can level a first-class blunderbuss. On the whole, I should think we were certainly in for fun of some sort."

"But if this is true," said Beth indignantly, "why are we going on? How do you know we shan't be held up before we get to Coggeshall?"

"Deduction, dear lady," explained Mr Campion obligingly. "There are two roads from Sanctuary to Coggeshall. You might have taken either. After Coggeshall you must go straight to Kelvedon, and thence by main road. I fancy they'll be patrolling the main road looking for us."

In spite of herself Penny was impressed. "Well, you're thorough, anyway," she said grudgingly.

"And clean," said Mr Campion. "In my last place the lady said no home was complete without one of these—hygienic, colourful, and only ten cents down. Get Campion-conscious to-day. Of course," he went on, "I suppose we could attempt to make a detour, but considering all things I think that the telephone wires are probably busy, and at the same time I'm rather anxious to catch a glimpse of our friends in action. I think the quicker we push on the better."

Penny nodded. "All right," she said without resentment. "We leave it to you."

The Case is Altered was a small and unpretentious red brick building standing back from the road and fronted by a square gravel yard. Mr Campion descended, and cautiously taking the suitcase from the dickey, preceded the ladies into the bar parlour, an unlovely apartment principally ornamented by large oleographs of *"The Empty Chair"*, *"The Death of Nelson"*, and *"The Monarch of the Glen"*, and furnished with vast quantities of floral china, bamboo furniture, and a pot of paper roses. The atmosphere was flavoured with new oilcloth and stale beer, and the motif was sedate preservation.

Val was standing on the hearthrug when they entered, a slightly amused expression on his face. Penny reddened when she saw him, and walking towards him raised her face defiantly to his.

"Well?" she said.

He kissed her.

"Honesty is the best policy, my girl," he said. "Have some ginger beer?"

Penny caught her brother's arm. "Val, do you realize," she said, "here we are, miles from home, with the—the *Thing* actually in a portmanteau. I feel as if we might be struck by a thunderbolt for impudence."

Val put his arm round her shoulders. "Leave it to Albert," he said. "He spotted your little game. He seems to have one of his own."

They turned to Campion inquiringly and he grinned.

"Well, look here," he said, "if you don't want to play darts or try the local beer or otherwise disport yourselves, I think the sooner we get on the better. What I suggest is that we split up. Penny, you and I will take the precious suitcase in the two-seater. Val and Miss Cairey will follow close behind to come to our assistance if necessary. Have you got enough petrol?" Penny looked at him in surprise. "I think so," she said, but as he hesitated she added, laughing, "I'll go and see if you like."

Mr Campion looked more foolish than before. "Twice armed is he who speeds with an excuse, but thrice is he whose car is full of juice," he remarked absently.

Penny went out, leaving the door open, and was just about

to return after satisfying herself that all was well, when the young man came out of the doorway bearing the suitcase.

"We'll get on, if you don't mind," he said. "Val's just squaring up with the good lady of the establishment. They'll follow immediately."

Penny glanced about her. "Where is the other car?" she demanded.

There was a Ford trade van standing beside the bar entrance, but no sign of a private car.

"Round at the back," said Campion glibly. "There's a petrol pump there."

He dropped the suitcase carefully into the back of the car and sprang in beside the girl. "Now let's drive like fun," he said happily. "How about letting me have the wheel? I've got testimonials from every magistrate in the county."

Somewhat reluctantly the girl gave up her place, but Mr Campion's driving soon resigned her to the change. He drove with the apparent omnipotence of the born motorist, and all the time he chattered happily in an inconsequential fashion that gave her no time to consider anyone or anything but himself.

"I love cars," he said ecstatically. "I knew a man once—he was a relation of mine as a matter of fact—who had one of the earliest of the breed. I believe it was a roller-skate to start with, but he kept on improving it and it got on wonderfully. About 1904 it was going really strong. It had gadgets all over it then: finally I believe he overdid the thing, but when I knew it you could light a cigarette from almost any pipe under the bonnet, and my relation made tea in the radiator as well as installing a sort of mechanical picnic-basket between the two back wheels. Then one day it died in Trafalgar Square and so—" he finished oracularly—"the first coffee-stall was born. Phoenix-fashion, you know. But perhaps you're not liking this?" he ventured, regarding her anxiously. "After all, I have been a bit trying this morning, haven't I?"

Penny smiled faintly at him.

"I don't really dislike you," she said. "No, go on. Some people drive better when they're talking, I think, don't you?"

"That's not how a young lady should talk," said Mr Campion reprovingly. "It's the manners of the modern girl I deplore most. When I was a young man—years before I went to India, don't you know, to see about the Mutiny—women were women. Egad, yes. How they blushed when I passed."

Penny shot a sidelong glance in his direction. He was pale and foolish-looking as ever, and seemed to be in deadly earnest.

"Are you trying to amuse me or are you just getting it out of your system?" she said.

"Emancipated, that's what you are," said Mr Campion, suddenly dropping the Anglo-Indian drawl he had adopted for the last part of his homily. "Emancipated and proud of yourself. Stap my crinoline, Amelia, if you don't think you're a better man than I am!"

Penny laughed. "You're all right, really," she said. "When does the fun begin?"

"Any time from now on," said Mr Campion gaily, as he swung the little car into the main road. Penny glanced nervously over her shoulder.

"There's no sign of the others yet," she said.

Her companion looked faintly perturbed.

"Can't help that," he said.

It was now about half-past eleven o'clock, and although a Friday morning, the road was not as crowded as it would become later in the day. Mr Campion drove fiercely, overtaking everything that presented itself. On the long straight strip outside Witham he once more broke into his peculiar brand of one-sided conversation.

"Then there's poetry," he said. "Here is to-day's beautiful thought:

> There was an ex-mayor in a garden
> A-playing upon a bombardon,
> His tunes were flat, crude,
> Broad, uncivic, rude,
> And—

"I don't like the look of that car which has just passed us. It's an old Staff Benz, isn't it? Sit still, and whatever you do don't try and hit anybody. If you lose your head it doesn't matter, but don't try to hit out."

On the last word he jammed on the brakes and brought the car to a standstill only just in time, as the old German staff car, heavy as a lorry and fast as a racer, swerved violently across the road in front of them and came to a full stop diagonally across their path so that they were hemmed in by the angle. The whole thing was so neatly timed that there was no escape. It was only by brilliant driving that Mr Campion had succeeded in pulling up at all.

What took place immediately afterwards happened with the speed and precision of a well-planned smash-and-grab raid. Hardly were the two cars stationary before five men had slipped out of the Benz, the driver alone remaining in his seat, and the sports car was surrounded. The raiding party swarmed over the little car. There was no outward show of violence, and it was only when Penny glanced up into the face of the man who had stationed himself on the running-board at her side that she fully realized that the newcomers were definitely hostile.

She shot a sidelong terrified glance at Mr Campion, and saw that the man upon his side had laid a hand in an apparently friendly fashion on the back of his neck, the only untoward feature of the gesture being that in the hand was a revolver.

A third man leaned negligently against the bonnet, his hand in the pocket of his coat, while a fourth, with remarkable coolness, stood by the back of the Benz to signal that all was well to any passing motorist who might stop, suspecting a smash.

They were all heavy, flashily dressed specimens of the type only too well known to the racecourse bookmaker.

Penny opened her mouth. She was vaguely conscious of other cars on the road. The man at her side gripped her arm.

"Hold your tongue, miss," he said softly. "No yelping. Now then, where is it?"

Penny glanced at Albert. He was sitting very still, his expression a complete blank.

"No—no," he said, in a slightly high-pitched voice, "I do not wish to subscribe. I am not a music lover. Go and play outside the next house."

The stranger's hand still rested caressingly on the back of his neck.

"Now then, no acting 'crackers'," he said. "Where is it?"

"You should take glycerine for your voice and peppermints for your breath, my friend," continued Mr Campion querulously. "Don't bellow at me. I'm not deaf."

His interlocutor summoned the man who leant so negligently against the bonnet. "There's nothing in the front of the car," he said. "Have a squint into the dickey."

"No!" Penny could not repress a little cry of horror.

The man with the gun, who seemed to be in charge of the proceedings, grinned. "Thank you kindly, miss," he said sarcastically. "A girl and a loony. It's like stealing a bottle from a baby."

"There's only my lunch in there," said Mr Campion, but Penny noticed that his voice betrayed nothing but nervousness.

"Is that so?" The third man lifted out the suitcase. "This is it," he said. "It weighs a ton. The rest of the car is empty, anyhow."

Too terror-stricken to speak, Penny glanced wildly up the road only to see a Rolls-Royce and a van being waved on by their persecutors.

"'Ere, these locks 'ave been bunged up," said a voice behind her. "Give us yer knife."

The man with the gun glanced down the road, apprehensively it seemed to Penny. "Stick it in the bus," he said. "There's nothing else here, anyhow. Now then, boys, scarpa!"

His four satellites were back in the Benz with the precious suitcase within ten seconds. The driver swung the car back with a roar, and the man with the gun gave up his position and leapt for it as it passed. They had chosen a moment when the coast was clear, and the whole astounding episode was over in a space of time a little under five minutes.

Mr Campion freed his brakes and started the engine, but instead of turning and following the retreating raiders as Penny had half hoped, half feared he would, he sent the car careering down the road towards London, and the speedometer finger crept round the dial like a stop watch.

It was not until they reached Witham and crawled through the narrow street that Mr Campion permitted himself a glance at his companion. Before then the car had occupied his whole attention. To his horror she was in tears. For the first time that day his nerve failed him.

CHAPTER TWELVE

Holding the Baby

"**A**ND HE NEVER STOPPED *once to beg pardon,*" said Mr Campion, as he swung the sports car neatly into the big yard at the back of the Huguenot's Arms at Witham and brought it to a stop within a yard of the pump.

Penny hastily dabbed away her tears. "What on earth are you talking about?"

"Poetry," said Mr Campion. "The highest within me. Soul juice, in fact. It's the last line of the Neo-Georgian sonnet I was declaiming to you when the rude gentleman with the acquisitive instinct stopped us. Don't you remember—about the civic person in the garden? I'd better recite the whole thing to you."

Penny put out her hand appealingly. "Don't," she said. "It's awfully good of you to try to cheer me up, but you can't realize, as a stranger, what this means. That suitcase contained the one thing that matters most in the world. I'm afraid I've lost my nerve completely. We must get to the police."

Mr Campion sat perfectly still, regarding her with owlish solemnity.

"You're the first person I've met to feel so sensibly about a couple of bottles of bitter," he said. "I had no idea you'd get het-up like this."

Penny stared at him, the truth slowly dawning upon her.

"Albert," she said, "you—"

He laid a hand upon her arm. "Don't spoil the fun," he said. "Look."

Even as he spoke there came the roar of an engine from outside and a trade van jolted slowly into the yard. The cab was facing them, and a gasp of mingled amusement and relief escaped Penny.

Val sat at the steering wheel, a peaked cap pulled well down over his eyes and a cheap yellow mackintosh buttoned tightly up to his throat. He had a strap buckled across one shoulder which suggested admirably the presence of a leather cash satchel. A pencil behind his ear finished the ensemble. The metamorphosis was perfect. Anyone would have been deceived.

The *chef-d' œuvre* of the outfit, however, was Beth. She had pushed her smart beret on to the back of her head, reddened her lips until they looked sticky, plastered a kiss-curl in the middle of her forehead, and had removed the jacket of her three-piece suit so that she was in a blouse and skirt. She was smiling complacently, her big dark eyes dancing with amusement. And in her arms, clasped tightly against her breast, was a precious bundle swaddled in white shawls with a lace veil over the upper part.

"There," said Mr Campion. "All done with a few common chalks. Our young Harry taking his missus and the kid for a trip during business hours. 'Domesticity versus Efficiency', or 'All His Own Work'."

Penny chuckled. "You're wonderful," she said. "And the baby, of course—?"

"Is worth his weight in gold. Let's leave it at that," said Mr

Campion. "Now, since this trip seems to have degenerated into a pub-crawl, suppose we go into the private room which Val I hope has booked on the phone and we'll shuffle and cut again."

Ten minutes later, in a small and stuffy room on the first floor of the old road house, Mr Campion made his apologies to Penny.

"I've behaved like a common or garden toot," he said with real penitence in his eyes. "But you see, there wasn't time to go into full explanations at Coggeshall—and then you might not have agreed. And I did so want to get a squint at Uncle Beastly's boy friends in action. I didn't think there'd be any real danger, and there wasn't, you know. Will you forgive me?"

Penny sat down in a rickety wicker arm-chair. "That's all right," she said weakly. "What happens next?"

Beth, who was standing before the mirror over the fireplace rearranging her make-up, turned to her friend.

"When we passed you and the man who was holding you up signed to us to go on, I thought I'd die," she said.

"If this had been a real baby I'd have squeezed the life out of it. They didn't suspect us for a moment, though, and later on, when you passed us again, we knew it was all right."

Penny passed a hand over her forehead. "Who worked it all out?" she said. "I suppose you had the shawls and stuff with you, Val?"

Her brother nodded. "When you went out to see if there was enough petrol we swapped the—contents of the suitcase for a couple of quart bottles of bitter, and then I explained to Beth. She's been wonderful."

He cast an admiring glance at the little dark-haired girl. Beth changed the subject.

"Did you find out what you wanted to know about the gangsters, Mr Campion?" she said. "I mean—did you recognize any of them?"

"Yes and no, as they say in legal circles," said Mr Campion. "The unsavoury little object who leant on our bonnet, Penny, was our Natty Johnson, an old thorn in Lugg's flesh. Two others were 'whizz boys'—pickpockets or sneak-thieves, you know—and the gentleman who did the talking and tickled my neck with a gun muzzle is 'Fingers' Hawkins, an old associate of 'Putnam' Sanderson. All sound reliable workmen whose services can be obtained for a moderate fee. The driver I was unable to see, although his was a nice professional piece of work. They're now probably swigging the beer and playing 'who says the rudest word'. That's why we needn't fear reprisals at the moment. They've got no personal animosity, if you get me. They'll wait for instructions before they do anything else. It doesn't tell us much, unfortunately."

Val lounged forward. "Now I suppose we send these two kids home?" he said.

"A remark that might have been better put," said Mr Campion mildly. "What I was hoping we could persuade our two young female friends to do is to catch the twelve-thirty to Hadleigh from the station opposite, while we sally forth to the city in their car with their treasure." He looked from one to the other of the two girls dubiously. "I suppose you're going to be furious?" he inquired.

Penny looked disappointed, but Beth chuckled. "I'll say they've got a nerve," she said. "Still, I guess we'll have to let them have their own way. This is strong man's work." She imitated Val's somewhat unctuous delivery, and the boy laughed.

"She's been getting at me all the way along," he said. "You wait till this thing's over and I'll show you the lighter side of country life."

Beth smiled. "It's had its moments already," she said, and placed the shawl-wrapped bundle in his arms.

"How about the van?" said Penny.

"That's all right," said Val. "I arranged with the man to

leave it. It belongs to Mudds', of Ipwich. Now, suppose we get along?"

He insisted that he would accompany the girls to the station opposite, while Mr Campion got out the car and invested in another suitcase.

"When will you be back?" inquired Penny in the doorway.

"To-morrow, if all goes well." Campion spoke lightly. "In the meantime rely on Lugg, my other ego. I don't think there's a chance of any trouble, but should the worst happen he's as good as a police force and about as beautiful. He's going to the nation when I die. Tell him not to wear my socks, by the way. Also my pullover in the School colours. I have spies everywhere."

She laughed and went out. Mr Campion looked after her reflectively. "Such a nice girl," he observed to the world at large. "Why in Heaven's name couldn't Marlowe Lobbett have waited a bit and picked on her instead of Biddy?"

He and Val were on the road again within twenty minutes. The younger man seemed much more cheerful than before.

"Do you know," he confided after a long period of silence, "there's something quite different about that girl, Beth. She's got a sort of charm. I've hated women for so long," he went on diffidently, "that it's marvellous to find one who breaks down your prejudices. In spite of your being such a funny bird you must know what I mean."

"You forget I am wedded to my art," said Mr Campion with great solemnity. "Since I took up woodcraft women have had no place in my life."

"I mean seriously," said Val, a little nettled.

A slightly weary expression entered Mr Campion's pale eyes behind his enormous spectacles. "Seriously, my dear old bird," he said, "Ophelia married Macbeth in my Hamlet. Now, for Heaven's sake get your mind on the business in hand."

Val leant back in the car. "You drive magnificently," he said. "I'm not sure if it's her voice or her eyes that are most attractive—which would you say?" he added irrelevantly.

Mr Campion did not reply immediately, and the little car sped on towards the city.

"We'll go straight there if you don't mind." It was almost an hour later when he spoke again as he turned the car deviously through Aldgate and made for that ancient and slightly gloomy section of the city which is called Poultry.

Val sat forward.

"Not at all—good idea," he said. "Although, I say, Campion, you're sure it's safe?"

Mr Campion shrugged his shoulders. "Melchizadek's safe enough," he said. "Patronized by all the best people since the first George, don't you know. And as silent as the grave. An old friend of mine, too. But, of course, I don't suppose he's bullet-proof if it comes to that. Still, I'd like his opinion on the chances of getting an indetectable copy made. Frankly, Val, how far back does this Chalice date?"

The younger man hesitated. "It's hard to say, really," he said at length. "It's pre-Conquest, anyhow."

Mr Campion all but stopped the car, and the face he turned towards his passenger was blank with astonishment. "Look here," he said, "you don't mean to say this thing we've got in the suitcase is a thousand years old, do you?"

"My dear fellow, of course it is." Val was a little hurt. "You know the legends about it as well as I do."

Mr Campion was silent, and the other went on. "Why the amazement?" he demanded.

"Nothing," said his companion. "The idea suddenly struck me all of a heap, that's all. Here have we been playing 'body in the bag' with it all the morning and its importance suddenly came home to me. Here we are, by the way."

He turned the car dexterously into a narrow blind alley

and pulled up outside a small old-fashioned shop, or rather a building with a shop window which had been half covered over with gold and black paint so that it resembled one of the many wholesale businesses with which the neighbourhood abounded. The heavy door with its shining brass trimmings stood ajar, and Mr. Campion dismounted, and lifting out the new suitcase walked into the building. Val followed him.

A small brass plate with the name "I. Melchizadek" engraved upon it was fixed directly beneath the old-fashioned bell-pull. Val noticed that there was no sign of any other business in the building. He followed Campion into a large outer office with a flimsy wooden barrier across it. It all seemed very quiet and deserted, and save for two or three small showcases containing beautifully worked replicas of obscure medals and diplomatic jewellery there was no indication of the business of the firm.

Immediately upon their arrival a slight, suave young man rose from behind a roll-top desk set in the far corner behind the barrier and came towards them. Mr Campion took a card from his pocket and handed it to him.

"Will you ask Mr Melchizadek if he can spare me a few moments?" he asked.

The young man took the card and repeated the name aloud.

"Mr Christopher Twelvetrees."

"Hullo," said Val, "you've made—"

To his astonishment Mr Campion signalled to him to be quiet and nodded to the clerk. "That's all right," he said. "Mr Melchizadek knows me."

As the young man disappeared Campion turned an apologetic face to his friend. "I ought to have warned you about my many *noms de guerre,*" he said. "It's just so that my best friends can't tell me. You won't forget, will you? I'm Christopher Twelvetrees until we get outside."

Considerably bewildered, Val had only just time to nod in silent acquiescence when the door of the inner office through which the clerk had disappeared re-opened to admit one of the most striking-looking old men he had ever seen.

Mr Israel Melchizadek was that miracle of good breeding, the refined and intellectual Jew. Looking at him one was irresistibly reminded of the fact that his ancestors had ancestors who had conversed with Jehovah. He was nearing seventy years of age, a tall, lean old fellow with a firm delicate face of what might well have been polished ivory. He was clean-shaven and his white hair was cut close to his head. He came forward with outstretched hand.

"Mr Twelvetrees," he said, "I am pleased to see you." His voice had a luxurious quality which heightened the peculiar Oriental note of his whole personality. Campion shook hands and introduced Val.

The boy was conscious of little shrewd black eyes peering into his face, summing him up with unerring judgement. In spite of himself he was impressed. Mr Melchizadek glanced at the suitcase.

"If you'll come into my office, Mr Twelvetrees," he said, "we can speak without being overheard or interrupted."

He led the way through the second doorway down a short corridor, and ushered them into a small luxurious room which served as a perfect frame for his remarkable personality.

The floor was covered with an ancient Persian rug, while the walls were hung with fine paintings; a David, a Zoffany, and, over the mantel, the head of a very beautiful woman by de Laszlo.

An immense table desk took up most of the room, and after setting chairs for his clients Mr Melchizadek sat down behind it.

"Now, Mr Twelvetrees," he said, "what can I do for you?"

He hesitated. "You wish me to make a copy, perhaps? Perhaps of a certain very famous chalice?"

Mr Campion raised his eyebrows.

"Taking the long road, sir?" he inquired affably.

The old man shook his head and for a moment, his thin lips parted in a smile.

"No, my friend," he said. "I have too many clients to follow any road but my own."

Campion sighed. "Thank Heaven for that," he said. "Well, of course, you're right. I see you appreciate the gravity of the situation. What we've got here is nothing more nor less than the Gyrth Chalice."

He picked up the suitcase and laid it reverently upon the desk. The old man rose and came forward.

"I have never seen it," he said, "although of course its history—or rather its legend—is quite well known to me. Really, this is going to be a most delightful experience for me, Mr Gyrth," he added, glancing at Val. "In the last two hundred years we have been privileged to handle many treasures, but even so this is a memorable occasion."

"Over a thousand years old," said Mr Campion profoundly, and, Val thought, a little foolishly, as if he were particularly anxious to impress the date on the old man's mind. "Over a thousand years."

He carefully unlocked the suitcase, and having first removed the motor rug, produced the Chalice, still in its wrapping of shawls.

Mr Melchizadek was surprised and even a little shocked, it seemed to Val, by this unconventional covering. However, he said nothing until Mr Campion took off the last shawl and placed the golden cup in his hands.

The picture was one that Val never forgot. The tall, austere old man appraising the magnificent workmanship with long delicate fingers. He turned the relic over and over, peering at it through a small jeweller's glass; glancing beneath it, inside it, and finally setting it down upon the desk, and turning to his visitors. He seemed a little puzzled, ill at ease.

"Mr Twelvetrees," he said slowly, "we are old friends, you and I."

Mr Campion met his eyes.

"Mr Gyrth here, and I," he said with apparent irrelevancy, "can swear to you that that is the Gyrth Chalice. What can you tell us about it?"

For the first time Val sensed that something was wrong, and rising from his chair came to stand beside the others.

Mr Melchizadek picked up the Chalice again.

"This is a beautiful piece," he said. "The workmanship is magnificent, and the design is almost a replica of the one in the church of San Michele at Vecchia. But it is not medieval. I am not sure, but I believe that if you will allow me to look up our records, I can tell you the exact date when it was made."

An inarticulate cry escaped Val, and he opened his mouth to speak angrily. Mr Campion restrained him.

"Hang on a bit, old bird," he murmured. "This thing's getting more complicated every minute. I fancy we're on the eve of a discovery."

The silence which followed was broken by Mr Melchizadek's quiet voice. "I would rather you did not take my word for it, Mr Twelvetrees," he said. "I should like a second opinion myself. I am an old man, and remarkable freaks of period do occur. I wonder, therefore, if you would allow me to introduce a friend of mine into this discussion? Quite by chance I have in the next room one of the most famous experts on this subject in the world. He was calling on me when you arrived, and did me the honour to wait until I should be disengaged. What do you say?" He turned from Campion to Val. The boy was scarlet and frankly bewildered. Mr Melchizadek coughed.

"You can rely upon his discretion as you would upon mine," he murmured.

"Oh, certainly," said Val hurriedly, and Campion nodded to the old expert, who went silently out of the room.

Val turned to Campion. "This is madness," he said huskily. "It—"

Mr Campion laid a hand upon his shoulder. "Hold on," he said, "let them do the talking. I believe I'm getting this thing straight at last."

He had no time for further confidences as Mr Melchizadek reappeared, and behind him came a slight, agile little man, with a high forehead and a pointed vandyke beard. His appearance was familiar to both of them, and they had recognized him even before Mr Melchizadek's opening words.

"This, gentlemen, is Professor Gardner Cairey, a great American authority. Professor Cairey, allow me to present to you Mr Gyrth and Mr Christopher Twelvetrees."

CHAPTER THIRTEEN

"I. Melchizadek Fecit"

THERE WAS A CONSIDERABLE pause after the introductions. Professor Cairey stood looking at the two young men, a slightly dubious expression in his eyes, and Val, for the first time, took good stock of him.

He was a little dapper old man, with the same delightful air of suppressed enjoyment that was so noticeable in his daughter. His face was keen and clever without being disconcertingly shrewd, and there was a friendliness about him which impressed the two immediately.

He was the first to speak, revealing a quiet, pleasant voice, with a definite transatlantic intonation which somehow underlined his appreciation of the oddity of the situation. He smiled at Mr. Melchizadek.

"This is a whale of a problem," he said. "Luck has caught me out. I'm not on speaking terms with Mr Gyrth's folk, and I owe him an apology, anyway."

Then he laughed, and instantly the tension relaxed. Val

would have spoken had not Campion rested a hand on his arm, and Professor Cairey continued.

"I've been what my daughter would call a Kibitzer," he said. "In fact, I even went so far as to trespass in your garden a day or two back, Mr Gyrth. I didn't think I was seen, but in case I was perhaps I'd better explain."

Val could not be restrained. "I'm afraid we did see you, Professor," he said. "You were looking into the chapel."

The old man grimaced. "I was," he said. "I was half-way through my new book, *The Effect of the Commonwealth on East Anglian Ecclesiastical Decoration*, and I don't mind telling you I was hoping—well, to get some assistance from you folk. But I got myself in wrong with your Pa somehow, and I was as far off from the inside of your chapel as I should have been if I'd stayed at home in Westport, N.J." He hesitated and glanced at them with bright, laughing eyes. "I stuck it as long as I could," he went on, "and then the other night, before I heard of your trouble, I felt I'd attempt to have a look and finish my chapter if it meant being chased by a gardener's boy."

Val reddened. "I haven't been at home," he said. "And, of course, I'm afraid my poor aunt made things rather difficult. I'd be delighted to take you over the place any time. As a matter of fact," he added transparently, "I came up to Town part of the way with your daughter."

Mr Campion, who had been silent so far during the interview, regarded the Professor with eyes that laughed behind his spectacles.

"Professor Cairey," he said, "you're the author of *Superstition before Cotton Mather*, aren't you?"

Professor Cairey positively blushed. "That's so, Mr Twelvetrees," he said, laying particular stress on the name. "I didn't think anyone on this side took any stock of it." Val had the uncomfortable impression that these two were getting at one another with a certain playfulness which he did not understand.

Mr Campion's manner then became almost reverential. "I owe you an apology, sir," he said. "I don't mind telling you we thought you were a bird of a very different feather. In fact," he added with alarming frankness, "we thought you were out after the Chalice." Mr Melchizadek looked horrified and muttered a word of protest. The Professor soothed him with a smile.

"So I was," he said, "in a way." He turned to Val and explained himself. "Of course, I've been familiar with the history of your great treasure, Mr Gyrth. It's one of the seven wonders of the world, in my estimation. I was naturally anxious to get a glimpse of it if I could. I had heard that there was one day in the week when it was displayed to the public, and I'd have availed myself of that, only, as I say, the Cup was hidden behind bars in a bad light and there was this mite of trouble between your aunt and Mrs Cairey, and while I was hoping that the little contretemps would blow over, your poor aunt met her death, and naturally I could hardly come visiting."

Val, who seemed to have fallen completely under the spell of the old man's charming personality, would have launched out into a stream of incoherent apologies for what he knew instinctively was some appalling piece of bad manners from the late Lady Pethwick, when Mr Melchizadek's suave gentle voice forestalled him.

"I think," he ventured, "that if you would allow Professor Cairey to examine the Chalice on the table he could give an opinion of interest to all of us."

"By all means." Mr Campion stepped aside from the desk and revealed the Cup. The Professor pounced upon it with enthusiasm. He took it up, turned it over, and tested the metal with his thumb.

"I'll take the loan of your glass, Melchizadek," he said. "This is a lovely thing."

They stood watching him, fascinated. His short capable fingers moved caressingly over the ornate surface. He appraised it almost movement for movement as Mr Melchizadek had done. Finally he set it down.

"What do you want to know about it?" he said.

"What is it?" said Mr Campion quickly, before Val could get a word in.

The Professor considered. "It's a church Chalice," he said. "The design is Renaissance. But the workmanship I should say is of much later date. It's about a hundred and fifty years old."

Val looked at Campion dumbly, and Mr. Melchizadek took the treasure.

"I thought so," he said. "If you will permit me, Mr Gyrth, I think I could prove this to you. I didn't like to suggest it before in case I was mistaken."

He took a small slender-bladed knife from a drawer, and after studying the jewelled bosses round the pedestal of the cup through his lens for some minutes, finally began to prise gently round the base of one of them. Suddenly an exclamation of gratification escaped him, and putting down the instrument he unscrewed the jewel and its setting and laid it carefully on the desk. As the others crowded round him he pointed to the tiny smooth surface that was exposed.

There, only just decipherable, was the simple inscription, engraved upon the metal:

I. Melchizadek fecit
1772

"My great-grandfather," said Mr. Melchizadek simply, "the founder of this firm. He invariably signed every piece that he made, although at times it was necessary for him to do so where it would not be seen by the casual observer."

"But," said Val, refusing to be silenced any longer, "don't

you see what this means? This is what has passed for the last—well, for my own and my father's lifetime—as the Gyrth Chalice."

For a moment the Professor seemed as stupefied as Val. Then a light of understanding crept into his eyes. He crossed over to Mr Campion.

"Mr Twelvetrees," he murmured, "I'd like to have a word with you and Mr Gyrth in private. Maybe there's somewhere where we could go and talk."

Mr Campion regarded him shrewdly from behind his heavy spectacles. "I was hoping that myself," he said.

Meanwhile Val, still inarticulate and bewildered, was standing staring at the handiwork of the Melchizadek great-grandparent as if he had never seen it before. Professor Cairey took the situation in hand. He bade farewell to the old Jew, with whom he seemed to be on intimate terms, the Chalice was repacked in the suitcase, and ten minutes later all three of them were squeezed into the two-seater worming their way from the City to the West End.

It did just occur to Val that this acceptance of Professor Cairey was a little sudden, to say the least of it. But the Professor was so obviously bona fide, and his disposition so kindly, that he himself was prepared to trust him to any lengths within ten minutes of their first meeting. However, Mr Campion had never struck him as being the possessor of a particularly trusting spirit, and he was surprised.

Before they had reached Piccadilly Campion had reintroduced himself with charming naïveté, and by the time they mounted the stairs to the flat they were talking like comparatively old friends.

Val, who had been considerably astonished by the open way in which Campion had approached the place, now glanced across at him as he set a chair for their visitor.

"Last time I came here," he remarked, "I understood from

you that I was liable to be plugged at any moment if I went outside the door. Why no excitement now?"

"Now," said Mr Campion, "the damage is done, as far as they're concerned. It must be obvious by this time to everyone interested that you and I are on the job together. To put a bullet through you would be only wanton destructiveness. The good news has been brought from Aix to Ghent, as it were. Your father knows there's danger, Scotland Yard knows, every 'tec in the country may be on the job. 'George's' minions may be watching outside, but I doubt it."

Professor Cairey, who had been listening to this conversation, his round brown eyes alert with interest and his hands folded across his waist, now spoke quietly.

"I haven't been able to help gathering what the trouble is," he remarked.

Val shrugged his shoulders. "After Mr. Melchizadek's discoveries," he said slowly, "the trouble becomes absurd. In fact, the whole thing is a tragic fiasco," he added bitterly.

The Professor and Campion exchanged glances. It was the old man who spoke, however.

"I shouldn't waste your time thinking that, son," he said. "See here," he added, turning to Campion, "I'll say you'd better confess to Mr Gyrth right now, and then perhaps we can get going."

Val looked quickly at Campion who came forward modestly. "The situation is a delicate one," he murmured. "However, perhaps you're right and now is the time to get things sorted out. The truth is, Val, I had my doubts about the Chalice the moment I saw the photograph of it. Before I looked you up, therefore, I paid a visit to my old friend Professor Cairey, the greatest living expert on the subject, who, I discovered, was staying next door to the ancestral home. This is not the coincidence it sounds, you see. The Professor has confessed why he rented the next place to yours. He couldn't tell me for certain from the photographs, although he had very grave doubts." He paused, and the American nodded. Campion continued:

"Since there was a little friction between your aunt and her neighbours, I couldn't very well introduce the Professor into the bosom of the family right away. I regret to say, therefore, that I called on him, and begged him to meet me up at Melchizadek's. You see, I knew it would take more than one expert opinion to convince you that the Chalice wasn't all it set itself up to be." He paused and stood looking hesitantly at the younger man. "I'm awfully sorry," he said apologetically. "You see, I was going to persuade you to bring it up to be copied, and then the girls pinched it so obligingly for us."

Val sank down in a chair and covered his face with his hands. "It's beyond me," he said. "It seems to be the end of everything."

The Professor leant forward in his chair, and the expression upon his wise, humorous face was very kindly.

"See here," he said, "I don't want to upset any family arrangement whereby you're told certain things at a certain age. Also I appreciate the delicacy of the matter I'm presuming to discuss. But, if you'll permit me, I'd like to tell you certain facts that occur to me as they might to anyone who looked at this matter from the outside without being hampered by a lifelong association with one idea."

He paused, and Val, looking up, listened to him intently.

"If you ask me," went on the Professor, "I'd say that that very lovely piece which you have in the case there, and which has been in your chapel for the last hundred and fifty odd years, is what might be called a 'mock chalice'. You see," he continued, warming up to his subject, "most ancient ideas were simple, obvious notions; uncomplicated methods of preserving the safety of a treasure. Now in my opinion that 'mock chalice', as we'll call it, is the last of many such—probably all different in design. The real Chalice has always been kept in the background—hidden out of sight—while the show-piece took its place to appease sightseers and thieves and so forth."

Val took a deep breath. "I follow you," he said, a glimmer of hope appearing in his eyes. "You mean that the real Chalice is too valuable to be on show?"

"Absolutely—when there were marauders like your great patriot Cromwell about." The Professor spoke with the hint of a chuckle in his voice. "There are two or three examples of this happening before. I've made a study of this sort of thing, you know. In fact," he added, "I could probably tell you more about the history of your own Chalice than anyone in the world outside your own family. For instance, in the time of Richard the Second it was said to have been stolen, and again just after the Restoration. But the Gyrths' lands were never forfeited to the Crown as they would certainly have been had the real Chalice been stolen. Queen Anne granted another charter, ratifying, so to speak, your family's possession of the genuine thing."

He paused at the boy's surprise, and Campion grinned.

"The Professor's a true son of his country—he knows more about ours than we do," he remarked.

Val sat back in his chair. "Look here," he said, "if this is the 'mock chalice', as you call it, why can't we let these infernal thieves, whoever they are, have it, and say no more about it?"

Mr Campion shook his head. "That's no good," he said. "In the first place they'd spot it from the thing itself, just as we have; and in the second place, unless this forfeiting business of lands and whatnot was at any rate discussed, they'd know they hadn't got the real thing and they wouldn't be happy until they had. Infernally tenacious beggars, 'Ethel' and 'George'. No, our original scheme is the only one. We've got to find the big fish and hook him."

"You see, Mr Gyrth," the Professor put in slowly, "everything that I have told you this morning would be perfectly obvious to an intelligent thief. I imagine the people you have to deal with are men of taste and discrimination. Once they had handled this Chalice themselves they'd be bound to come to the same conclusion as I have. Unfortunately it has been described by several ancient writers. Modern delinquents have much more opportunity of finding out historical facts than their medieval counterparts."

"My dear old bird," said Mr Campion, "don't look so funereal. They don't know this yet, rest assured of that. There are probably only five people in the world at present aware of the existence of the second Chalice, and in order to preserve the secret of the real one we must hang on to the 'mock chalice' like a pair of bull pups."

"Yes, I see that." Val spoke slowly. "But where is the real Chalice—buried somewhere?"

The Professor cleared his throat. "As an outsider," he began, "I hardly like to put forward the suggestion, but it seems perfectly obvious to me—allowing for the medieval mind—that that point will be made quite clear to you on your twenty-fifth birthday."

Val started violently. "The *Room!*" he said. "Of course."

For a moment he was lost in wonderment. Then his expression changed and there was something that was almost fear in his eyes.

"But that's not all," he said huskily. It was evident that the subject so long taboo had rankled in his mind, for he spoke with eagerness, almost with relief, at being able at last to speak his pent-up suspicions.

"The room in the east wing," he said solemnly, "contains something terrible. Do you know, Campion, I may be crazy, but I can't help feeling that it's no ordinary museum exhibit. All my life my father has been over-shadowed by something. I mean," he went on, struggling vainly to express himself, "he has something on his mind—something that's almost too big for it. And my grandfather was the same. This is not a subject that's ever spoken of, and I've never mentioned it before to a soul, but there *is* something there, and it's something awe-inspiring."

There was a short silence after he had spoken, and the Professor rose to his feet. "I don't think there's any doubt," he said quietly, "that the real Chalice, which is made of English red gold, and is probably little bigger than a man's cupped hand, has a very terrible and effective guardian."

CHAPTER FOURTEEN

Fifty-seven Varieties

"ALL THESE THINGS are ordained, as the old lady said at the Church Congress," observed Mr Campion. "Everything comes to an end, and we're certainly getting a bit forrader. We shall have another expert opinion in a moment or so. My friend Inspector Stanislaus Oates is a most delightful cove. He'll turn up all bright and unofficial and tell us the betting odds."

He sank down in an arm-chair opposite Val and lit a cigarette. His friend stirred uneasily.

"We *are* having a day with the experts, aren't we?" he said. "I say, I like the Professor. Why did you keep him up your sleeve so long?"

Mr Campion spread out his hands. "Just low cunning," he said. "A foolish desire to impress. Also, you must remember, I didn't know you very well. You might not have been the sort of young person for him to associate with. Besides that, Mrs Cairey—a most charming old dear, by the way—and your aunt were playing the old feminine game of spit-scratch-and-run among the tea-cups. Sans 'purr' seems to have been your aunt's motto."

Val frowned. "Aunt Di," he said, "was what Uncle Lionel's brother Adolphe used to call a freak of Nature. I remember him saying to me: 'Val, my boy, you never get a woman who is a complete fool. Many men achieve that distinction, but never a woman. The exception which proves that rule is your Aunt Diana'. He didn't like her. I wonder what she said to Mrs Cairey. Something offensive, I'll bet."

"Something about the 'Pilgrim Fathers being Nonconformists, anyhow,' I should think," said Mr Campion judicially, as he adjusted his glasses. "Hullo," he added, pricking up his ears, "footsteps on the stairs. 'And that, if I mistake not, Watson, is our client.' He's early. As a rule they don't let him out till half-past six."

He did not trouble to rise, but shouted cheerfully: "Enter the Byng Boy! Lift the latch and come in."

A long silence followed this invitation. Mr Campion shouted again. "Come right in. All friends here. Leave your handcuffs on the hook provided by the management."

There was a footstep in the passage outside, and the next moment the door of the room in which they sat was pushed cautiously open, and a small white face topped by a battered trilby hat peered through the opening. Mr Campion sprang to his feet.

"Ernie Walker!" he said. "Shoo! Shoo! Scat! We've got a policeman coming up here."

The pale unlovely face split into a leer. "That's all right," he said. "I'm out on tick. All me papers signed up proper. I got something to tell yer. Something to make yer sit up."

Mr Campion sat down again. "Come in," he said. "Shut the door carefully behind you. Stand up straight, and wipe the egg off your upper lip."

The leer broadened. "I can grow a moustache if I like,

can't I?" said Mr Walker without malice. He edged into the room, revealing a lank, drooping figure clad in dingy tweeds grown stiff with motor-grease. He came towards Campion with a slow self-conscious swagger.

"I can do you a bit o' good, I can," he said. "But it'll cost yer a fiver."

"Just what they say in Harley Street, only not so frankly," said Mr Campion cheerfully. "What are you offering me? Pills? Or do you want to put me up for your club?"

Ernie Walker jerked his thumb towards Val. "What about 'im?" he demanded.

"That's all right. He's the Lord Harry," said Campion. "No one of importance. Carry on. What's the tale?"

"I said a fiver," said Ernie, removing his hat, out of deference, Val felt, to the title his friend had so suddenly bestowed upon him.

"You'll never get a job on the knocker like that," said Mr Campion reprovingly. "Get on with your fanny."

Ernie winked at Val. "Knows all the words, don't 'e?" he said. "If 'e was as bright as 'e thinks 'e is 'e'd 'ave spotted me this morning."

Mr Campion looked up. "Good Lord! You drove the Benz," he said. "You'll get your papers 'all torn up proper' if you don't look out."

"Steady on—steady on. I wasn't doin' nothin'. Drivin' a party for an outin'—that's wot I was up to." Ernie's expression was one of outraged innocence. "And if you don't want to know anything, you needn't. I'm treatin' yer like a friend and yer start gettin' nasty." He put on his hat.

"No need to replace the divot," said Mr Campion mildly. "You were hired for the job, I suppose?"

"That's right," said Ernie. "And I thought you might pay a fiver to find out who hired me."

Mr Campion sighed. "If you've come all this way to tell

me that Matthew Sanderson doesn't like me," he said, "you're a bigger fool than I am, Gunga Din."

"If it comes to callin' names," said Mr Walker with heat, as he struggled to repress his disappointment, "I know me piece as well as anybody."

Campion raised a hand warningly. "Hush," he said, indicating Val. "Remember the Aristocracy. Is that all you have to offer?"

"No, it ain't. Certainly Matt Sanderson engaged me, but he's working for another feller. While I was tuning up the car I kept me ears open and I 'eard 'im talkin' about the big feller. You never know when a spot of information may be useful, I says to meself."

Mr Campion's eyes flickered behind his big spectacles. "Now you're becoming mildly interesting," he said.

"It's five quid," said Ernie. "Five quid for the name o' the bloke Sanderson was workin' for."

Mr Campion felt for his note-case. "It's this cheap fiction you read," he grumbled. "This thinking in terms of fivers. Your dad would come across for half a crown." He held up five notes like a poker hand.

"Now," he said, "out with it."

Ernie became affable. "You're a gent," he said, "that's what you are. One of the nobs. Well, I 'eard Sanderson say to a pal of 'is—a stranger to the game—'I shall 'ave to answer to The Daisy for this.' That was when we was drinkin' up the beer you left in the bag. Mind yer—I didn't know it was you until I saw yer in the car. You 'ad the laugh of 'em all right. They was wild."

"The Daisy," said Mr Campion. "Are you sure?"

"That was the name. I remember it becos Alf Ridgway, the chap they used to call The Daisy, was strung up two years ago. At Manchester, that was."

"Oh," said Mr Campion, and passed over the notes, "How's the car business?"

"As good as ever it was." Mr Walker spoke with enthusiasm. "I sold a lovely repaint in Norwood last week. My brother pinched it up at Newcastle. Brought it down to the garage and we faked it up lovely—registration book and everything. I was the mug, though. The dirty little tick I sold it to—a respectable 'ouseholder, too—passed a couple o' dud notes off on me. Dishonest, that's what people are half the time."

"Hush," said Mr Campion, "here comes Stanislaus."

Ernie pocketed the notes hastily and turned expectantly towards the doorway. A moment later Inspector Stanislaus Oates appeared. He was a tall, greyish man, inclined to run to fat at the stomach, but nowhere else.

"Hullo," he said, "do you always leave the front door open?" Then, catching sight of Ernie, he added with apparent irrelevancy: "O—my—aunt!"

"I'm just off, sir." Indeed, Ernie was already moving towards the door. "I come up 'ere visitin'. Same as you, I 'ope," he added, cocking an eye slyly at his host.

Campion chuckled. "Shut the door behind you," he said pointedly. "And remember always to look at the watermark."

"What's that?" said Inspector Oates suspiciously. But already the door had closed behind the fleeting figure of the car thief, and they were alone.

Campion introduced Val, and poured the detective a whisky-and-soda. The man from Scotland Yard lounged back in his chair.

"What are you doing with that little rat?" he demanded, waving his hand in the direction of the door through which Mr Ernest Walker had so lately disappeared. He turned to Val apologetically: "Whenever I come up to see this man," he said, "I find someone on our books having a drink in the kitchen or sunning himself on the mat. Even his man is an unreformed character."

"Steady," said Mr Campion. "The name of Lugg is sacred.

I'm awfully glad you've turned up, old bird," he went on. "You're just the man I want. Do you by any chance know of a wealthy, influential man-about-the-underworld called 'The Daisy'?"

"Hanged in Manchester the twenty-seventh of November, 1928," said the man from Scotland Yard promptly. "Filthy case. Body cut in pieces, and whatnot. I remember that execution. It was raining."

"Wrong," said Mr Campion. "Guess again. I mean a much more superior person. Although," he added despondently, "it's a hundred to one on his being an amateur."

"There are fifty-seven varieties of Daisy that I know of," said Mr Oates. "If you use it as a nickname. But they're small fry—very small fry, all of 'em. What exactly are you up to now? Or is it a State Secret again?"

He laughed, and Val began to like this quiet, homely man with the twinkling grey eyes.

"Well, I'm taking the short road, as a matter of fact," said Mr Campion, and added, as his visitor looked puzzled, "as opposed to the long one, if you get my meaning."

The Inspector was very silent for some moments. Then he sighed and set down his glass. "You have my sympathy," he said. "If you go playing with fire, my lad, you'll get burnt one of these days. What help do you expect from me?"

"Don't you worry," said Mr Campion, ignoring the last question. "I shall live to be present at my godson's twenty-first. Nineteen years hence, isn't it? How is His Nibs?"

For the first time the Inspector's face became animated. "Splendid," he said. "Takes that Mickey Mouse you sent him to bed with him every night. I say, you understand I'm here utterly unofficially," he went on hurriedly. "Although if you haven't already lost whatever you're looking after why not put it in our hands absolutely, and leave it at that?" He paused. "The trouble with you," he added judicially, "is that you're so infernally keen on your job. You'll get yourself into trouble."

Mr Campion rose to his feet. "Look here, Stanislaus," he said, "you know as well as I do that in ninety-nine cases out of a hundred the police are the only people in the world to protect a man and his property. But the hundredth time, when publicity is fatal, and the only way out is a drastic spot of eradication, then the private individual has to get busy on his own account. What I want to talk to you about, however, is this. You see that suit-case over there?" He pointed to the new fibre suit-case resting upon a side table. "That," he said, "has got to be protected for the next few days. What it contains is of comparatively small intrinsic value, but the agents of our friends of the long road are after it. And once they get hold of it a very great State treasure will be in jeopardy. Do you follow me?"

The Inspector considered. "Speaking officially," he said, "I should say: 'My dear sir, put it in a bank, or a safe deposit, or the cloakroom of a railway station—or give it to me and I'll take it to the Yard'."

"Quite," said Mr Campion. "But speaking as yourself, personally, to an old friend who's in this thing up to the hilt, then what?"

"Then I'd sit on it," said the Inspector shortly. "I wouldn't take it outside this door. This is about the safest place in London. You're over a prominent police station. I'd have a Bobby on the doorstep, a couple in old Rodriguez's cookshop, and a plain-clothes man on the roof. You can hire police protection, you know."

"Fine," said Mr Campion. "How do you feel about that, Val? You stay up here with the suit-case with a small police force all round you, while I go down to Sanctuary and make an intensive effort to get a line on The Daisy?"

Val nodded. "I'll do anything you like," he said. "I'm completely in your hands. There's one thing, though. You've only got four days. Next Wednesday is the second."

"That's so," said Mr Campion. "Well, four days, then. Can you fix up the body guard, Stanislaus?"

"Sure." The Inspector picked up the telephone, and after ten minutes' intensive instruction set it down again. "There you are," he said. "Endless official forms saved you. It'll cost you a bit. Money no object, I suppose, though? By the way," he added, "hasn't an order come through to give you unofficially any assistance for which you may ask?"

Campion shot him a warning glance and he turned off the remark hastily. "I probably dreamt it," he said. He looked at Val curiously, but the boy had not noticed the incident.

"That's settled, then," said Mr Campion. "I'll wait till you're all fixed up, and go back to Sanctuary to-morrow morning. You'll find everything you want here, Val. I suppose it'll be all right with your pater?"

Val grinned. "Oh, Lord, yes," he said. "He seems to have taken you for granted since the first time he heard of you, which is rather odd, but still—the whole thing's incomprehensible. I've ceased to marvel."

The Inspector rose and stood beside his friend. "Take care," he said. "Four days isn't long to nail down a chosen expert of *Les Inconnus* and write full-stop after his name. And besides," he added with unmistakable gravity, "I should hate to see you hanged."

Mr Campion held out his hand. "A sentiment which does you credit, kind sir," he said. But there was a new solemnity beneath the lightness of his words, and the pale eyes behind the horn-rimmed spectacles were hard and determined.

CHAPTER FIFTEEN

Pharisees' Clearing

WHEN MR CAMPION sailed down the drive of the Tower at about ten o'clock the next morning, Penny met him some time before he reached the garage. She came running across the sunlit lawn towards him, her yellow hair flopping in heavy braids against her cheeks.

Campion stopped the car and she sprang on to the running-board. He noticed immediately a certain hint of excitement in her manner, and her first words were not reassuring.

"I'm so glad you've come," she said. "Something terrible has happened to Lugg."

Mr Campion took off his spectacles as though to see her better.

"You're joking," he said hopefully.

"Of course I'm not." Penny's blue eyes were dark and reproachful. "Lugg's in bed in a sort of fit. I haven't called the doctor yet, as you said on the phone last night that you'd be down early."

Mr Campion was still looking at her in incredulous

amazement. "What do you mean? A sort of fit?" he said. "Apoplexy or something?"

Penny looked uncomfortable and seemed to be debating how much to say. Eventually she took a deep breath and plunged into the story.

"It happened about dawn," she said. "I woke up hearing a sort of dreadful howling beneath my window. I looked out, and there was Lugg outside on the lawn. He was jumping about like a maniac and bellowing the place down. I was just going down myself when Branch, whose room is over mine, you know, scuttled out and fetched him in. No one could do anything with him. He was gibbering and raving, and very puffed." She paused. "It may seem absurd to say so, but it looked to me like hysterics."

Mr Campion replaced his glasses. "What an extraordinary story," he said. "I suppose he hadn't found the key to the wine cellars, by any chance?"

"Oh, no, it wasn't anything like that." Penny spoke with unusual gravity. "Don't you see what happened? He'd been down to Pharisees' Clearing. He saw what Aunt Di saw."

Her words seemed to sink into Mr Campion's brain slowly. He sat motionless in the car in the middle of the drive staring in front of him.

"My hat," he said at last. "That's a step in the right direction, if you like. I only meant to keep the old terror occupied. I had no idea there'd be any serious fun toward."

He started the car and crawled slowly forward, the girl beside him.

"Albert," she said severely, "you didn't tell him to go down there at night, did you? Because, if so, you're directly responsible for this. You didn't believe me when I told you there was something fearful there. You seem to forget that it killed Aunt Di."

Mr Campion looked hurt. "Your Aunt Diana and my

friend Magersfontein Lugg are rather different propositions," he said. "I only told him to improve the shining hour by finding out what it was down there. I'll go and see him at once. What does Branch say about it?"

"Branch is very discreet," murmured Penny. "Look here, you'd better leave the car here and go straight up."

Mr Campion raced up the narrow staircase at the back of the house which led to the servants' quarters, the expression of hurt astonishment still on his face. He found Branch on guard outside Mr Lugg's door. The little old man seemed very shaken and his delight at seeing Campion was almost pitiful.

"Oh, sir," he said, "I'm so glad you've come. It's all I can do to keep 'im quiet. If 'e shouts much louder we shan't 'ave a servant left in the 'ouse by to-night."

"What happened?" said Mr Campion, his hand on the door knob.

"I doubt not 'e went down to Pharisees' Clearing, sir." The Suffolk accent was very apparent in the old man's voice, and his gravity was profound. Mr Campion opened the door and went in.

The room was darkened, and there was a muffled wail from a bed in the far corner. He walked across the room, pulled up the blind, and let a flood of sunshine into the apartment. Then he turned to face the cowering object who peered at him wildly from beneath the bed quilt.

"Now, what the hell?" said Mr Campion.

Mr Lugg pulled himself together. The sight of his master seemed to revive those sparks of truculence still left in his nature. "I've resigned," he said at length.

"I should hope so," said Campion bitterly. "The sooner you clear out and stop disgracing me the better I shall like it."

Mr Lugg sat up in bed. "Gawd, I 'ave 'ad a night," he said weakly. "I nearly lost me reason for yer, and this is 'ow yer treat me."

"Nonsense," said Campion. "I go and leave you in a respectable household, and you bellow the place down in the middle of the night and generally carry on like an hysterical calf elephant."

The bright sunlight combined with the uncompromising attitude of his employer began to act like a tonic upon the shaken Lugg.

"I tell yer what, mate," he said solemnly, "I lost me nerve. And so 'ud you if you'd seen what I seen. Lumme, what a sight!"

Mr Campion remained contemptuous. "A couple of owls hooted at you, I suppose," he observed. "And you came back and screamed the place down."

"A couple o' blood-curdling owls," said Mr Lugg solemnly. "And some more. I'll tell you what. You spend the night in that wood and I'll take you to Colney 'Atch in the morning. That thing killed Lady Pethwick, the sight of it, that's what it did. And she wasn't no weakling, let me tell yer. She was a strong-minded woman. A weak-minded one would 'ave burst."

In spite of his picturesque remarks there was an underlying note of deadly seriousness in Mr Lugg's husky voice, and his little black eyes were frankly terror-stricken. Secretly Mr Campion was shocked. He and Lugg had been through many terrifying experiences together, and he knew that as far as concrete dangers were concerned his aide's nerves were of iron.

"Just what are you driving at?" he said, with more friendliness than before. "A white lady with her head under her arm tried to get off with you, I suppose?"

Mr Lugg glanced about him fearfully.

"No jokin' with the supernatural," he said. "You may laugh now, but you won't later on. What I saw down in that wood last night was a monster. And what's more, it's the monster that chap in the pub was tellin' me about. The one they keep in the secret room."

"Shut up," said Campion. "You're wrong there. I told you to forget that."

"All right, clever," said Mr Lugg sulkily. "But what I saw wasn't of this world, I can tell you that much. For Gawd's sake come off yer perch and listen to this seriously or I'll think I've gone off me onion."

Such an appeal from the independent, cocksure Lugg was too much for Campion. He softened visibly.

"Let's have it," he suggested. "Animal, vegetable, or mineral?"

Mr Lugg opened his mouth to speak, and shut it again, his eyes bulging, as he attempted to recall the scene of his adventure.

"I'm blowed if I know," he said at last. "You see, I was sittin' out in the clearing, like you said, smoking me pipe and wishin' it wasn't so quiet like, when I 'eard a sort of song—not church music, you know, but the sort of song an animal might sing, if you take me. I sat up, a bit rattled naturally. And then, standin' in the patch of light where the moon nipped in through the trees, I see it." He paused dramatically. "As filfy a sight as ever I clapped eyes on in all me born days. A great thin thing with little short legs and 'orns on its 'ead. It come towards me, and I didn't stay, but I tell yer what—I smelt it. Putrid, it was, like somethink dead. I lost me 'ead completely and come up to the house at forty miles an hour yelping like a puppy dawg. I expec' I made a bit of a fool of meself," he added regretfully. "But it 'ud put anyone into a ruddy funk, that would."

Mr Campion perched himself on the edge of the bedrail. Lugg was glad to see that his animosity had given place to interest.

"Horns?" he said. "Was it a sort of animal?"

"No ordin'ry animal," said Lugg with decision. "I'll tell yer what, though," he conceded, "it was like a ten-foot 'igh goat walkin' on its 'ind legs."

"This has an ancient and fishlike smell," said Mr Campion. "Are you sure it wasn't a goat?"

"You're trying to make me out a fool. I tell you this thing was about nine foot 'igh and it 'ad 'uman 'ands—because I saw 'em. Standin' out black against the sky.

Mr Campion rose to his feet. "Lugg, you win," he said. "I apologize. Now get up. And remember, whatever you do, don't breathe a word of this to the other servants. And if they know you saw a ghost, well, it was nothing to do with the room, see? Don't you breathe a word about that. By the way, I met a friend of yours in Town. Ernie Walker."

"Don't you 'ave nothin' to do with 'im." The last vestige of Mr Lugg's hysteria disappeared. "No soul above 'is work—that's the sort of bloke Ernie is. A dirty little shark 'oo'd squeal on 'is Ma for a packet o' damp fags."

Mr Campion grinned. "It seems as if you can't see a ghost in the place without my getting into bad company in your absence, doesn't it?" he said affably. "Now get up and pretend you've had a bilious attack."

"Oi, that's not quite the article," said Mr Lugg shocked. "'Eart attack, if you don't mind. I 'ave my feelings, same as you do."

Campion went out and stood for a moment on the landing, the inane expression upon his face more strongly marked than ever. He went to Sir Percival's sanctum on the first floor, and remained there for twenty minutes or so. When he came out again he was more thoughtful than ever. He was about to set off downstairs when a figure which had been curled up on the windowsill at the far end of the corridor unfolded itself and Penny came towards him.

"Well?" she said. "I hope you're convinced about Lugg now."

To her astonishment Mr Campion linked her arm through his.

"You are now, my dear Madam, about to become my Doctor Watson," he said. "You will ask the inane questions, and I shall answer them with all that scintillating and superior wisdom which makes me such a favourite at all my clubs. They used to laugh when I got up to speak. Now they gag me. But do I care? No, I speak my mind. I like a plain man, a straightforward man, a man who calls a spade a pail."

"Stop showing off," said Penny placidly, as they emerged into the garden. "What are you going to do?"

Mr Campion stopped and regarded her seriously. "Look here," he said, "you haven't quarrelled with Beth or anything?"

"Of course not. Why? I was on the phone to her last night. She naturally wanted to know all about Val staying in Town. They seem to have got on astoundingly well together, you know."

"Quite old friends, in fact," said Mr Campion. "I noticed that yesterday. Oh, I'm not so bat-eyed as you think. A youthful heart still beats beneath my nice new chest-protector and the locket containing the old school cap. No, I only asked about Beth because we are now going to visit her father, who is a very distinguished person in spite of the fact that he is a friend of mine. I ought to have told you that before, but there you are."

"Be serious," the girl begged. "You seem to forget that I don't know as much about things as you do."

"We're going to see Professor Cairey," continued Mr Campion. "Not charioted by Bacchus and his pards but via the footpath. You see," he went on as they set off across the lawn, "you're getting a big girl now, and you may be useful. The situation is roughly this. I've got three days before Val's birthday. Three days in which to spot the cause of the trouble and settle up with him. The only line I've got on the gent in question is that his pet name is 'The Daisy'."

Penny looked dubious. "It's hardly possible, is it?" she said.

Mr Campion did not answer her, but proceeded equably. "It's perfectly obvious to me," he continued, "and probably to you, my dear Watson, that there's something fishy in Pharisees' Clearing—something very fishy if Lugg is to be believed. I have a hunch that if we can lay that ghost we'll get a line on The Daisy."

"But," said Penny, "if The Daisy, as you call him, is responsible for the ghost and Aunt Di was frightened intentionally, why should the creature go on haunting?"

"That," observed Mr Campion, "is the point under consideration. Of course Lugg may have gone batty and imagined the whole thing."

Penny shot a quick glance at him. "You don't believe that," she said.

Mr Campion met her gaze.

"You," he said, "believe it's something supernatural." The girl started violently and the colour came into her face.

"Oh," she burst out suddenly, "if you only knew as much about the country folk as I do, if you'd been brought up with them, listened to their stories and heard their beliefs, you wouldn't be so supercilious about things that aren't, well, quite right things. Of course," she went on after a pause, "I'm not saying anything definite. I don't know. But ever since Aunt Di's death more and more Gypsies have been pouring into the district. They say there's a small army of them on the heath."

Mr Campion raised his eyebrows. "Good old Mrs Sarah," he said. "Always do all you can for the Benwell tribe, Penny; the finest chals and churls in the world."

Penny was mystified. "You seem to know something about everything," she said. "Why are we going to see the Professor?"

"Because," said Mr Campion, "if our bogle in Pharisees'

Clearing is a genuine local phenomenon you can bet your boots Professor Cairey knows all there is to know about it. Besides that, when dealing with the supernatural there's nothing quite so comforting as the scientific mind and a scientific explanation."

They found the Professor at work in a green canvas shelter in the garden of his attractive Tudor house, whose colour-washed walls and rusty tiled roof rose up in the midst of a tangle of flowers. The old man rose to meet them with genuine welcome in his face.

"This is delightful. You've come to lunch, I hope? Mrs Cairey is somewhere in the house and Beth with her."

Penny hesitated awkwardly, and it was Mr Campion who broached the all-important matter in hand.

"Professor," he said, "I'm in trouble again. We've come to you for help."

"Why, sure." The Professor's enthusiasm was indubitable. "Judge Lobbett, one of my greatest friends, owes his life to this young man," he added, turning to Penny. "Now what can I do for you two?"

"Have you ever heard of the ghost in Pharisees' Clearing?" said Penny, unable to control her curiosity any longer.

The Professor looked from one to the other of them, a curious expression in his round, dark eyes.

"Well," he said hesitantly, "I don't know what you'll think of me, but I've got a sort of idea that I've a photograph of it. Come into the library."

CHAPTER SIXTEEN

Phenomenon

IN THE DEPTHS of the Professor's study, a cool old-fashioned room with stamped plaster walls striped with unstained oak beams, Penny and Mr Campion listened to an extraordinary story.

"I don't want you to get me wrong," said the Professor, as he knelt down before an exquisite old lowboy and unlocked the bottom drawer. "I admit I've been poking my nose into other people's business and I've been trespassing. Way over across the water we don't mind if we do set our feet in a neighbour's back garden," he added slyly.

Penny looked profoundly uncomfortable. "Don't tease us about that, Professor," she said pleadingly. "That was just an unfortunate accident. Aunt Di made it awkward all round, and Father was silly about the Gypsies."

The Professor paused with his hand on the drawer handle.

"You don't say it was that?" he said. "Well, your father had one up on me that time. I've lost half a dozen pedigree hens to those darn hobos. I sent them off my land yesterday morning when I saw they were back again."

Penny hardly heard him. "The—the ghost," she said. "Is it a real one?"

The Professor looked at her curiously and did not answer directly. "You'll see," he said. "As I was saying, I've been trespassing. I heard this yarn of a ghost long before your poor aunt passed over, and naturally I was interested. You see, I'm something of an authority on medieval witchcraft and magic—it's my hobby, you know—and there were certain peculiarities about the tales I heard that got me interested. I sat up waiting in your father's wood for several nights and I can't say I saw anything. Still, I had a gun with me and maybe that had something to do with it."

He paused and looked at Penny searchingly. "You probably know these stories better than I do," he said.

She nodded. "I've heard several things," she admitted. "But the photograph—?"

"I was coming to that," said the Professor. "I don't know if you know it, but there's a way that folks have for setting a trap to photograph animals at night. It's a dandy little arrangement whereby the animal jerks a string stretched across its path, that releases a flashlight and snaps open the camera lens. I set a thing like this two or three nights, and finally, about a fortnight back, I got a result. Now I'll show you."

He rose to his feet carrying a big envelope. While they watched him he raised the flap and produced a large shiny reproduction.

"I had it enlarged," he said. "It's not good—I warn you it's not good, but it gives you an idea."

Mr Campion and Penny bent forward eagerly. As in all flashlight photographs taken in the open at night, only a certain portion of the plate bore a clear picture, and the snapshot conveyed largely an impression of tangled leaves and branches shown up in vivid black and white. But on the edge of the circle of light, and largely obscured by the shadows, was something that was obviously a figure turned in flight.

It was horned and very tall. That was all that was clear. The rest was mostly hidden by the undergrowth and the exaggerated shadows thrown by the foliage. In the ordinary way the photograph might have been dismissed as a freak plate, an odd arrangement of light and shadow, but in view of the Professor's story and Lugg's horrific description it took on a startling significance. Seen in this light, every blur and shadow on the figure that might have passed as accidental took on a horrible suggestion of unnamable detail.

Campion looked at the Professor.

"Have you got a nice satisfying explanation for all this?" he said.

Professor Cairey's reply was guarded. "There is a possible explanation," he said, "and if it's the right one it'll be one of the most interesting examples of medieval survival I've ever heard of. Naturally I haven't cared to bring this matter up, nor to go trespassing lately. You'll appreciate that the situation was a little delicate."

"Well," said Mr Campion, straightening his back, "first catch your ghost. A cheery night's work for our little Albert."

The Professor's face flushed with enthusiasm. "I'm with you," he said. "I've been itching to do just that for the last month."

There was something boyish in the old man's heartiness which Penny hardly shared. "Look here," she said quietly, "if you really mean to go wandering about in Pharisees' Clearing to-night I think I can put you on to the man to help you. Young Peck. He works for you, doesn't he, Professor? He and his father know more about the countryside than all the rest of Sanctuary put together."

Professor Cairey beamed.

"I was just about to suggest him myself," he said. "As a matter of fact, old Peck has been my chief source of information in this affair. A fine old chap," he added, turning to Mr Campion. "It took me three weeks to find out what he was talking about, but we get on famously now. He has a cottage on the edge of my willow plantation, and he spends all his days sitting in the sun 'harkening in', as he calls it. His son's put him up a radio. See here," he went on, "if you'll stay to lunch we'll go down there afterwards and get the youngster on the job."

"Oh, we can't force ourselves on you like this," Penny protested. But the luncheon gong silenced her and the Professor bore them off in triumph to the dining-room.

Mrs. Cairey, a gracious little woman with grey eyes and white shingled hair, received the unexpected addition to her luncheon table with charming equanimity. Whatever her quarrel with Lady Pethwick had been, she did not allow its shadow to be visited upon the young people. Mr Campion appeared to be an old favourite of hers, and Penny was a friend of Beth's. By her pleasant personality the meal was made a jolly one in spite of the sinister business which lay in the background of the minds of at least three of the party.

"I'm real glad Albert is no longer a secret," said she as they settled themselves at the fine Georgian table in the graceful flower-filled room. "Beth and I kept our promise to you," she went on, smiling at the young man. "Not a word about us knowing you has passed our lips. I thought this was a quiet old-fashioned county. I never dreamed I'd have so much mystery going on around me."

The Professor grinned. "Mother likes her mysteries kept in the kitchen," he said.

His wife's still beautiful face flushed. "Will I never hear the end of this teasing, Papa?" she said. "He's making game of me," she added, turning to the visitors, "because when I came over here and saw this house I was so charmed with the old brick oven and the pumps and the eighteenth-century brewhouse that I just made up my mind I wouldn't have the electric plant we planned, but I'd set up housekeeping as they did in the old days, and I'd bake and brew and I'd make Devonshire cream in the right old-fashioned way." She paused and spread out her hands expressively. "I had six girls in the kitchen before I'd finished, and not one of them could I get to do the necessary chores."

The Professor chuckled. "We bought a brewing licence down at the Post Office," he said. "But do you think one of the lads on the farm would drink the home-made stuff? Not on your life. They'd rather have their fourpence to go to the pub with."

"It was the refrigerator that did it," said Beth.

Little Mrs Cairey laughed. "How you manage to exist without ice I don't know," she said to Penny. "I stuck it out for a long time, just so Papa wouldn't get the laugh on me. Then one day Beth and I went into Colchester and got just what we wanted—all worked by paraffin. Half the village came to see it, and the tales we heard about illnesses that could only be cured by an ice cube you wouldn't believe."

Penny grinned. "They're terrible," she said. "For goodness' sake don't let yourself in for too much fairy god-mothering. You see," she went on, "all the little villages round here are really estates that have got too big and too expensive for the Squires to take care of. Death duties at ten shillings in the pound have rather spoilt the feudal system. But the people still expect to be looked after. If they live on your land they consider themselves part of the family."

"You can get very fond of them, though," said Mrs Cairey placidly. "Although they like their 'largesse', as they call it."

The meal passed, and as they rose and went out on to the

lawn Penny felt as though a peaceful interlude in a world of painful excitement had passed.

The Professor had a word with Campion in private under the pretence of showing him a magnificent rambler.

"I guess we ought to keep the ladies out of this," he said.

Mr Campion nodded. "Emphatically," he agreed. "But I don't know about Penny. She's a strong-minded young woman, and, as I take it, an old friend of the worthy gentleman we're just about to visit. I don't think she'll want to come ghost hunting, but her influence with the Pecks may be useful."

The Professor hesitated. "If it's what I think it is," he said, "it's no business for a woman. Still, as you say, Miss Gyrth may be a deal of help just at first. If you'll excuse me I'll have a word with Mother."

Five minutes later the remarkable old gentleman had succeeded in allaying both the fears and the curiosity of the feminine part of his establishment, and the three walked down the shady gravel path of his flower garden and through a tiny wicket gate into a broad green meadow beyond, which was a belt of marshy land where a clump of slender willows shook their grey leaves in the sunlight.

They were unusually silent for the best part of the way but just before they entered the clearing Penny could contain her fears no longer.

"Professor," she said, "you know something. Tell me, you don't think this—phenomenon, I suppose you'd call it—is definitely supernatural?"

The old man did not answer her immediately.

"My dear young lady," he said at last, "if it turns out to be what I think it is, it's much more unpleasant than any ghost."

He offered no further explanation and she did not like to question him, but his words left a chill upon her, and the underlying horror which seems always to lurk somewhere beneath the flamboyant loveliness of a lonely English countryside in the height of summer, a presence of that mysterious dread, which the ancients called panic, had become startlingly apparent.

Peck's cottage was one of those picturesque, insanitary thatched lath-and-plaster dwellings which stir admiration and envy in the hearts of all those who do not have to live in them. The thatch was moss-covered, and the whole building almost obscured by the high grass and overgrown bushes with which it was surrounded. A weed-grown brick path led up to the front door which stood open, revealing an old man in a battered felt hat seated on a low wooden chair beside an atrocious loud-speaker, which was at this moment murmuring a nasal reproduction of the advertising gramophone music from Radio Paris.

The old man cocked an eye at their approach, and rising with evident regret, switched off the instrument. Mr Peck senior was by no means an unhandsome old man, with a skin like red sandstone and a rugged toothless face, on the lower promontory of which he had raised a very fine tuft of bristly white hair. He was dressed in an odd assortment of garments, chiefly conspicuous among which were a pair of well-patched white canvas trousers and a red and green knitted waistcoat, obviously designed for a much larger man. His knuckles were swollen with rheumatism, and the backs of his hands were almost as furry as bears' paws.

"Old Man 'Possum," said Mr Campion, *sotto voce.*

"Be quiet," said Penny reprovingly, and went forward to greet her friend. He touched his hat to her solemnly. "Mornin', miss," he said.

"Good morning," replied Penny politely but inaccurately. "Is your son anywhere about?"

Mr Peck glanced over his shoulder. "Perce!" he bellowed. "Gentry be 'ere."

"I'm now comin'," a voice replied from the depths of the cottage, and the next moment a tall, loose-limbed young countryman appeared from an inner doorway. He was in shirt-sleeves and waistcoat, and was collarless. Smiling and unembarrassed, he indicated the seats in the cottage porch.

"If you don't mind settin' there, sirs," he said, "I'll get Miss Penny a chair."

They sat down, and instantly the little gathering took on the air of a conspiracy. Young Perce hovered behind his father's chair, his quick brown eyes watching their visitors, waiting for them to come to the object of their call.

"My j'ints be bad," Mr Peck senior put forward as an opening gambit.

"I'll send you down some of cook's linament," Penny offered.

"Huh," said Mr Peck, without pleasure or reproach.

"Don't take no notice on 'im," said Percy, reddening for his father's delinquencies. "'E's as right as ever 'e was, ain't yer, Father?"

"No I ain't," returned his father uncompromisingly, and added irrelevantly, "I 'ear that were a quiet buryin'. Yer aunt was pison to some on us. Still, I 'ont speak ill o' the dead."

A violent kick at the back of his chair almost upset him, and he sat quiet, mumbling, his lips together. His two subjects of conversation having been turned down, he was inclined to let people speak for themselves.

The formalities of the call being over, it was Penny who broached the all-important matter in hand.

"Percy," she said, "I want you to take Mr Campion and Professor Cairey down to Pharisees' Clearing to-night. They think there's—there's an animal there wants snaring. Do you understand? You wouldn't be afraid, would you?"

"No, miss. I shouldn't be scared." The boy spoke readily enough, but a shadow had passed over his face.

His father grunted. "That ain't no animal, miss," he said. "That's a spirit, like I told Master Cairey."

His tone was so matter-of-fact that Mr Campion shot an inquiring glance at him. The Professor spoke hastily.

"Of course, we won't want any tales told about this, Peck, you understand?"

The boy laughed. "Us don't talk, sir," he said. "Was you thinkin' of trappin' that, now, or do you want to shoot ut?"

"Oh, trap it certainly," said the Professor firmly.

Penny looked up.

"Percy," she said, "do you remember when Val and I were kids we helped you and young Finch to catch an old ram that had gone wild down in Happy Valley?"

"That was with a stack net, warn't ut?" The idea evidently appealed to Mr Peck junior. "Yes, us could do that. Allowin' that's real," he added, practically.

"You 'on't catch nothin'," observed his father, accepting a fill of tobacco gratefully from the Professor's pouch. "That's a spirit. You'll drop a net, and that'll go right through ut, like that was water. You can make fules of yourselves ef you like: that ain't nothin' to me. Oi won't hurt."

"Look here," said Mr Campion, breaking into the conversation for the first time. "Is the ghost in Pharisees' Clearing a new affair or has it been going on for some time?"

The elder Peck considered. "There's allus been summat strange down there," he said. "It ain't been reg'lar. Off and on, as you might say. I mind when I was a boy the whole village were quaggly about ut. Then that died down. Then about five years agoo someone seen un, and there ain't no one been there of a night time sence. I reckon' that's a spirit."

Penny looked at the younger man. "What do you think about it?" she said.

"I don't know, miss." The boy was puzzled. "I never rightly thought on ut. That never interfered with me. But I never were there at night. That's a mystery, that's what that is. Still," he added cheerfully, "I ain't afraid of ut. I fixed up that wireless for the old 'un and if I can rule that I can rule any ghost. Seems like that's magic," he observed naïvely, indicating the mass of crazy looking machinery behind the old man's chair.

The Professor rose. "Then you'll be down at Tye Hall at about eleven-thirty, with a stack net?" he said.

Mr Peck junior touched an imaginary hat. "I will, sir."

"I 'on't," said his father complacently. "I'll be harkening to a band then from Germany; they don't be so set on the Sabbath as we are 'ere, the 'eathens. And if you're wise," he added with sudden vigour, "you'll stay in yer beds, same as I do. There be more goes on at night than us thinks on. You stay out of ut, miss. That ain't no wild sheep down in Pharisees. And whatever comes on ut," he concluded solemnly, "it won't be no good."

"I'll be there," said his son, escorting them down the path. As they turned into the field the strains of the Soldiers' Chorus came floating to them across the tangled garden.

CHAPTER SEVENTEEN

The Stack Net

"IF THAT OWL CRIES again I shall have hysterics," said Beth nervously.

There were all four of them, the two girls, Professor Cairey and Mr Campion, seated in the candle-lit library at Tye Hall, waiting for half-past eleven and the arrival of young Perce with his stack net. Mrs Cairey had retired, but nothing the Professor or Mr Campion could say would persuade the two girls to follow her example.

Earlier in the evening Campion had been pleasantly fatuous, but now, as the actual moment approached, even he seemed to have become sobered by the eeriness of the occasion. The Professor was the virtual leader of the party. His boyish enthusiasm of earlier in the day had given place to a brisk, commanding mood, and he prepared for the expedition in a business-like manner.

"Torch, travelling rug, and a hip flask," he said, setting them on the table. "I shouldn't take a gun in case you're tempted to loose off. I wish you two girls would go to bed and keep out of it."

"Nonsense," said Beth stoutly. "We're going to hold the fort for you. Whether you see a ghost or not you'll be glad of something hot when you come in."

Mr Campion, who had been standing in the window, turned. "We shall have a little moon," he said. "I wish I knew what you were getting at, Professor. Am I to expect a wailing manacled figure, or are chains distinctly *passé?*"

The Professor shook his head. "I'm not going to make guesses," he said, "in case my hunch is absolutely wrong. However, the girls will be all right up here. There won't be any clutching hands or spooks blowing out the candles. It's extraordinary how these old houses do creak at night, though," he observed involuntarily.

Beth perched herself on the arm of Penny's chair. "We shall hold each other's hands till you come back," she said. "It's hot to-night, isn't it?"

As soon as she had spoken, the oppressive warmth of the night seemed to become almost unbearable. It was a breathless evening, and the garden outside was uncannily silent, so that when an owl screamed it sounded almost as if the terrifying noise were in the room.

Long awkward silences fell on the company as they waited, and even the most casual sentence seemed jerky and nervous.

A sharp tap on the window startled them violently, and it was only when a husky Suffolk voice outside remarked confidentially: "I be 'ere, sir," that they realized that the party was complete.

Next moment Mr Peck junior's head and shoulders appeared in the open half of the casement. He looked a little distrait himself, and his grin was inclined to be sheepish. He had paid special attention to his coiffure in honour of going ghost hunting with the gentry, with the result that his brown curling locks were brushed up to a stupendous quiff on the top of his head, which gave him the startling appearance of having his hair standing on end with fright.

"I see a light, so I come 'ere, sir," he said. "Not wishin' to startle the maids, like. Am I right for time?"

It was evident that he was endeavouring to appear as calm as though the trip were the most usual one in the world. The Professor hastily gathered his things together.

"We'll go out by the side door," he said to Campion. "Wait there a minute, will you, Peck? We'll come round to you."

"Good luck," said Penny.

Mr Campion followed the alert and still youthful Professor out into the stone-flagged corridor and down to the half-glass garden door. They stepped out on to a soft lawn and the Professor led the way round to the side of the house, where young Peck's gaunt figure stood silhouetted against the window. As they approached, something stirred in the darkness at their feet.

"'Tis Neb, sir," said Peck in reply to the Professor's muttered exclamation. "My owd dog. I reckoned I'd bring 'un with me. For company, like. He'll be as quiet as a meece, won't you, boy?" The last words were addressed to the dog, as he stooped and patted a shape that was rapidly becoming visible as their eyes grew accustomed to the darkness. Neb turned out to be a large, lank creature with a huge head, no tail, and ears like a calf. He moved like a shadow behind his master, being trained with that astonishing excellence that is often regarded with suspicion in those parts of the country where men preserve game.

"Have you got the net?" said Mr Campion as they crossed the grass and made for the footpath to the coppice.

"'Ere it be, sir. 'Tis a piece of an old 'un. I reckoned we couldn't managed a whole heavy 'un." He half-turned, showing a large and heavy roll of stout interlaced cords which he carried slung over his shoulder. "I brought a hurricane with me, too," he added, turning to the Professor, "but I didn't light 'un by the house."

"You can leave that," said the Professor. "I've got a torch."

Mr Peck clung to his lantern.

"I reckon I'll keep that, if you don't mind, sir," he said.

As they went through the darkness, the heavy silence closed in upon them, broken only by the rustle of their own feet in the grass.

Presently young Peck detailed his idea of their procedure.

"Since you left the trappin' of ut to me, sirs," he ventured, "I thought maybe you'd like to know how I be settin' out. I reckoned I'd find a good tree with a branch stickin' out on ut, and I'd set on that with the net, and when the thing come beneath then I'd drop that over ut."

The simplicity of this plan seemed to fill the young man with pride and delight. Mr Campion and the Professor were hardly so struck by it.

"Suppose it doesn't come under your tree?" said Mr Campion.

But the younger Peck was prepared for this emergency. "I doubt not that will, sir," he said. He paused, and after a moment or two of consideration volunteered an enlightening remark. "That chases people, sir. I was talking to the old 'un, tea-time. 'E told I that, and I thought ut out that if I was up the tree, sir, you could sort of lead that under I. Of course," he went on cheerfully, "us can't tell if that'll be there, can us?"

Mr Campion chuckled. "I see," he said. "We're the bait and the poor fish too."

Mr Peck shook with silent mirth at this sally. "That's so, sir," he whispered. "Now, if you don't mind, us'll keep quiet. I'll go first, if you please."

He slipped in front of them, treading silently as a cat, and behind him the great mongrel picked his way furtively. For some time they plodded on in silence. Mr Campion had removed his spectacles, a habit of his when action was indicated. The heat had become almost unbearable. There was only a waning moon visible, although the stars shone brightly enough.

The belt of trees which they were rapidly approaching was ink black and curiously uninviting, and the little Belgian owls with which that part of the country is infested hooted dismally from time to time. They followed the path and entered the Professor's wood, which corresponded to the larger one belonging to the Tower on the opposite side of the clearing, and through which Penny had conducted Mr Campion on the morning of Lady Pethwick's death only a week before.

Young Peck straightened himself and pushed on doggedly as the branches over his head rendered his path almost completely black. Suddenly Neb began to snuffle, his great head bowed to his master's heels. Presently he stopped dead and emitted a suppressed whinnying sound which brought the youth to a standstill.

"What is ut, boy?" whispered Peck. The dog turned silently from the path and disappeared into the darkness, to return a moment or so later with something hanging from his jaw. The youth squatted down on his heels and lit a match. The tiny flare showed the great yellow dog with a young rabbit in his mouth. The animal was quite dead, a piece of wire drawn tightly round its neck.

Peck took it from the dog and the Professor produced his torch.

"Ah," whispered the boy contemptuously as he threw the rabbit down. "There's someone about don't fear no ghosts. That ain't been snared above a 'alf-hour."

He rose to his feet, and with the dog walking obediently behind him set off once more into the silent depths of the wood. The path was one left by woodcutters in the winter, and led directly through the scrub into open space beyond.

Pharisees' Clearing was uncanny enough in the daytime, but at night it was frankly awe-inspiring. The narrow stony strip between the woods was ghostly in the starlight, and here, hemmed in between the long line of trees, the air was suffocating.

The Professor nudged Mr Campion's arm. "Almost too good to be true," he murmured.

Campion nodded. "So much for background," he whispered. "This is the place and the hour all right. When does the performance begin?"

But if Campion could be light-hearted, Mr Peck was certainly not in the same mood. As they halted in the shadows on the edge of the clearing his voice came to them husky and alarmed.

"Reckon this is the place. You draw that under 'ere and I'll catch un," he murmured, indicating the oak beneath which they stood. Then he disappeared like a shadow into the blackness, and they heard the soft scrape of his rubber shoes on the bole of the tree. He climbed like a monkey, no mean feat in the darkness with two stone of ropes tied round him, and they heard him grunt softly as he pulled himself up. A few moments later a whisper came from just above their heads.

"I'll rest 'ere time that comes."

"Where's the dog?" said the Professor softly.

"That's at the foot of the tree. That won't move."

Mr Peck seemed to have made his arrangements complete.

"What does A do now?" murmured Mr Campion.

There were faint, almost indetectable sounds all round them in the wood, minute rustlings like stifled breathings in the dark. Neither was insensible to the eeriness of the moment, but each man had his own particular interest in the matter.

"I think," the Professor whispered, "that if you'll work round the left side I'll go round the right. I got my photograph from the point where the Colonel's woodpath reaches the clearing. If we all three wait at equal distances round the oval, our quarry can't very well escape us, if it appears at all."

"I wish I'd brought my twig of rowan," said Mr Campion with apparent feeling, as he set off in the direction indicated. He moved along the side of the wood, keeping well in the shadow of the overhanging trees. Apart from the breathtaking moment when he disturbed a hare at his very feet, there were no thrills until he reached a spot about thirty yards, or so he judged, from the entrance to the Tower Wood. Here he sat down in the long grass and waited.

From the absolute silence in the clearing he guessed that the Professor had reached his point of vantage somewhere across the faintly lit stretch opposite him. The thought that there were three men and a dog watching anxiously for something unknown to appear among those loose stones and sparse clumps of coarse grass in front of him made the scene slightly more terrifying. He hunched his knees to his chin and composed himself for a long wait. He had not underestimated his vigil.

The minutes passed slowly. Once or twice a sleepy squawk sounded from the wood behind him, and, as his ears became attuned to the quietness, somewhere far away in the Tower garden a nightjar repeated its uncouth cry like an old-fashioned policeman's rattle.

And then, for the first time, Mr Campion became conscious that someone was moving clumsily in the depths of the wood behind him. He turned his head and listened intently. There was certainly nothing supernatural about this. The movements were those of a man, or some animal quite as heavy. For a minute or so he was puzzled, but a single sound reassured him, the sharp metallic click of a spring trap being set.

He listened to the rustling going farther and farther away, with occasional pauses as other traps were set. Someone evidently paid very little respect to the horror which had killed Lady Pethwick and driven Lugg into hysterics.

Once again all was silent. The illuminated hands on his watch showed half-past twelve. He sighed and settled down once more. His face in the darkness still wore his habitual expression of affable fatuity. His eyes were half-closed.

"Angels and ministers of grace defend me, I hope," he remarked under his breath, and turned up his coat to obscure the whiteness of his collar.

The oppressive warmth of the night was giving place to the first cool breath of dawn when his senses, which had gradually become drowsy, were startled into tingling life by one of the most terrible sounds he had ever heard. It was not very loud, but its quality made up for any deficiency on that score.

It was a noise that could only be described as a gentle howling, coming swiftly through the trees, and he was reminded unpleasantly of Mr Lugg's description, "The sort of song an animal might sing". Not even among native races, of whom he had some little experience, had he ever heard anything quite so blood-curdling. Quite the most terrifying point about the noise was that the sound was rhythmic. It rose and fell on a definite beat, and the pitch was high and quavering.

The sound came nearer and nearer, and quite suddenly he saw the figure.

It had advanced not from the Colonel's path, as they had expected, but from the narrow opening at the northern end of the clearing, and now stood silhouetted against the lightening sky.

Mr Campion rose to his feet, only vaguely aware of his numbed and aching limbs. The creature, whatever it was, certainly had points of elemental horror about it. It was immensely tall, as Lugg had said, and almost inconceivably thin. Long caprious horns crowned its head, and its body showed grotesque and misshapen.

It advanced down the clearing, still wailing, and Campion caught a clearer glimpse of the front of it as it came nearer.

He felt suddenly sick, and his scalp tingled.

Almost at the same moment the creature came to windward of him, and he was aware of the aroma of putrefaction, strong and unclean in his nostrils.

He darted out of his hiding-place. The figure halted and turned towards him. As it did so he caught sight of a single dead eye, blank and revolting.

Mr Campion stood his ground, and the figure came nearer. From somewhere beyond it Peck's dog had begun to howl piteously. Mr Campion gave way cautiously, edging round towards the sound, allowing the apparition to gain a little upon him as he did so. Every time it came a step forward he retreated, leading it unerringly towards the trap.

Suddenly it made a rush at him, and he turned and ran for the opening, his long thin figure a picture of terror in the night. The horned thing padded after him.

He passed the whimpering dog, and for a giddy moment the creature seemed almost upon him. There was a rustle above his head and something seemed to hover for an instant in the air like a great bat. Then the weighty stack net dropped over his pursuer and a terrible half human howl went shattering through the leaves.

"Call off the dog!" shouted the Professor as he come running up. "For God's sake call off the dog!"

CHAPTER EIGHTEEN

Survival

As HE LEVELED his torch, the Professor's hand shook violently.

The dog, after its first frenzied attack, crouched cowering by the tree trunk, while Mr Campion bent over the struggling mass in the heavy net.

The almost blinding beam of light after the intense darkness seemed paradoxically to add to the confusion. The creature, whatever it was, had ceased to struggle and lay motionless in the net, shapeless and hairy under the tangle of ropes.

The fact that the "ghost" actually lay captured at their feet brought home to both men how slender their hopes of success had been the previous evening. Yet there it lay, still incomprehensible, a grotesque and reeking mass.

Peck dropped to the ground from his branch, and they caught a glimpse of his face, pale, and glistening with great beads of sweat.

"Lumme," he kept whispering to himself pathetically. "Lumme."

The Professor bent over the net, and when he spoke there was more excitement than horror in his tone.

"I knew it," he said. "I'm right. This is one of the most remarkable survivals I've ever heard of. Do you know what we've got here?"

"A woman," said Mr Campion.

"A witch," said the Professor. "Look out—gently now. I'm afraid she has collapsed."

Very carefully he began to lift off the net. Young Peck, fighting his terror with what was, in the circumstances, real heroism, set about lighting the hurricane with hands that trembled uncontrollably.

Mr Campion and the Professor gently removed the tangle of cords. The figure on the ground did not move.

"Lands sake! I hope the shock hasn't killed her!" There was real concern in the Professor's voice. "Bring that lantern over here, will you, Peck? That's fine. Now hold this torch."

And then, as the light fell uninterruptedly upon their captive, the horror of Pharisees' Clearing lay exposed.

In many respects it differed from the conventional ghost, but chiefly it did so in the fact that none of its horror was lost when it was clearly seen.

The figure was that of a woman, old, and scarcely clad at all save for great uncured strips of goatskin draped upon her gaunt yellow form. Her headdress was composed of the animal's skull to which the hair still clung, and her face was hidden by a mask of fur, slits having been cut for the eye-holes. Her bony arms appeared to have been smeared with blood and the effect was unspeakable.

The Professor bent down and removed the headdress, picking it up gingerly by the horns. Mr Campion turned away for a moment, sickened. When he looked again a fresh shock awaited him. The woman's head lay exposed, and above her closed eyes her forehead seemed to stretch back unendingly. She was perfectly bald.

Young Peck's voice, husky with relief, answered the question in both their minds.

"'Tis owd Missus Munsey," he said. "The old un said she were a witch, but I never took no heed on ut. Lumme, who'd 'a' thought ut? I never believed them tales."

The Professor produced his travelling rug. "Since we know who it is, it makes it much simpler," he said. "Where does she live? Alone, I suppose?"

"She lives with 'er son, sir—Sammy," put in Mr Peck, whose courage was reviving apace at the discovery that the "spirit" had human substance. "'E's a natural. They ain't neither on 'em right."

"Can you lead us to the cottage?" said Campion. "Is it far? We shall have to carry this woman."

"No, that ain't no distance. One thing, that's some way from any other house."

The Professor in the meantime had succeeded in disengaging the old woman from her grisly trappings and had wrapped her in the rug.

"It occurs to me," he said, "that if we could get this poor thing to her house before we attempt to revive her it may be better for all concerned. The discovery of herself still out here surrounded by her regalia—and us—might send her raving."

Young Peck, who had stolen off some moments before, now reappeared with a light wooden hurdle, part of the boundary fence between the two estates. "I thought I seen this," he observed. "Now, if you're ready, sirs, our best way is to set 'er on 'ere and cut through the clearin'. It ain't above a 'alf mile."

They lifted the repellent figure on to the rough stretcher and set out. Since the first outburst no one had spoken. This extraordinary finish to an extraordinary expedition had silenced them for the time being. Peck took the head of the procession.

The hurricane clanked at his side, throwing a fitful distorted light on his path. His dog ran behind him, beneath the hurdle, and the Professor and Campion brought up the rear, stumbling along on the uneven ground.

For some time the Professor seemed lost in thought, but as the track led them up through the northern exit from the clearing he glanced at Campion.

"Do you get it?" he said.

"Vaguely," said Campion. "I shouldn't believe it if I hadn't seen it."

"I suspected it all along," the older man confided. "The goat horns, and those yarns of the curious chantings put the idea in my head at once. It's an interesting case. There hasn't been one approaching it for fifty years that I know of. It's an example of a blind spot. Modern civilization goes on all over the country—all over the world—and yet here and there you come across a patch that hasn't been altered for three hundred years. This woman's a lunatic, of course," he added hastily, as he became aware of Peck's large red ears strained back to catch every word. "But there's no doubt at all in my mind that she's descended from a regular line of practising witches. Some of their beliefs have been handed down to her. That costume of hers, for instance, was authentic, and a chant like that is described by several experts. She's a throw-back. Probably she realizes what she's doing only in a dim, instinctive sort of fashion. It's most interesting—most interesting."

"Yes, but *why?*" said Campion, who was more rattled than he cared to admit. "Had she any motive? Did any one put her up to it?"

The Professor considered. "We must find that out," be said. "I should say, since her nocturnal trips were so frequent, she must have had some very powerful reason. But doubtless that will emerge. Of course," he went on almost hopefully, "this may have gone on for years. Her mother may have done the same sort of thing. You'd be astonished to discover what a lot of witchcraft has been practised in this country, and my own, in the last three hundred years. It wasn't so long ago that the authorities stopped burning 'em. A couple of years before I was born, D. D. Home was expelled from Rome as a sorcerer. A lot of it survives to this day in one superstition or another. You come across extraordinary stories of this sort in the police court reports in local newspapers."

"Still, this is a bit unusual, isn't it?" said Mr Campion, indicating the shrouded figure on the hurdle they carried.

"Oh, this?" said the Professor. "I'd say so. This is a survival of one of the early forms of witchcraft, but, after all, if you find these country folk sitting on three hundred year old chairs and using Elizabethan horn spoons to mix their puddings, why shouldn't you find them—very, very rarely, I admit—practising the black rites of three or four centuries back? We'll learn a lot more when we get her home, no doubt."

"I hate to be unfeeling," said Mr Campion, straightening his back and changing his grip on the hurdle, "but I certainly wish the good lady had provided herself with a broomstick."

"We're now there," observed Peck, joining naturally in the conversation. "That's just over this rise."

Five minutes' plodding brought them to the top of the field. It was now nearing dawn, and in the east the sky was almost white. The light from the hurricane lantern was beginning to yellow.

The old woman's cottage was faintly visible, therefore. It was a mere shed of a building, quite obviously an outhouse belonging to a cottage that had long since collapsed. As they came nearer they could make out the heterogeneous collection of boards, mud and tarred sheeting of which it was composed. It was surrounded by a patch of earth trodden bare, upon which several lean fowls nestled uneasily. Some six feet from the door young Peck turned.

"Reckon us 'ad better set un down 'ere, sir," he suggested, "while us find out if Sammy's t'home. Will you wait 'ere?"

He set his end of the hurdle down gratefully, and they followed suit, easing their strained backs. Mr Peck, lantern in hand, advanced towards the crazy door, his dog at his heels. He tapped upon it softly, and receiving no answer, opened it and entered.

Almost immediately there was a terrified twittering sound from within, and a figure fled out of the doorway and disappeared into the shadows round the back of the hut. The incident was so unexpected that it jolted the nerves of the two who waited almost more than any of the foregoing adventures of the night.

"Gee! what was that?" said the Professor huskily.

He was answered by Peck, who appeared a little shame-facedly in the doorway. "That's Sammy," he said. "That didn't 'alf give I a turn. Shall us carry 'er in? 'Tis a wonderfully dirty place."

Between them they lifted the hurdle once more and bore it into the dwelling. Peck hung the lantern from a hook in the roof and it shed its uncertain light on one of the most squalid of all human habitations.

A poverty-stricken collection of furniture was strewn about the low-ceilinged room. There was a bed in one corner, and a door leading into another apartment revealed a second couch. A fireplace in which there were still the relics of a fire was built in the outer wall on the left of the door, and the floor was strewn with debris.

The Professor looked about him with distaste. "I'll say this shouldn't be allowed," be said. "Though it's hard to interfere always, I know. If you'll help me, Campion, I'll put her on the couch here."

They lifted the ragged old creature, still in the rug, and set her down on the tousled bed.

"Whose land is this?" he inquired.

"That don't rightly belong to anyone, sir," volunteered Peck. "'Tis a bit o' waste, as you might call ut. They've lived 'ere years, she and 'er mother afore 'er. There ain't nobody 'ereabouts as can do anything with 'er."

The Professor produced his flask, and pouring a little brandy into the cupped top, forced it between the old woman's lips. She stirred uneasily and mumbled a few unintelligible words.

"Take care, sir. I doubt not she'll curse you." Peck could not repress the warning.

The Professor grinned. "I doubt not," he said.

It was at this point that a shadow appeared in the doorway, and they were conscious of a white, frightened face with a straggling growth of beard on its chin peering in at them.

"Come in," said Mr Campion in a quiet, matter-of-fact voice. "Your mother fainted in the wood."

Sammy Munsey came into the room shyly, moving from side to side like a timid animal. Finally he paused beneath the light, revealing himself to be an undersized, attenuated figure clad in ragged misshapen garments. He stood smiling foolishly, swinging his arms.

Suddenly a thought seemed to occur to him, and he whimpered: "You seen 'er—you seen 'er in the wood. Don't you touch me. I won't 'ave 'em after me. I ain't done nothin'."

He exhausted himself by this outburst, and Mr Peck, who had been poking about the cabin, suddenly came forward with a pair of scarcely cold hares in his hand. Sammy snatched them from him and put them behind his back like a child, and he stood there quivering with fear and a species of temper.

"Snared," said Mr Peck with righteous indignation. "That's why they don't do no work," he added, turning to the Professor. "It's been a miracle down in the village how they lived."

Sammy looked round for some means of escape, but his

path to the doorway was blocked by his accuser. He swore vehemently for some moments, and then as though he realized his helplessness, he turned wildly to the figure on the bed.

"Mother, they've found us!" he shouted, shaking the old creature. "They've found us out!"

The old woman opened her eyes, pale, and watery, with bloodshot rims.

"I'll curse 'em," she murmured with sudden venom. "They don't none of 'em dare come near me." She turned her head and caught sight of the Professor, and raising herself upon an elbow she let out such a stream of filthy abuse that in spite of his interest he was quite obviously shocked. As he did not fly before her, however, her mood changed.

"Leave I alone," she wailed. "I ain't hurt ye. I ain't done nothin'. I 'on't hurt ye, if ye go."

It was Sammy who cut in upon her wailings, and his fear was piteous. "They've found us out," he repeated. "They've found us out."

The words seemed to sink into the old creature's mind only after some moments. She began to moan to herself.

"I couldn't 'elp ut."

It dawned upon Mr Campion that she was by no means the mental case that her son was. There was a glimmer of intelligence in the old red-rimmed eyes. As they rolled round they seemed to take in the situation pretty completely.

"Did you frighten people out of Pharisees' Clearing so that your son could poach in the wood?" he said.

She looked at him shrewdly. "You 'on't take un away if I tell ye?"

"I won't touch him," said Mr Campion. "I only want to know why you dressed up like that."

The guileless expression upon his face seemed to lull the old creature's suspicions, for her voice grew quieter.

"'E ain't right," she said. "'E couldn't catch nothing if 'e was interfered with. 'E don't know 'ow to take care of 'isself. 'E warn't afraid of I. But the others—I scared 'em." She laughed, sucking the breath in noisily between her gums.

The Professor bent over her. "Who taught you to do this?" he said.

She seemed to scent a challenge in his remark, for she snarled at him. "I larnt ut when I were young. I know more'n you think. Where be my robe?"

The Professor started. "If you mean your goatskins, they're in the wood."

The old woman attempted to stumble out of bed. "I must get they," she insisted. "There be power in they—more than you know on."

"Soon," promised Mr Campion. "Soon. Lie down now, till you're stronger."

Mrs Munsey lay back obediently, but her glance roved suspiciously about the room, and her mouth moved without words.

Mr Campion bent forward again. "Why did you set upon Lady Pethwick?" he said. "She wouldn't have stopped anyone poaching."

The old woman sat bolt upright, making a fearsome picture with her bald head and her toothless gums bared like an animal's.

"I di'nt," she said huskily.

"Then perhaps it was Sammy?" suggested Mr Campion quietly.

Mrs Munsey's red-rimmed eyes became positively venomous. She rose up in her bed and stood there, towering above them, clutching the rug about her attenuated form.

"I curse ye," she said with concentrated hatred in her voice which was uncommonly disconcerting. "I curse ye by a right line, a crooked line, a simple and a broken. By flame, by wind, by water, by a mass, by rain, and by clay. By a flying thing, by a creeping thing, by a sarpint. By an eye, by a hand, by a foot, by a crown, by a crost, by a sword and by a scourge I curse ye. *Haade, Mikaded, Rakeben, Rika, Rita lica, Tasarith, Modeca, Rabert, Tuth, Tumch.*"

As the last word left her lips she sank down upon the bed again, where she lay breathing heavily.

The Professor, who had listened to this wealth of archaic invective with unabashed delight, took a small notebook from his pocket and scribbled down a few words.

Mr Campion, who had received the full brunt of the lady's ill-wishes, stood his ground. Now that she was proving herself strong enough for the interview he felt more at ease.

"You frightened Lady Pethwick to death," he said, speaking with slow, careful deliberation as though he were talking to a child. "Afterwards, when you saw what you had done, you folded her hands and closed her eyes. Why did you do it? If it was an accident, tell us."

Sammy, who had been listening to this harangue with his mouth hanging open, now spoke in a misguided effort to exonerate his mother from what he realized vaguely was a serious charge.

"She hid from the gentry afore Daisy told 'er about 'er Ladyship. Afore then she only chased the country folk."

"Don' you listen to un!" screamed his mother, dancing up and down on the bed in her fury. "'E don't know nothin'. 'E's lyin' to 'ee."

But Mr Campion had heard quite enough to interest him.

"Who's Daisy?" he demanded, repressing every shade of interest in his voice. "Now, Sammy?"

"You can't blame Daisy!" shouted Mrs Munsey. "She didn't mean for her to die. She said for to frighten 'er, so's maybe she'd take to 'er bed for a day or two. She ain't done nothin'."

"Who *is* Daisy?" persisted Mr Campion. His pale eyes were hard, and for once there was no vacuity in his face.

"You can't blame Daisy." Mrs Munsey repeated the words vehemently. "I made the image on 'er Ladyship, I named ut, and I burnt ut."

She made this startling announcement without pride or remorse, and the Professor caught his breath.

"Was it a clay image or a wax image?" he said involuntarily.

"It was mud," said Mrs. Munsey sulkily.

Mr Campion did not hear this part of the conversation: his mind was entirely taken up with Sammy. Once again he repeated his question.

The half-wit would not look at him, but bending his head, he mumbled a few almost unintelligible words.

"That's Miss Daisy she means," he said. "My Father worked for 'er one time when 'e was alive."

It was Peck who came forward and supplied the final startling piece of information.

"Excuse me, sir," he said.

"That's Mrs Daisy 'e means. Mrs Daisy Shannon, as keeps the 'orses. 'Er they call Mrs Dick."

"Damn!" said Mr Campion, for once taken aback.

CHAPTER NINETEEN

"What Should A Do?"

"I'D SAY THAT'S ONE of the most remarkable experiences of my life," remarked the Professor to Mr Campion, as they walked back over the fields together from Mrs Munsey's cottage to the Tye Hall. "Of course, it mustn't come out," he went on. "I understand that all right. There'd be endless complications. But I shall cite you as a witness if ever I write a book of reminiscences. I suppose that boy Peck will hold his tongue?"

Mr Campion seemed to drag his thoughts back from some vague and foolish calculation. "Eh?" he said, recalling the old man's last words to his mind with a conscious effort. "Oh, Lord, yes, he'll be as silent as the grave. In the first place, I don't think he believes it happened. Besides," he added as his eye caught the top of the Tower rising above the trees in the distance, "they're used to keeping secrets round here. Old Mr Peck may hear something, but no one else."

They walked on in silence for some moments. It was now full dawn and the air was fresh and cool, and the heavy dew made the myriads of tiny cobwebs with which the grass was covered stand out in delicate tracery.

"A genuine case," the Professor repeated. "Did you hear what she said about her robe, and the image she'd made? The notion of making a clay figure of an enemy and breaking or maiming it to ensure that the same evils fall on the human is one of the oldest ideas in the world, an authentic traditional practice. And that curse she put upon you, Campion. Pure traditional magic. Each symbol, the right line and the "sarpint" and so on—each represents a different evil spirit. I shall set that down if I can when I get in."

Mr Campion shrugged his shoulders. "You might counteract it with a suitable blessing while you're about it," he said. "I hope to goodness it doesn't come off. If it does, I'm for a parroty time, as far as I remember. And just at the moment I need the angels on my side."

The Professor shot him a sly glance. "That remarkable accusation against a lady called Shannon," he said. "You're not taking that seriously, are you?"

The pale young man at his side vouchsafed no reply. His face was as expressionless as ever, and he seemed if anything a little tired. The Professor shook his head.

"A woman like Mrs Munsey might say anything," he said, and went on thoughtfully: "You can see just how it happened. There they were, friendless and practically destitute, and the boy not wise enough to go trapping satisfactorily unless he was completely undisturbed. Then his mother thinks out in that twisted, tortuous brain of hers how best she can help him, and there comes to her the memory of what her mother had taught her when she was a girl—all the old beliefs, the peculiar power of the goat. The strange half-forgotten shibboleths come crowding back into her mind, and instinctively she turns it to her own use. It wasn't the keepers she had to fear, you see. I don't preserve, so there was no man patrolling my wood. It was the other poachers. Every man's hand was against Sammy. This isn't the first or last country community that has no sympathy with the weak-minded." He laughed shortly. "It's a real primitive story, illustrating, probably, one of the earliest reasons for witchcraft—the terrorization of the strong by the weak. Most interesting."

"What'll happen to them?" said Mr Campion.

"I've been thinking that out." The Professor's face was very kindly. "The parson down here is a very decent old man. His name's Pembroke. He and I get on very well together. He's a scholar, but a man who hasn't let the teachings of the spirit blind him to a knowledge of the world. I'll see him about these two. Maybe something can be done for them. They want looking after, and they must be looked after. Lands sakes! If Mother had seen that woman it might have scared her out of her wits. I guessed more or less what was coming, but it gave me a turn."

"A turn?" said Mr Campion. "I was dizzy before we'd finished. Poor old Lugg! One more shock like that and he'll sign the pledge. I wonder why Mrs Munsey took so much trouble to rearrange Lady Pethwick's body?"

"Instinct again," said the Professor. "That old woman scarcely thinks. She works by instinct and superstition. There's an old belief that if you leave the dead with their eyes wide open they watch you ever after."

They had reached the lattice gate at the end of the garden by this time. "We'll keep most of this story to ourselves," he remarked.

"Of course," Mr Campion agreed. "I'll collect Penny and go back to the Tower."

There was a fire in the library when they went in, and a scratch meal appeared upon the table. Beth and Penny were burning with excitement, but their hollow eyes and pale cheeks betrayed that their vigil had not been without its terrors. Beth kissed her father.

"Golly, I'm glad you're back," she said. "When it got so late Penny and I were afraid the ghost had decamped with you. Did you find anything?"

The Professor contented himself with a very brief outline of the story.

"It was simply an old woman wandering around trying to frighten folks so her son could do a bit of poaching," he said, accepting the coffee she handed to him with gratitude. "Nothing to get alarmed about."

"Mrs Munsey?" said Penny quickly.

The Professor raised his eyebrows. "What gives you that idea?" he murmured.

"It sounded like her," said Penny cryptically.

"It sounds rather flat to me," remarked Beth, a tinge of disappointment in her voice. "If you'd seen the things that we've *imagined* sitting up here alone you'd have a different tale to tell."

Mr Campion rose to his feet. "I think, Penny," he observed, "you and I had better get back to the Tower. To come to lunch and stay till breakfast next morning is not quite the article. Lugg will be shocked. His book of etiquette considers over-long calls definitely low."

Penny agreed readily. "I'll come at once," she said, and in spite of the Professor's protestations they gently insisted on returning.

The Professor shook Campion's hand in the hall. "You can leave all this to me," he murmured. "I'll see to it."

As they passed out of the garden Penny turned to Mr Campion suspiciously. "Now," she said, "out with it. What really did happen?"

"Undue curiosity in females should be curbed on all occasions as the evidences of it are invariably distressing to the really well-bred," said Mr Campion morosely. "That's in the etiquette book, too. Page four. It's illustrated."

"How dare you behave like this," said the girl with sudden spirit, "when you both came in looking as though you'd been through hell fire together? Mrs Munsey, was it? Did she go for Aunt Di of her own volition, or did someone put her up to it?"

Mr Campion eyed her speculatively. "It wasn't nice," he said. "Even Peck's dog was shocked. It was frightened to death and kept howling about the place like an old lady at a wake. The Professor was strong and silent, of course, but Mrs Munsey's sartorial efforts blanched even his cheek. We took her to her residence, whereupon she told my fortune, in a rather pessimistic vein, I thought. Then we shook hands all round and came home. There you are, there's the whole story, hot from the horse's mouth."

"All right," said Penny, "I'll find out all the details. You needn't worry."

"I bet you will," said Campion with contempt. "Beth will worm the lurid story from her poor doting father, and you two, little Annie Mile and little Addie Noid, will gloat over them together like the two little nasties you are."

Penny was silent for some time.

"Anything about The Daisy?" she ventured at last.

Mr Campion shot a quick glance at her. "I say," he said. "I forgot I'd told you about that. Look here, Penny, this is deadly serious. By the bones of my Aunt Joanna and her box, swear to me that you will never breathe a word about The Daisy to a living soul, especially not to Beth and her father. Because although Mrs Munsey gave your aunt the scare that killed her, it was The Daisy who engineered the whole thing. I don't think murder was intended, but…I don't know."

There was an unusual earnestness in his face and Penny, regarding him steadily, was surprised and a little flustered to see an almost imploring expression in his eyes.

"Promise," he repeated.

"All right," she said ungrudgingly. "You found out some-thing, then?"

Campion nodded. "It may or may not be important," he said. "Frankly, I hope it isn't."

Penny did not reply, but walked along beside him, her hands clasped behind her and her yellow head bent.

"I say," he said suddenly, "when I had a word with your father yesterday to assure him that Val would be home for his birthday the day after to-morrow he didn't say anything about the general procedure. What usually happens on these occa-sions?"

Penny considered. "It was a great day, years ago, I believe," she said dubiously. "The family was quite wealthy in my grand-father's time, you know. Mother used to tell us that on Father's twenty-fifth birthday they had a terrific set-out with a Church service, theatricals, a house party, and a dance for the tenants in the evening. Daddy had to keep out of the fun, though, because of the midnight ceremony of the Room, when his father and the chaplain initiated him into the secret. Of course," she said quickly, "we don't talk about that."

"I see," said Mr Campion slowly. "I suppose they dispense with a chaplain these days?"

"Well, we haven't got a private chaplain, if that's what you mean," she said, grinning; "although old Mr Pembroke, the vicar here, had rooms in the east wing when Father was away at the War. That was when we were children. I think he'll dine with us on the birthday night. There won't be any other cele-brations, partly because we haven't got much money, and also because of poor Aunt Di. Of course," she went on, "I dare say you think Father has been rather curious about this whole ter-rible business—the way he's kept out of it all—but you can't possibly understand about him if you don't realize that he is a man with something on his mind. I mean," she added, drop-ping her voice, "I wouldn't say this to anyone but you, but the secret absorbs him. Even when he thought the Cup was missing it didn't seem to rouse him to frenzy. You do follow me? That's why he's so odd and reserved and we see so little of him."

She paused and looked at Campion appealingly. The young man with the pale face and absent air turned to her.

"I'm not nearly the mutt I look," he said mildly.

A wave of understanding passed over her face. "I believe you and Father are pretty thick," she said. "Usually he loathes strangers. Do you know, you're quite the most remarkable person I've ever met?" She looked up at him with all the admiration of her age showing in her young face.

"No vamping me," said Mr Campion, nervously. "My sister— her what married the Squire—would be ashamed of you."

"That's all right," said Penny cheerfully. "I haven't got any designs on you. I think Val and Beth are heading for the altar, though. Val seemed to have got over his anti-woman complex with a vengeance last time I saw him."

"You'll be a danger," said Mr Campion, "in a few years' time. I'll come and sit at the back of the church when you're married and weep violently among all the old maids. I always think a picturesque figure of that sort helps a wedding so. Don't you?"

Penny was not to be diverted from the matter in hand.

"You've got something on your mind," she said.

She linked her arm through his with charming friendliness.

"In the words of my favourite authoress: 'Is it a woman, my boy?' Or aren't you used to late hours?"

To her surprise he stopped dead and faced her. "My child," he said with great solemnity, "in the words of the rottenest actor I ever heard on mortal stage: *The man who raises his hand against a woman save in the way of kindness is not wor-*

thy of the name.' Which is to say: 'Don't knock the lady on the head, Daddy, or the policeman will take you away.' This is the most darned awkward situation I've ever been in in my life."

Penny laughed, not realizing the significance beneath the frivolous words. "I should give it her," she said, "whoever she is. I'll stand by you."

Mr Campion permitted himself a dubious smile.

"I wonder if you would?" he murmured.

CHAPTER TWENTY

Trunk Call

"'ERE, WAKE UP, SIR. Inspector Stanislaus Oates, 'imself and personal, on the phone. Now we shall 'ave a chance of seein' that lovely dressin'-gown o' yours. I've bin wondering when that was comin' out."

Mr Lugg put his head round the door of his master's room and spoke with heavy jocularity. "'E's bin ringin' you all day," he added, assuming a certain amount of truculence to hide his apprehension. "There's a couple o' telegrams waitin'. But I didn't like to rouse yer. Let 'im 'ave 'is beauty sleep, that's what I said."

Mr Campion bounded out of bed, looking oddly rakish in the afternoon light. "Good Heavens," he said, "what's the time?"

"Calm yerself—calm yerself. 'Alf-past four." Mr Lugg came forward bearing a chastely coloured silk dressing-gown. "Pull yerself together. You remind me o' Buster Keaton when you're 'alf awake. Brush yer 'air before yer go down. There's a lady 'elp what's taken my fancy 'anging on to the phone."

Mr Campion bound the dressing-gown girdle tightly round his willowy form and snatched up his spectacles.

"What's this about phoning all day?" he said. "If this is true I'll sack you, Lugg."

"I've got to keep you alive. My job depends on it," observed his valet sententiously. "Staying out all night ghost 'untin' ain't done you no good. You look like an 'arf warmed corpse as it is. That's right—knock me about," he added, as Mr Campion brushed past him and pattered down the stairs to the side hall where the phone was situated.

The chubby little servant girl, evidently a captive to the charms of Mr Lugg, was clinging to the receiver, which she relinquished to Campion. She stood back and would have remained at a respectful distance, if by no means out of ear-shot, had not Mr Lugg waved her majestically kitchen-wards.

"Hallo," said a faint voice at the far end of the crackling wire, "is that you? At last. I was on the point of coming to you. I'm terribly sorry, old boy, but they've got it."

Mr Campion remained silent for some moments, but in response to a sharp query from the other end of the phone he said weakly: "Oh, yes, I can hear you all right. What do you want—congratulations?"

"Go easy," came the distant voice imploringly. "It was a most ingenious stunt. You'd have been sunk yourself. About two o'clock this morning a whole pack of drunks got hauled into Bottle Street Station, and about thirty of their friends arrived at the same time. There was a terrific fight, and the man on duty on your doorstep joined in, like a mutt. In the confusion someone must have peeled up your stairs and raided the flat. I've been trying to get on to you ever since. What have you been doing? Dabbling in the dew?"

In spite of the lightness of his tone it was evident to Mr Campion that his old friend was desperately worried. "We're doing all we can," came the voice, "and some more. Can you give us a line?"

"Half a minute," said Mr Campion. "What about young Hercules?"

"Oh, Gyrth? That's half the trouble," whispered the distant voice. "They knocked him on the head, of course, but the moment our man on the roof dropped through the skylight he pulled himself together and shot down after his property. Frankly, we can't find him. There was a free fight going on in the street, you see, and you know what a hopeless place it is. We've rounded up the usuals, but they don't seem to know anything. We've got a dozen or so of the rowdies too. Clever men most of 'em. Have you got anything we can go on?"

Mr Campion considered. He was now fully awake. "Have you got a pen there?" he said. "Listen. There's two whizzboys, Darky Farrell and a little sheeny called Diver. They may or may not be concerned, but I've seen them in the business. Oh, you've got them, have you? Well, put them through it. Then there's Natty Johnson, of course. The only other person I can think of is Fingers Hawkins, the Riverside one. How's that?"

"A nasty little list." The far-away voice spoke with feeling. "Righto, leave it to us. You'll stay there, will you? I'll ring you if anything happens. We're pretty sick up here, of course. They're a hot lot; all race-gang people, I notice."

"That had occurred to me," said Mr Campion. "Don't get your head bashed in for my sake. Oh, and I say, Stanislaus… kiss that bobby on the door for me."

He replaced the receiver and turned wearily away from the instrument to come face to face with his aide, the sight of whom seemed to fill him with sudden wrath.

"Now you've done it," he said. "If we muck this whole thing up it'll be directly due to your old-hen complex. Bah! Go and keep mushrooms!"

Mr Lugg remained unabashed.

"You've mixed us up with a nice set, 'aven't yer?" he said. "I've known ticket o' leave men who'd blush to 'ear theirselves associated with them names you've mentioned over the phone. Fight with razors and broken bottles, they do. It's the class o' the thing I object to. No one can call me a snob—not reely—but a gent 'as to draw 'is line somewhere."

But for once Mr Campion was not mollified by this attitude.

"Put on a bath, get out the car, find a map, and go and lose yourself," he said, and stalked off upstairs, leaving Mr Lugg speechless and startled out of his usual gloomy truculence.

A little over an hour later Penny, seated by herself in the spacious faded drawing-room whose broad lattice-paned windows overlooked the drive, was somewhat surprised to hear the door of her father's room across the hall close softly, and to see Mr Campion in a motoring coat and hatless run down the steps from the open front door, and, climbing into his car which stood waiting for him, hurtle off down the drive at an alarming speed.

She had imagined that he would have been down shortly to take tea with her, and she was just about to put her pride in her pocket and ring for Lugg and information, when Branch appeared carrying a bulky envelope on a salver.

"Mr Campion was wishful for me to give you this, miss," he said, and withdrew.

With her curiosity considerably piqued, Penny tore open the stout manilla and shook its contents out upon the Chesterfield beside her. To her astonishment there lay disclosed upon the faded brocade a folded sheet of paper, another envelope, and a small bag made of cheap red silk. The paper was closely written in broad distinctive writing.

Dear Penny, I have gone to pay a friendly call to show off my new suit. I may be so welcome that they

*won't want to part with me, so don't expect me until you
see me. I leave Lugg with you as a sort of keepsake. Three
meals a day, my dear, and no alcohol.*

*I wonder if you would mind giving him the enclosed
note, which I have stuck down to show my ill-breeding.
No doubt he will show it to you. But I don't want him to
have it until I am safely on my journey, since he is trained
to follow a car. The rather garish bag, which you will see
is not made to open, contains, as far as I know, a portion
of the beard of a very old friend of mine (a prophet in a
small way). That is for Lugg too.*

*Remember your promise, which only holds good
while I'm alive, of course. Don't get the wind up whatever happens. If in doubt, apply to the Professor, who is
a mine of information and the best sort in the world.*

*Such clement weather we are having for the time of
year, are we not? 'The face is but the guinea's stamp. The
heart's the heart for a' that.'*

Believe me, Sincerely yours, W. Shakespeare.
[Bill, to you.]

The girl sat turning the paper over on her knee until
Branch re-entered with the tea-wagon. But although she was
burning with curiosity, it was not until a good half-hour had
elapsed that she sent for Lugg. Colonel Gyrth never took tea,
and she was still alone when the door opened to admit the
troubled face and portly figure of Mr Campion's other ego.

The big man had a horror of the drawing-room, which he
crossed as though the floor were unsteady.

"Yes, miss?" he said suspiciously.

Penny handed him the envelope in silence. He seized
upon it greedily, and, quite forgetting all Branch's training of
the past few days, tore it open and began to read, holding the
paper very close to his little bright eyes.

"There," he said suddenly. "Wot did I tell yer? Now we're for it. 'Eadstrong, that's what 'e is."

He caught sight of Penny's face, and, remembering where he was, was about to withdraw in an abashed and elephantine fashion when she stopped him.

"I had a letter from Mr Campion too," she said. "He said I was to give you this." She handed him the red silk bag, and added brazenly: "He said you'd probably show me your letter."

Mr Lugg hesitated at first, but finally seemed relieved at the thought of having a confidante.

"There you are," he said ungraciously. "That'll show yer what a caution 'e is. He tossed the note into her lap. "It may be a bit above yer 'ead."

Penny unfolded the missive and began to read.

> *Unutterable Imbecile and Cretin. Hoping this finds you as it leaves me—in a blue funk. However, don't you worry, cleversides. Have had to resort to the Moran trick. If I am not back by to-morrow morning get somebody to take the beard of the prophet to Mrs Sarah on Heronhoe Heath. Don't have hysterics again, and if the worst comes to the worst don't forge my name to any rotten references. You'd only be found out. Leave the Open Sesame to Sarah and the Chicks. Yours, Disgusted.*

Penny put the note down. "What does it all mean?" she said.

"Ask me another," said Mr Lugg savagely. "Sneaked off on me, that's what 'e's done. 'E knew I'd 'ave stopped 'im if 'e didn't. This 'as torn it. I'll be readin' the Situations Vacant before I know where I am. 'E ain't even left me a reference. Lumme, we are in a mess."

"I wish you'd explain," said Penny, whose patience was beginning to fail her. "What's the Moran Trick, anyhow?"

"Oh, that," said Mr Lugg. "That was silly then. It's sooi-cide now. We was up against a bloke called Moran, a mur-derer among other things, 'oo kep' a set o' coloured thugs around 'im. What did 'Is Nibs do when we couldn't get any satisfaction from 'im but walk into 'is 'ouse as cool as you please—forcin' 'em to kidnap 'im, so's 'e could find out what they was up to. 'Curiosity'll kill you, my lad,' I said when I got 'im out. 'A lot of satisfaction it'll be to you when you're 'arp-ing to 'ave a pile of evidence against the bloke who's bumped you off.' "

Penny sprang to her feet. "Then he knows who it is?" she said.

"O' course 'e does," said Mr. Lugg. "Probably known it from 'is cradle—at least, that's what 'e'll tell you. But the fac' remains that we don't know. Gorn off in a silly temper and left me out of it. If I ever get 'im back from this alive I'll 'ave 'im certified."

The girl looked at him wildly. "But if the Cup's safe with Val, what's he doing it for?" she wailed.

Lugg cocked a wary eye at her. "Depend upon it, miss, there's a lot o' things neither of us 'ave been told. All we can do is to carry out 'is orders and 'ope fer the best. I'll tell yer wot, though, I'll get my lucky bean out to-night—blimey if I don't."

Penny returned to the letter. "Who is Mrs Sarah?" she demanded.

"The Mother Superior of a lot o' gippos," said Mr Lugg disconsolately. "It's either nobs or nobodies with 'im, and I loathe the sight o' both of 'em—begging yer pardon, miss."

Penny looked up quickly. "We'll take the token together to-morrow morning," she said. "Heronhoe Heath is about five miles from here across country. Mrs Shannon has her racing stables on the far side of it. We'll drive over."

Lugg raised an eyebrow. "Mrs Shannon? Is that the party

as come snooping round 'ere the day after yer aunt died?" he said. "Powerful voiced, and nippy like?"

"That's right," said Penny, smiling in spite of herself.

Mr Lugg whistled. "I 'ate women," he said, with apparent irrelevance. "Especially in business."

CHAPTER TWENTY-ONE

The Yellow Caravan

HERONHOE HEATH, A BROAD strip of waste land bordered by the Ipswich road on one side and Heronhoe Creek on the other, was half covered with gaudy broom bushes when Mr Lugg and Penny bumped their way across it in the two-seater on the morning after Mr Campion's departure. The sunshine was so brilliant that a grey heat haze hung over the creek end of the heath, through which the flat red buildings of Mrs Shannon's stables were faintly discernible. There was not another house for three miles either way.

The Gypsy encampment was equally remote from the world. It lay sprawled along the northern edge of the strip like a bright bandana handkerchief spread out upon the grass by the side of a little ditch of clear water which ran through to the creek.

When they were within hailing distance of the camp the track, chewed up by many caravans' wheels, became unnegotiable. Penny pulled up. "We'll have to walk this bit," she said.

Mr Lugg sighed and scrambled out of the car, the girl following him. They made an odd pair.

Penny was in a white silk jumper suit and no hat, while Mr Lugg wore the conventional black suit and bowler hat of the upper servant, the respectability of which he had entirely mined by tilting the hat over one eye, thereby achieving an air of truculent bravado which was not lessened by the straw which he held between his teeth. He grumbled in a continuous breathy undertone as he lumbered along.

"Look at 'em," he said. "Vagabonds. 'Ut dwellers. Lumme, you wouldn't catch me spendin' my life in a marquee."

Penny surveyed the scene in front of her with approval. The gaily painted wagons with their high hooped canvas tops, the coloured clothes hanging out on the lines, and the dozens of little fires whose smoke curled up almost perpendicularly in the breathless air were certainly attractive. There was squalor there, too, and ugliness, but on the whole the prospect was definitely pleasing, the sunlight bringing out the colours.

What impressed the girl particularly was the number of wagons and caravans; there seemed to be quite forty of them, and she noticed that they were not settled with the numerous little odd tents and shacks around them as is usual in a big encampment, but that the whole gathering had a temporary air which was heightened by the presence of a huge old-fashioned yellow char-a-banc of the type used by the people of the fairs.

Although she had known the Gypsies since her childhood she had never visited them before. Their haunts had been forbidden to her, and she knew them only as brown, soft-spoken people with sales methods that would put the keenest hire-system traveller to shame.

It was with some trepidation, therefore, that she walked along by the disconsolate Lugg towards the very heart of the group. Children playing half-naked round the caravans grinned at her as she approached and shouted unintelligible remarks in shrill twittering voices. Mr Lugg went on unperturbed.

A swarthy young man leaning over the half-door of one of

the vans, his magnificent arms and chest looking like polished copper against the outrageous red and white print of his shirt, took one look at Lugg and burst into a bellow of delight that summoned half the clan. Heads popped out from every conceivable opening, and just for a moment Penny was afraid that the reception was not going to be wholly friendly.

Mr Lugg stood his ground. "Party, name o' Mrs Sarah," he demanded in stentorian tones. "I got a message for 'er. Private and important."

The name had a distinctly quietening effect upon the crowd which was gathering, and the young man who had heralded their arrival opened the low door of his wagon and clattered down the steps.

"Come here," he said, and led them across the uneven turf to the very heart of the assembly, where stood a truly magnificent caravan, decorated with a portrait of the King and Queen on one side and four dolphins surrounding a lurid representation of the Siamese Twins on the other. The brasswork in the front of this exquisitely baroque chariot was polished until it looked like gold. It formed a little balcony in front of the wagon, behind which, seated in the driver's cab, was a monstrously fat old woman, her head bound round with a green and yellow cotton scarf, while an immense print overall covered her capacious form. She was smiling, her shrewd black eyes regarding the visitors with a species of royal amusement.

Their guide made a few unintelligible remarks to her in some peculiar "back slang" which the girl did not follow. The old woman's smile broadened.

"Come up, lady," she said, throwing out a hand to indicate the coloured steps which led into the darkness of the wagon. As she did so the sunlight caught the rings on her hand, and the blaze of real stones dazzled in the heat.

Penny clambered up the steps and took the seat opposite the old woman, while Mr Lugg lumbered after her and perched himself gingerly on the topmost step of the ladder. The crowd still hung about inquisitively. Penny was aware of eager derisive brown faces and shrill chattering tongues making remarks she could not hope to understand.

The monstrous old lady, who appeared to be Mrs Sarah, turned upon the crowd, her smile gone. A few vitriolic sentences, at the sense of which Penny could only guess, dispersed them like naughty children. With the ease of a duchess Mrs Sarah then returned to her guests.

"Who sent you, lady?" she said in her sibilant persuasive, "party" voice.

Mr Lugg produced the red silk bag, which he handed to Penny, who in turn gave it to the old lady. The plump brown fingers seized upon it, and with her long blackened fingernails Mrs Sarah jerked at the cotton which bound the topmost edge of the bag. Next moment the contents lay in her hand.

Penny regarded it with curiosity. It was an old-fashioned hair ring, made of countless tiny plaits woven together with microscopic intricacy. She held it up and laughed.

"Orlando!" she said with evident delight. "Don't worry, lady. Sarah knows. To-morrow," she went on slowly. "Yes, he said the day after. Very well. We shall be ready. Good-bye, lady."

Penny, considerably mystified, looked startled. "Orlando?"

Mr Lugg nudged her. "One of 'is names," he said sepulchrally. "Come on. The court is adjourned."

He was obviously right: the old woman smiled and nodded but did not seem disposed to converse any further. Penny had the impression that their hostess had received a piece of information for which she had been waiting. As the girl descended the steps, however, the affable old goddess leaned forward.

"You've got a lucky face, my dear," she said. "You'll get a nice husband. But you won't get Orlando."

Considerably startled by this unexpected announcement, Penny smiled at her and started after Lugg, who was making for the little car as fast as his dignity would permit.

"'E calls 'isself Orlando among the gippos," he said. "A funny old party, wasn't she? See 'er groinies?—Rings, I mean. Close on a thousand quid's worth there, I reckoned. All made from poor mugs like us. One of 'em told my fortune once. A journey across the water, she said. I was in Parkhurst inside of a month."

Penny was not listening to him. "But what does it mean?" she said. "What's he got them to do?"

Mr Lugg made an exaggerated gesture of despair. "They're old friends of 'is," he said. "'E goes off with 'em sometimes. 'E don't take me—leaves me at 'ome to mind the jackdaw. That's the sort of man 'e is. You got to face these things. I can see a rough 'ouse afore we've finished."

They had reached the car by this time, and Penny did not answer, but as she climbed into the driver's seat yet another caravan passed them heading for the camp. She glanced across the heath to where the stables lay just visible in the distance. For a moment a gleam of understanding appeared in her eyes, but she did not confide her thoughts to Lugg.

They drove home through the winding lanes to Sanctuary.

"'Ere! Wot's this we're in?" said Mr Lugg, after some seventeen sharp turns. "A blinkin' maze?"

Penny, who had grown used to his artless familiarity, smiled. "It's a long way round by road, I know," she said. "It's only five miles across the fields. This road dates from the time when one had to avoid the wealthy landowners' property."

As they passed Tye Hall Beth and the Professor were at the gate. They waved to her, and Penny pulled up and got out.

"Look here," she said to Lugg, "you take the car back to the Tower. I'll walk home."

Still grumbling a little, Mr Lugg obeyed, and Penny went back along the white dusty road to where her friends were waiting.

"We're waiting for the post," said Beth cheerfully. "Where's your funny little friend this morning?"

"Goodness only knows," said Penny awkwardly. "He went off last night, leaving a note to say he was going visiting. I believe he knows something."

The Professor, very coolly and sensibly dressed in yellow shantung and a panama hat, stroked his neat little beard with a thin brown hand. "Is that all he said?" he inquired. "I'll say that sounds very odd."

"To walk out at a time like this," said Beth. "It's not like him."

"I think he's up to something," said Penny, anxious to dispel any wrong impression. "He left Lugg and me a most extraordinary errand to do. That's where we've been. We've taken a red silk bag to an old lady who looked like that figure of Hotei in your drawing-room, Professor, all wrapped up in coloured print. She's a sort of Gypsy Queen, I suppose. There's a whole crowd of them camping on Heronhoe Heath."

The Professor's round brown eyes widened perceptibly. "Well, now, isn't that strange?" he said, and appeared to relapse in deep thought.

"She seemed to understand what it was all about, anyhow," Penny went on, "which was more than I did. And she said something about to-morrow, as if he'd made a date or something. He's an extraordinary person, you know."

Beth opened her mouth to agree, but she was silenced by an apparition which had just appeared leaning over the field gate which split the high hedge directly opposite the Tye Hall drive. A startled exclamation escaped her, and all three of them turned and stared at the dishevelled figure which clutched the topmost bar of the gate for support.

"Val!" Beth darted across the road, the other two behind her. The young man was deathly pale. He looked ill, and as he made a move towards them he swayed drunkenly. The Professor unhooked the gate, and, hitching the boy's arm round his own shoulder, half led, half dragged him across the road and up the path to the house.

"Don't chatter to him now, girls." The Professor spoke firmly, silencing a chorus of questions. "He looks real bad to me. Beth, cut up to the house and get out some brandy and ice water. Penny, my dear, give me a hand with his other arm."

"I'm all right," said Val weakly. "I've been doped, I think. Only just came to myself—heard you talking and staggered out. I'm a silly ass, that's what I am."

"Hold on. Don't talk for a bit," the Professor advised, as he led the little party into the house by the side door from the lawn. "No, it's all right," he said to an excited maidservant who met them. "Don't alarm Mrs. Cairey. Young Mr Gyrth has come over a bit faint, that's all."

The girl vanished with a startled "yessir," and the Professor turned his charge into the library, where Beth was already waiting with the brandy and water.

Val would not be silenced any longer. "I asked for it and I got it," he said, as he sank down gratefully into a deep saddle-back. "Gosh! I've got a head like fifty champagne suppers."

"But what's happened?" said Penny and Beth in chorus. "And," added his sister as the thought suddenly burst upon her, "where's the Cup?"

Val's clouded eyes grew hard for a moment, and he tried to struggle to his feet as the recollection returned to him. Next moment, however, he had sunk back again helplessly.

"They've got it," he said apathetically. "Where's Campion?"

Penny made an inarticulate noise in her throat and then sat down by the table, white and trembling.

Beth seemed more concerned about Val than any Chalice, however. Beneath her kindly ministrations the boy began to recover rapidly. He looked at her gratefully.

"I'm giving you an awful lot of trouble," he said. "I don't know how I got in that field. I woke up and heard you talking and staggered out, and here I am."

"Now, my boy," said the Professor, "what happened? Can you remember?"

Val considered. "I was at Campion's flat," he said. "I sat up late, reading, with the Chalice in the suitcase actually on my lap. A damn silly place to put it, I suppose. I hadn't undressed—I didn't mean to go to bed. Early in the morning, about two or three I suppose it was, I heard a fiendish noise going on out-side. I looked out of the window and saw a sort of free fight in progress round that Police Station downstairs. I was wonder-ing what was up when I heard someone in the flat behind me. He must have had a pass-key, I suppose."

He paused reflectively as he tried to piece together the jumbled events in his mind. "Oh well, then," he said at last, "—curse this headache, it's blinding me—then I got a crack over the skull, but not before I'd caught a glimpse of the fellow who swatted me. I recognized him. When I was down and out," he added awkwardly, "I went into all sorts of low eating houses. And there was one off Berwick Street, in Soho, just by the market, you know, where I used to see a whole lot of odd fishy characters going in and out. I think they had a room at the back. Well, this chap who hit me was a man I'd seen there often. I spotted him at once. He'd got a most obvious sort of face with a curious lumpy nose."

He stopped again and the Professor nodded comprehend-ingly.

"Then you were knocked out?" he suggested.

"That's right," Val agreed. "But I don't think I was out more than a couple of minutes at the most. I remember getting in a hell of a temper and charging downstairs; the only thing clear in my mind was that dirty little dive off Berwick Street. Outside there was still a young battle going on, and I charged through it. I think I sent a bobby flying in the process. Of course, I ought to have taken a few of them with me, but that didn't occur to me at the time. They had their hands full, anyhow."

"And when you got to Berwick Street?" said Beth, who had listened to this recital of her hero's with wide-eyed enthusiasm.

"Well, that was about all," said Val. "I charged into the place like a roaring bull and asked the proprietor chap for the man I wanted. He took me into the back room, where I waited, fuming, until a great lout of a fellow came in and before I knew what had happened I got a towel full of ether or chloroform or something in my face. That's all I remember, until I found myself sitting in the hedge in the field outside here, feeling like a half resuscitated corpse.

"I say," he added suddenly, "what's to-day? I mean—?"

"You're twenty-five to-morrow," said the Professor. "By the look of you you've been lying in that hedge since early this morning. Thank goodness it's dry weather."

"How did I get there?" said Val in bewilderment. "I tell you, I was laid out in a filthy little dive off Berwick Market last night—no, it couldn't have been last night. The night before, then. I suppose they injected something. Chloroform wouldn't have kept me under all that time. Here—where's Campion? I must let him know. Although," he added morosely, "I suppose he's heard all about it from the police by now."

"Albert's gone," wailed Penny. "And we've lost the Chalice. And yet," she added, suddenly sitting up, "that accounts for it. Someone was phoning Albert up all day yesterday. I was in bed at the time, but Mary told me this morning. That's why he went off. He didn't want to scare Father or me, I suppose."

She was interrupted by the arrival of Mrs Cairey, who put her head round the door.

"Papa dear," she said, "the postman's here. There's that special mail you've got to pay for, and I wondered if you'd like your letters too, Penny, my dear. He'll give them to you if you come. Lands above!" she added, coming into the room, all her motherly instincts aroused, "you do look ill, Mr Gyrth. Is there anything I can do for you?"

Penny went out with the Professor almost mechanically. Her brain was whirling with the complications of this new and apparently final development. Why on earth could no one realize that the Chalice had gone?

The postman, a scarlet-faced and perspiring East Anglian, was standing at the front door leaning gratefully on his bicycle.

"Two letters for you, miss," he remarked, as he completed his transaction with the Professor. "Your brother ain't 'ere by any chance, is 'e?" he added, raising a hopeful blue eye in her direction.

"He is, as a matter of fact," said Penny, considerably startled by the coincidence of such a question.

"Ain't that lucky? The only other thing for the Tower is this parcel for 'im. If you wouldn't mind, miss—?" The man was already unbuckling the prodigious canvas bag on his carrier, and the next moment he had dumped a large and heavy parcel in her arms. "It's lucky you got it," he said. "It feels like it's over the regulation weight to me. Good morning, miss."

He touched his ridiculous hat and swung on to the bicycle.

Penny, with the parcel in her arms, walked slowly back to the study. Just as she entered the room something about the weight and size of her burden sent a curious thrill through her.

"Val," she said breathlessly, "open this. I think—oh, I don't know—anyhow, open it."

There was something so imperative in her tone that the boy's interest was mused.

"What in the name of—" he began. "Oh, it's my birthday to-morrow. It's probably something stupid from one of the relations."

Nevertheless he accepted the knife Beth handed him and ripped up the cords, displaying a stout cardboard box of the type usually used to pack large bottles. Something of his sister's excitement seemed to be conveyed to him, for the hand that unfastened the slotted end of the carton shook violently.

Next moment he had pulled out a wad of straw packing and an exclamation escaped him. The Professor, Mrs Cairey and Beth bent forward, and very gently he drew out the long, slender golden cup that Mr Melchizadek's great grandfather had made.

"The Chalice!" said Penny, a sob in her voice. "Oh, Val, it's all right."

The faces of the other two women reflected her delight, but the Professor and Val exchanged glances.

"How—?" said Val breathlessly. "This is incredible. Is there any message? Who addressed it?"

A frenzied search revealed that there was no other enclosure, and that the address was printed in block capitals. The postmark was illegible.

The Professor cleared his throat. "I guess I can understand this," he said, tapping the relics of the parcel. "But how you arrived in that field this morning is completely beyond my comprehension. Who set you there, and why? It doesn't make sense."

Penny, who had been staring at her brother during the last few minutes, suddenly stretched out her hand.

"Val!" she said. "Your buttonhole!"

Instinctively the boy put up his hand to the lapel of his collar and an expression of astonishment came into his face as he detached a drooping wild flower bud from the slit and stared at it.

"Funny," he said. "I certainly don't remember putting it there. It's fairly fresh, too."

Penny snatched it from him. "Don't you see what it is?" she said, her voice rising. "There's hundreds of them in that field where you woke up. It's a white campion. There's only one person on earth who would think of that."

CHAPTER TWENTY-TWO

The Three-Card Trick

MR CAMPION STOPPED his car among the high broom bushes on Heronhoe Heath that evening and sniffed the air appreciatively. He seemed if anything a little more inane than usual, and in spite of his evident anxiety, there was something about him which conveyed that he was definitely pleased with himself.

Although he had been driving most of the day there was no trace of weariness in his tall loose-limbed figure. He locked the car, slipped the key into his pocket, and stood for a moment with his hand on the bonnet. "The highwayman's farewell to his horse," he remarked aloud to the empty air, and then, turning abruptly, strode off across the springy turf.

Behind him the lights of the Gypsy camp glowed in the dusk, and for a moment he hesitated, half drawn by their inviting friendliness. He turned away resolutely, however, and contented himself by hailing them by a long drawn-out whistle that might easily have come from one of the myriad seabirds on the creek. He paused to listen, the heath whispering and rustling around him. Almost immediately the cry was returned, two melodious whistles that sounded pleasantly reassuring. Mr Campion appeared satisfied and strode on his way almost jauntily.

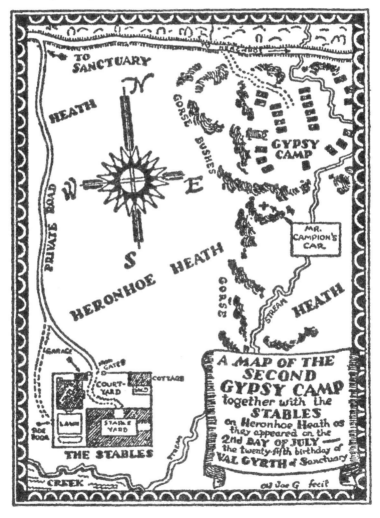

Mrs Dick's stables were only just discernible, a dark rectangular patch in the greyness. He had miscalculated the distance a little, and the walk was longer than he had anticipated. When he reached the buildings at last he stood for a moment in the shadow of a high wall listening intently. There was no sound from within, and, convinced that his approach had not been observed, he began to work slowly round the walls, moving silently and using his torch at intervals.

The building was much as he had expected. A high red wall enclosed the whole of the establishment, forming a large rectangular block, only one side of which was skirted by the rough private track which he had been so careful to avoid in his journey from the main road.

The large iron gates which formed the entrance from the track were locked. Peering cautiously through them, he was relieved to find the place in darkness. The dwelling-house and garden took up the western third of the rectangle. Directly in front of him was a square court with a cottage on his left, while the stables occupied the remaining portion of the whole block. They were built on all four sides of a square, two storeys high, with big wooden gates to the courtyard and a second entrance giving on to the heath on the eastern side, at right-angles to the creek. The drive led on a gentle curve past the front door of the house to the wooden gates of the stable yard.

Alone in the darkness, Mr Campion became suddenly intensely alert. Somewhere in the house he fancied he could hear the murmur of voices. He made no attempt to enter until he had been all round the buildings, however, and by the time he had returned to the front gates once more he was considerably wiser.

The place was in appalling repair and many of the bricks had begun to flake badly under the influence of the salt air. Mr Campion put his spectacles in his pocket, and, having chosen a suitable spot by the kitchens of the house where an overgrown creeper hung down, began to climb. It was by no means an easy ascent, for the wall was high, and it was surmounted by broken glass which the creeper only just masked. He accomplished it, however, and slid noiselessly to the ground on the other side. Once again he paused to listen, holding his breath. Still there was no noise but the continued murmur of voices somewhere on the opposite side of the house.

Having replaced his spectacles, he set off once more on his perambulation. There were no dogs nor grooms to be seen, and after careful inspection of the stable yard, the wooden doors of which stood ajar, Mr Campion was convinced that the information which he had gathered on one of his many visits that afternoon in London was substantially correct. Mrs Dick's racing stables could hardly be regarded as a going concern. Although there were boxes for twenty horses, only one of them appeared to be occupied.

The cottage by the stable gates was empty also, and evidences of decay were on all sides. Only the lawn and the courtyard were trim. The garden was a wilderness.

Very cautiously he approached the one lighted aperture in the whole establishment: two glass doors giving out on to the lawn. He had been careful to avoid the beam of light which they shed on to the lawn, but now he ventured up to it, the grass deadening his footsteps.

There was a thin net curtain over the windows, but the light inside rendered it transparent as he came nearer. In the relics of what had once been a fine room, five men and a woman were grouped round a table at which a hand of poker was in progress.

"Not a nice lot," Mr Campion reflected as he glanced from face to face. There was Matthew Sanderson, looking more astute than ever as he dealt the cards; the horse-faced "Major", and Fingers Hawkins, who had held him up on the road, a little ill at ease among his social superiors, but nevertheless in shirt-sleeves. Then there was a grey-headed, narrow-eyed man he did not recognize, and a little insignificant Japanese half-caste that he did, and whose presence bewildered him.

Mrs Dick dominated the group by sheer force of personality. As usual, she was strikingly smart; her black and white dress contrived to be almost theatrical in its extreme yet austere fashionableness. Her white face was twisted in a half-smile. Her hair was close-cropped like a man's, displaying her curiously lobeless ears. A heavy rope of barbaric crimson beads was coiled round her throat, and the feminine touch looked bizarre upon her angular, masculine form.

"Not staying, Major?" she said, as the red-faced man threw down his cards. "You never have the courage to see a thing through. Sandy, I've been watching you. You're playing all you know."

Sanderson threw down his cards. "I wonder someone hasn't strangled you, Daisy," he said, with more admiration than resentment in his tone.

Mrs Dick was unabashed. "My husband tried," she observed.

"You got him first, I suppose?" said the Major, laughing.

The woman fixed him with her peculiarly insolent stare. "He used to say the whisky wasn't strong enough," she said. "I often think it was the methylated spirits we used to pep it up with that killed him."

Sanderson turned away. "You put the wind up me," he said. "The way you talk I wonder you're not afraid of the 'Blacking'."

Mrs Dick laughed. "I'd like to see any man who's got the guts to blackmail me," she said. "Make it five, Tony."

"No 'Blacking'," said Fingers Hawkins from the other side of the table. "But we'll get our do's."

"You'll get your dues and more." Mrs Dick was inclined to be contemptuous. "I'll make it the limit, Tony. You won't stay? Thanks. Mine."

She threw down her hand as Mr Campion tapped on the window.

The gentle noise startled everyone save Mrs Dick, who hardly looked up from the cards she was collecting. "Open that window, Fingers," she murmured. "There's something scratching on it."

The big man went forward cautiously, and, raising the catch, jerked the half-door open, jumping smartly sideways as he did so.

Mr Campion, pale, smiling and ineffably inane, was revealed on the threshold.

"Good evening, everybody," he said, coming into the room. "Anybody got a good tip for the Ascot Gold Cup?"

Fingers Hawkins side-stepped behind him and passed out into the darkness. "'E's alone," he remarked, and coming back into the room, relocked the window.

At this piece of information the spirits of the company, which had been momentarily uncertain, now became almost uproarious. Sanderson began to laugh.

"All on his own," he said. "Isn't that sweet and confiding? We were telling Daisy she ought to invite you for a nice quiet rest until the fun was over, and here you are."

"Look out. P'raps there's a cartload of busies outside," said the half-caste nervously.

Sanderson turned on him. "Shut up, Moggie," he said viciously. "How many times have I told you the police aren't in this business? What d'you think they're going to get you for— being alive?"

"Well, I could understand that," remarked Mr Campion affably. "Still, everyone to his taste, eh, Mrs Shannon?"

Mrs Dick did not deign to look in his direction. "What

have you come here for?" she said, reshuffling the cards. "I don't think I know you."

"Nonsense," said Mr Campion. "We met at the dear Vicar's. You must remember. I was passing round the biscuits. You took two. Then we both laughed heartily."

Mrs Dick raised her eyes and regarded him coldly. "You seem to be even more of a fool than I took you for at first," she said, her stentorian tones blaring at him across the card table. "What are you doing here?"

"Calling," said Mr Campion firmly. "That must be obvious to the meanest intelligence."

"Sandy," said Mrs Shannon, "put this creature out."

"Not on your life." Sanderson spoke with enthusiasm. "Daisy under-estimates you, Campion. I shall feel all the safer with you as a guest here for the next few days. Got a gun?"

"No," said Mr Campion. "I don't like firearms. Even pea-shooters are dangerous in my opinion."

"No fooling. I've got mine trained on you."

Mr Campion shrugged his shoulders and turned to Fingers. "Do your stuff," he said, raising his arms above his head. "I love to see a professional at work."

"You stow it," said the pickpocket uneasily. Nevertheless he complied with Mr Campion's request, and stood back a moment or so later shaking his head.

Sanderson's amusement increased.

"Well, this *is* friendly," he said. "What d'you think you're doing? You've done some balmy things in your life, but now you've stepped clean over the edge. What's the idea?"

"You look out for 'im," said the gentleman addressed as Moggie. "'E's as slippery as an eel. 'E's got something up his sleeve, you betcher life. Probably that great bull pup Lugg's about somewhere."

"Write that down, sign it, send it to our head office, and we present you with a magnificent fountain pen absolutely free," said Mr Campion. "Every testimonial, however humble, is docketed and on view at any time."

Mrs Dick stacked the cards up neatly and turned in her chair to survey her visitor once more. "Why have you come here, young man?" she said. "You're beginning to bore me."

"Just you wait," said Mr Campion. "Wait till I get my personality over. I do hope you don't mind. I've been looking over your stables. There's one thing I didn't quite get. So many boxes but only "a" horse's. I suppose the pretty creature has a different home each day, like Alice at the mad tea party."

The woman's expression did not change, but her strong bony hands ceased to play with the cards.

"Perhaps you had better stay here for a day or two," she said. "Lock him up in one of the boxes, Sandy, and then for Heaven's sake stick to the game."

"We'd better see if he *is* alone, first," said Sanderson. "I shan't be surprised if he is. He's conceited enough for anything."

"If you find anyone outside he's nothing to do with me," said Mr Campion. "Absolutely no connexion with any other firm. No; as I told you before, I'm making a perfectly normal formal call. I climbed the wall by a honeysuckle bush. Up and down, quite unaided. Moggie couldn't have done it better. Frankly," he went on, turning towards that worthy, "I don't see what a cat burglar is doing in this."

"You don't have to," cut in Sanderson quickly. "You don't have to think about us. It's your own skin you've got to watch. Fingers, you and the Major go and have a scout round."

"That's right," said Mr Campion. "And whistle all the time. Then we'll know it's you. Meantime, perhaps I could show you some card tricks?" he added, eyeing the pack on the table wistfully. "Or I'll tell your fortune, Mrs Shannon. You've got a lucky face."

To everyone's surprise Mrs Dick threw the pack in his

direction. Mr Campion picked them up and shuffled with great solemnity.

"You cut three times towards me and wish," he said. His pale eyes were mild and guileless, and there was an infantile expression upon his face. She cut the cards, the half-amused, half-derisive smile still twisting her small thin mouth.

Mr Campion set about arranging the cards with a portentous air. "I see a lot of knaves about you," he remarked cheerfully. "One fat one," he added, eyeing the retreating form of the "Major".

Sanderson laughed. "You're a cool customer," he said, a tinge of admiration in his voice. "Carry on."

"I see a great understanding," said Mr Campion, planking down the cards one after the other. "And a lot of trouble. Oh, dear, dear, dear! All black cards. It looks as if there's a hanging in it for somebody."

"Shut up," said Sanderson, stretching out a hand as if to sweep the cards off the table. "He's playing for time, or something."

"Hush," said Mr Campion. "I'm going to have my palm crossed with silver for this—I hope. Now here's a whole stack of money—I might almost say a pot of money. Ah, don't be led astray by riches, lady. Here comes the luck card. It's very close but it doesn't quite touch. There's a fair young man in between. I should watch out for him, Mrs Dick."

He prattled on, apparently oblivious of his surroundings.

"There's an old woman and her son who'll give the game away if you don't take care—a silly old woman and a sillier son. You'll have a lot to answer for there," he said presently, and was interrupted by the return of the two searchers.

"All the gates fast. Not a soul on the heath. He's alone," said the Major. "Shall we take him along now?"

"Don't interrupt," said Mr Campion reprovingly. "The gentleman is suffering from second sight and must not be disturbed until the fit is passed. Now, let me see." He sat for a moment looking at the cards which he had arranged in a half circle in the table. They lay so that one broken end faced Mrs Dick and the other was beneath his hand.

"Oh, yes," he said at last, as though a new thought had occurred to him. "And then there's journeys." He bent across the table and planted a single card before the woman some distance from the rest, so that the whole formation resembled a rough question mark.

"I see a far journey," he remarked. "Why yes, most certainly. *You take the long road.*" And then, as she stared at the table, he swept the cards carelessly aside and rose to his feet.

"The seance is ended," he said. "Any more for the information bureau? Sanderson, let me tell you your past."

An explosive giggle from the "Major" was silenced by a single savage glance from the gentleman addressed. "You'll stop mucking about," Sanderson said. "Where shall I put him, Daisy? In the loft, I suppose."

"Looks to me as though he's askin' for it a bit obvious," said Moggie. "What price we chuck 'im out on 'is ear?"

It was Mrs Dick who settled the discussion. "Put him in the gate loft," she said. "Let him cool his heels for a couple of days."

Sanderson grinned. "I thought you'd see reason," he remarked complacently. He put his hand on Campion's shoulder and jerked him towards the door. Fingers Hawkins seized his other arm, and thus, with all ignominy, was Mr Campion escorted to the stables which he had so lately examined; but although he protested the whole way, it should perhaps be recorded that on the whole he felt distinctly satisfied.

CHAPTER TWENTY-THREE

"Madame, Will You Talk?"

AT EIGHT O'CLOCK on the evening of July the second, Val Gyrth's twenty-fifth birthday, Mr Campion languished in the room over the gateway of Mrs Shannon's stableyard. It was an effective prison. The windows were barred to prevent an entry rather than an exit, but they were equally efficient in either case. The two doors which led into other first storey rooms on either side were locked. Even had he desired to escape, the process would have been difficult.

The atmosphere was suffocating under the low penthouse roof, and his couch, which consisted of a blanket thrown over a heap of straw, was not altogether comfortable. Yet he was by no means disheartened. He had had frequent visitors during the day, but so far the one person he had come to see had studiously avoided him.

While Sanderson seemed fidgety with curiosity, Mrs Dick had not yet appeared.

This was the one factor in his plans that had so far miscarried, and here he was completely in the dark. And he realized clearly that upon Mrs Dick's character everything depended.

During the day he had ascertained that there were considerably more men at the lady's command than he had encountered at the poker game, but he felt grateful at the thought of the yellow caravan across the heath.

He rose to his feet and glanced out of the window. Great dark blue streaks of cloud were beginning to creep across the golden sky in the west. A clatter in the yard sent him over to the opposite window, and he stood looking down at just such a scene as Sanderson had described to the uninterested little group in the Cup House on the day after Lady Pethwick's death.

Mrs Dick, assisted by a terrified stable-boy and the equally unhappy "Major", was engaged in transferring her remaining pedigree mare from one box to another. They made an extraordinary picture; the woman, tall, angular and more mannish than ever in her rat-catcher riding-breeches and gaiters, and her white shirt buttoned tight to her neck and finished with a high stock tie of the same colour. Her cropped head was bare, and the evening light fell upon her pale, distorted face. The beast, a beautiful creature with a coat like black satin save for a single white stocking, was both nervous and bad-tempered. She was as heavy as a hunter and very tall, and as she moved the great muscles rippled down her shoulders like still water ruffled by the wind.

She refused the second box, and reared, pawing savagely with her forefeet. Mrs Dick, one hand gripping the bridle rein, lashed out with her whip. Again and again the mare refused, clattering over the yard till the bricks echoed. But the woman was indomitable; a dozen times she seemed to save herself by sheer skill and the single steel wrist by which she held the animal.

Mr Campion remembered the horse's name, "Bitter

Aloes". As the words came back to him the battle outside came to a sudden end. The mare, charging savagely at her mistress, had been rewarded by a vicious punch on her velvet nose from a small but very forceful feminine fist, and as she clattered back from this unexpected attack the woman seized her opportunity and ran her back unprotesting into the box. Mrs Dick emerged a moment later, grim and triumphant, superbly conscious of her victory. She accepted the "Major's" clumsy congratulations with a tart bellow of "Don't be a fool," which reached Mr Campion clearly in his prison, and once again the yard was deserted.

He remained standing by the window for some time, vaguely troubled. The presence of Moggie, the little Japanese half-caste, puzzled him. And there was the grey-headed man too. There was no telling to what particular branch of the profession he might belong.

For the rest, however, he was content to wait. If Mrs Dick had any spark of femininity in her make-up she would come to see him after the fortune-telling episode. He was a little surprised that she had not come before. The burning question of the moment, as far as he was concerned, and the sole reason for his present position, was the problem of whether Mrs Dick was alone the employee of the *"Société Anonyme"*, the amateur who, with the professional assistance of Matthew Sanderson and his associates, was directly responsible for the whole adventure of the Gyrth Chalice, the employee whose death according to the rules of the society would constitute the only reason for the abandonment of the quest.

For his own sake as much as hers Mr Campion trusted fervently that this was not the case. Both he and Val had mentally shelved this aspect of the affair, concentrating doggedly on the immediate protection of the Chalice. But always this question had been lurking in the background, and now, it seemed to Campion, it clamoured for recognition.

In spite of himself he shied away from the subject and turned his thoughts towards the Tower. He imagined the sedate and rather solemn little dinner-party now in progress; Sir Percival at the head of the table with Val on his right, Penny opposite her brother, and Pembroke, the old parson, beside her. The conversation would be constrained, he felt sure, in spite of the intimate nature of the gathering. The shadow of the secret room would hang over them all relentlessly; the secret room which held the real Gyrth Chalice, and something else, that something which never seemed to leave Sir Percival's thoughts. He wondered if Val would react in the same way as his father had done, or if the sharing of the secret would lighten the burden on the old man's mind.

He was disturbed in his reflections by the sound of a motor engine in the courtyard, and, glancing out of the opposite window to that by which he had been standing, he saw Sanderson bringing out a car from the garage.

Something about this most ordinary action alarmed him unreasonably.

There was a storm blowing up, and the heat, which had been oppressive all day, was now positively unbearable. Sanderson went into the house, and Campion was able to stare at the car at his leisure. Lying over the front seat he saw a coil of very flexible rope, knotted at intervals. He was puzzled, and his pale face peering through the bars of the window wore an expression of almost childlike discomfort. There was a distinct atmosphere of preparation abroad; something was about to happen.

The sound of a key turning in a lock behind him made him spin round.

Mrs Dick stepped briskly into the room. She wore the costume in which he had seen her in the yard, and the short-handled whip was still in her hand. She stood with her back to the door, her legs slightly straddled, and regarded him insolently.

Immediately Mr Campion sensed the extreme force of her personality, for the first time, directed upon him alone. He had met forceful and unpleasant personalities before in the course of a short and somewhat chequered career, but never in a woman, and it was this fact which robbed him for the moment of his usual urbanity.

"You haven't shaved this morning," she said suddenly. "I like men to be clean. I don't want you in this loft any longer. Get in here, will you?"

Mr Campion looked hurt as he complied with her command, and suffered himself to be driven through a succession of similar lofts until he came to a full stop in a hay-strewn apartment which was, if anything, more hot and dusty than the one he had just left, in spite of the fact that there was a small open grating overlooking the heath in lieu of a window in the outer wall.

Mrs Dick followed him into the room and shut the door behind her.

"I want you in here because both doors bolt on the outside," she remarked. "Now, young man, what did you come here for?"

Mr Campion considered. "You hurt me about not being shaved," he said. "None of your friends would trust me with a razor. I used to have a beard once. I called it 'Impudence'—'Persuasion' out of 'Cheek', you see. Rather neat, don't you think?"

Mrs Dick permitted herself one of her sour smiles.

"I've been hearing about you," she said. "Impudence seems to be your strong point. I'm sorry you've got yourself mixed up in this. You might have been amusing. However," she went on, "since you've evidently got nothing to say, it's quite obvious to me what you're doing here. Since you are a prisoner like this, it gives you an excellent excuse to explain to your employers why you've failed. I recognize that fact."

Mr Campion grinned. "I say," he said, "that's a good idea. How did you come to that startling conclusion?"

Mrs Dick remained unmoved. "It was quite clever," she said judicially. "What a pity you'll never be able to use it. Sandy thinks you know much too much to get away with it. I've never paid blackmail, and I'm certainly not going to begin."

"It must be the people you associate with," said Mr Campion with dignity. "My Union doesn't allow blackmail. I had no idea I was going to be a perpetual guest," he added cheerfully. "I do hope you won't expect me to wear an iron mask."

Mrs Dick raised her eyebrows expressively, but she did not speak, and he went on.

"I suppose your present intention is to keep me here until you fix everything up with your London agents?"

The woman shot a penetrating glance at him. "You know very well we haven't succeeded yet," she said. "You were very clever, Mr Campion, making all that fuss about your spurious Chalice. A little childish, perhaps, but quite effective. You made us waste a lot of time."

Mr Campion's pale eyes flickered behind his spectacles. The blow had gone home.

"So you've found that out, have you?" he said. "You've been pretty quick. Little Albert has been taking things too easily, I see. Dear, dear, dear! What are you going to do next? Have a lovely treasure hunt and give prizes? I'll come and tell you when you're getting warm."

"I'm not amused by nonsense," said Mrs Dick. "In fact," she added with devastating frankness, "I have very little sense of humour."

"Well, that's original, I can't say fairer than that," said Mr Campion politely. "May I make you a suggestion? Take the Chalice you already have. It has been in the Cup House at the Tower ever since it was made. Present it to your employers, if they cavil at it you can answer sincerely that as far as you know it is the only Gyrth Chalice in existence. I fancy that they'd pay up."

"Now you're beginning to be genuinely amusing." said Mrs Dick. She lit a cigarette from a yellow packet which she drew from her breeches' pocket. "You don't seem to be very well informed. The spurious cup was sent back to the Tower the day before yesterday. I know perfectly well where the real Chalice is and I'm going to get it."

"With Matt Sanderson, Fingers Hawkins, Natty Johnson, the Major, old Uncle Tom Moggie and all," said Mr Campion. "You won't get much of a look-in on the pay roll, will you? Mother, is it worth it? Father's got to have his share, you know."

Mrs Dick stopped smoking, the cigarette hanging limply between her thin lips.

"I'm managing this," she said. "I was approached and the responsibility as well as the reward is entirely mine."

Mr Campion was silent for some moments. Then he coughed, and raising his eyes to hers, he regarded her solemnly. "If you're really responsible for this little lot," he said gravely, "the situation becomes exceedingly uncomfortable and difficult. In fact, to put it crudely, to end the matter satisfactorily, one or both of us will have to retire from the picture pretty effectively."

"That," said Mrs Dick absently, "has already occurred to me. You won't get out of here alive, my friend."

"Threats!" said Mr Campion, his light-heartedness returning. "Isn't it time you hissed at me? You have an advantage over me by being dressed for the part, you know. Give me a pair of moustachios and I'll be a villain too."

The light was gradually going, though he could still distinguish her white face across the loft, but he felt himself all the more at a disadvantage inasmuch as the finer shades of expression on it were lost to him.

"It would interest me," she said suddenly, "to know who employed you. The Gyrths, I suppose. How did they get wind of it in the first place? Well, I'm sorry they've wasted their money. Heaven knows they've got little enough."

"I suppose you need money yourself," said Campion quietly.

"Naturally. I've spent two fortunes in my time," said Mrs Dick without boast or regret. "That's why I've got to get hold of another. You don't think I'm going to allow a little rat like you to interfere?"

"You under-estimate me," said Mr Campion with firm politeness. "Manly courage, intelligence and resource are my strong points."

He raised his voice during the last words for the first time during the interview. Instantaneously there was a clatter of hoofs beneath his feet, followed by several thunderous kicks on the woodwork which shook the building.

"Bitter Aloes," said Mrs Dick significantly. "She's in the box beneath here. You're in good company. Keep your voice down, though…she's vicious with strangers."

"Not too matey with the lady of the house," observed Mr Campion more quietly. "I saw you playing together in the yard like a pair of kittens. I thought she'd get you with her forefeet."

"She killed a boy last year." Mrs Dick's voice was brisk but expressionless. "I was supposed to have her shot but I wangled out of it. The little beast came on her unexpectedly. I saw it happen. It wasn't a pretty death. Those forefeet of hers were like steel hammers."

Mr Campion hunched his shoulders. "You have a curious taste in pets," he observed. "Fingers Hawkins and Bitter Aloes make a very fine pair. But suppose we cut the melodrama and come back to business? In the first place—merely as a matter of curiosity, of course—how do you hope to get away with it?"

"What can prevent me?" said Mrs Dick with placid assurance. "You seem to forget why I was invited to enter into the business at all. My position is unassailable. I can go where I like with impunity, and surround myself with as many rough customers as I like without rousing any suspicion. That's the advantage of a profession and a reputation like mine."

"I see," said Mr Campion. "And this reputation of yours plus the state of your financial affairs which rendered you practically desperate, got you the contract, as we say in big business? But what I meant was, how do you expect to get clear away—go on living here, for example?"

"Why not? Mere suspicion can't upset a standing like mine. Even if the police arrested me, what possible reason could I have for stealing a gold cup? It isn't saleable, you know, and I'm not the sort of person to collect drawing-room ornaments. The police are not the people to press the question of my employers. Once I have hold of it I can do exactly as I please. The Gyrths daren't blare their loss abroad. Frankly, I don't see how the police would come into it, and ordinary county feeling has long since ceased to affect me. I assure you I've come through worse scandals than this will ever cause."

Mr Campion was silent, and she shot him an inquisitive glance through the gloom. "Well?" she said.

"I was thinking how clever they are, these employers of yours," he said slowly. "You're right. You're unassailable. In fact, there's only one danger point in your whole scheme."

"And that?"

"Me," said Mr Campion modestly. "You see, I know the rules of the society as well as you do. You, I take it," he went on quietly, "are thinking of killing me?"

"It would be absurd of me to let you interfere with my affairs," said Mrs Shannon. "You might possibly have been useful to me, but as it is you're a damned little nuisance. I'm not thinking of killing you. I'm preparing to kill you."

"So this is Suffolk," said Mr Campion. "Commend me to Chicago. I hate to keep raising objections, but won't you find my body about the place more than just a social nuisance? I know the police are forgiving, friendly people, but they do draw the line at a body. Perhaps you're going to bury me in the garden or throw me in the creek? Do tell."

The woman made no reply, and he went on.

"Before you get busy, however, I must do my singing exercises. Listen to this for an E in Alt."

He threw back his head, and the shrill bird cry that had sounded over the heath the previous evening now echoed through the little room. The grating above Mr Campion's head was open to the heath, and the sound escaped clearly to the sky beyond. Again he shouted, and the horse below clattered and kicked violently in her stable.

Mrs Dick began to laugh.

"If you've been relying on that pack of Gypsies," she said, "it's kindest to tell you that I had sent them off the heath this morning. You're alone. You seem to have played your cards very badly. In fact," she added with sudden seriousness, "you're such a damn failure that you're beginning to irritate me."

Mr Campion's eyes were hard and anxious behind his spectacles, but his expression of charming inanity had never wavered.

"Talking of failures," he said, "where's your success? You're no better off than when you started. You haven't got the Chalice."

"It's perfectly obvious where it is," said Mrs Dick slowly. "I was a fool not to think of it before. In that secret room in the east wing they make such a fuss about, of course. That was clear to me as soon as I found the cup in the chapel was spurious. I shall have the Chalice to-night."

She spoke with complete assurance, a tone that dismissed any other possibility as absurd. Mr Campion stiffened.

"I see," he said softly.

He took off his spectacles and put them in his pocket. It was growing very dark in the loft, and although he was not altogether unprepared for what followed, the suddenness of her attack caught him unawares. He saw the flash of the woman's arm in its white shirt-sleeve upraised, and the next moment the thong of her whip caught him full across the face and sent him staggering back against the wall beneath the grating.

He was vaguely aware of voices outside, but he had no time to think clearly. Mrs Dick was lashing at him with the same cool skill and deadly accuracy with which she had subdued the mare who was trampling wildly in the box beneath them. He threw up his arms to shield his face, and reeled backward as she drove him into the corner.

She came after him, feeling in the hay-strewn floor with her foot. At last she found what she sought. With a single vicious twist of her heel she shot back the iron bolt of the hay-shoot, precipitating the young man into the maelstrom of flying hoofs below.

Instinctively he threw out his hands to save himself, and his fingers caught at the edge of the trap.

For a sickening moment he swung suspended in the air. Mrs Dick, bending down to draw up the trap again, kicked his fingers from their grasp as if she were flicking a stone out of her way.

Then she drew up the door by the slack rope and slipped the bolt home.

CHAPTER TWENTY-FOUR

Bitter Aloes

BITTER ALOES WAS as frightened by the sudden intrusion into her box as was Mr Campion by his equally sudden descent. She started back, rearing and screaming, her forefeet beating wildly in the air. It was this momentary respite which saved Mr Campion's life.

Set across the corner of the stable, some four feet below the ceiling, was an old-fashioned iron hay-basket, just low enough to allow the horse to pull out mouthfuls of fodder as she desired, while saving the bulk from being fouled on the ground or in the manger.

When Mrs Dick kicked Mr Campion's fingers from their grasp, he dropped, and was actually in the low wooden manger when Bitter Aloes reared above him. Pressing himself back into a corner to save himself as much as possible from the flying hoofs, his head brushed against the bars of this hay-basket. The mare, frenzied with fear and with bad temper, rose up on her hind legs once more, pawing frantically in the gloom.

Campion leapt for the iron basket, drawing himself up

into it, and at last crouched, his head and shoulders battened down beneath the rebolted trap and Bitter Aloes snapping at him not six inches below his feet. Even at that moment he could not help marvelling at the simple villainy of Mrs Dick's arrangements. A stranger found savaged to death and probably unrecognizable in a racehorse box would convey only one thing to a jury's mind, especially if the lady supplied any necessary details to show that he had entered the stable for some nefarious purpose. Twelve good Suffolk men and true would consider it a case of poetic justice.

With his head and shoulders still smarting from her whip and his body growing numb in its unnatural position which he knew he could not hold for long, he listened intently. Bitter Aloes had quietened considerably, but he could still hear her snorting angrily and the swishing of her tail in the darkness. Outside he was vaguely aware of a bustle in the yard. Mrs Dick and her party of raiders were about to set out. He realized that she must have some very definite plan of action, and his heart failed him as he thought of the Tower completely unprotected save for Val and a handful of servants, all of whom would be taken by surprise. It would not only be robbery with violence, but robbery by a group of picked men, each a master in his own particular line. Such a party could hardly fail, since they had such a very good notion where to look for their spoil. The difficulty of tracing them once the coup was made would be unsurmountable even for Scotland Yard, since the treasure itself could never be traced.

Savage with himself as much as with the woman, Campion raised himself cautiously in his perilous cradle and tried to force the trapdoor up, against the hinge, by the whole strength of his head and shoulders. There was an ominous creak and he felt to his horror that it was the staples that supported the hay-basket and not the trapdoor which were giving.

He ceased his futile efforts and crouched down once more, while Bitter Aloes, alarmed by the noise, reared again.

It was at this moment that he became aware of footsteps above his head. Someone was moving stealthily across the loft. He crouched back in the corner, fearing for an instant that Mrs Dick had returned to make sure that the mare had done her work. His alarm increased as the bolt of the trap was shot safely back and the door began to descend.

The next moment a shaft of light from an electric torch cut through the gloom and sent Bitter Aloes rearing and kicking against the outer wall of the stable. Mr Campion remained very still, racked by a thousand cramps.

The trap opened a little wider, and a soft American voice murmured:

"Say, Campion, are you there?"

The young man started so violently that the staples creaked beneath him.

"Professor Cairey!" he whispered.

"Oh, you're there, are you?" The torch was turned full on his face. "I thought she'd got you. Hold on a minute while I let this door down. Then you can pull yourself up."

The trapdoor descended, Mr Campion keeping his head low. A minute later, assisted by the Professor, he was dragging himself up into the loft once more. The American pulled up the trap behind him and shot the bolt.

"I'll say it was time I dropped in," he remarked. "What's happened to your face? Did the horse do that?"

"No, that's its mistress," said Mr Campion bitterly. "You've saved my life, Professor. How on earth did you land here?"

The old man rose to his feet and dusted his knees before replying. It was lighter in the loft than in the stable, and Campion could see his dapper little figure, still in his shantung suit, and the sharp triangle made by his white vandyke beard.

"Something occurred to me," he remarked softly. "A point

I thought maybe you'd overlooked. So I just came along on a bicycle on the off-chance of finding you." He paused. "I figured out where you were when Penny told me she'd been to see those Gypsies. I trailed around the heath until I found your car. Then I was sure. By the way, your tyres have been slashed."

Mr Campion was still looking at him as if he could hardly believe his eyes, and the Professor's voice continued with the same gentle precision, for all the world as if he had been carrying on a most normal conversation in his own library.

"I called on the lady this afternoon," he went on. "Sent in my card and said I'd come about some yearlings that I thought might interest her. She sent word that she couldn't see me, and the man I saw let me out of the front door. Fortunately there was no one around. I guessed they'd keep you a prisoner, and looking at the stables I thought what a grand prison they'd make. So I nipped into an empty loose box. I've been here about two hours." He paused, and then added quietly: "You see, in my opinion it's vitally necessary for you to go back to the Tower to-night."

"How did you get *here?*" said Campion, still amazed by the astounding matter-of-fact attitude of the old gentleman.

The Professor chuckled. "I waited in a horse-box until I saw that woman fooling about with a horse. Land sakes! I thought she was going to put it in on top of me. So I nipped up a ladder on to the top floor, and I hadn't been waiting there above fifteen minutes when I heard you talking to her in here. My hearing isn't altogether what it used to be and I didn't quite make out what either of you was up to. But I heard you fall through the trap and I heard her go out. Then I had some difficulty getting the door open and it wasn't for some time that I realized where you were. The rest you know. I don't like to be disrespectful to ladies, but that woman seems an honest to God hell-cat to me."

Mr Campion felt the weal on his face. "I'm inclined to agree with you," he said.

The Professor touched his arm. "You must hurry," he said. "Don't worry about me. I'll get back all right. If they're going to make an attack on the genuine Chalice they'll do it to-night. That's why I came along. There's a bit of tradition that it occurred to me you might not know. I'm interested in these things; that's why it stayed in my mind. Old Peck put me wise months ago. I meant to tell you before, but what with one thing and another it slipped my mind."

He lowered his voice still more. "That secret room at the Tower has a window, but no apparent door, as you know. Now, on the night of the heir's twenty-fifth birthday there's a light burns in the window from sunset to cockcrow. You see," he hurried on, ignoring Campion's smothered exclamation, "in the old days there was always a big party on, so that every window in the house would be ablaze, but this time there isn't any party. The position of that room will be clear to anyone who cares to look from ten o'clock till dawn. Get me? That's not all, either," he added. "There's sure to be special preparations made to disclose the door to-night. If anyone raided the Tower now they'd find pretty clear indications of where the Room was, I'm thinking, provided they knew on what floor and in what direction to look. It may be thirty years before this opportunity occurs again. I think you ought to be on hand."

Mr Campion was silent for some moments. "I guessed there'd be a light, of course," he said at last, "but it never dawned on me it'd be on for so long. I didn't know the tradition. You're right. It's the time I've misjudged." He hurried to the window. "I suppose they've gone already."

The stable-yard was deserted, but he caught a glimpse of the big car still standing before the house. "We must get out," he said. "We'll go the way you came in."

The Professor led the way down the ladder in the adjoining loft and into the empty box below. Next moment an exclamation of annoyance escaped him.

"We're bolted in," he said. "We shall have to nip back and get round on the top storey. If we're fixed in here we're sunk."

"There's a window in that front room over the gate," said Campion thoughtfully. "I've been locked in there all day. I could get out of that, I think."

Fortunately, the communicating doors between the two storey lofts were unlocked, and they pushed right round the square until they emerged once more into the room over the gateway. Here Mr Campion stopped dead, and the Professor, panting a little, caught up with him. From somewhere outside there had arisen a most extraordinary noise.

"Heck!" said the Professor. "What's that?"

But Mr Campion was already at the window.

"Good old Mrs Sarah!" he said breathlessly. "I thought that was all guff about turning them off the heath." He caught the Professor's arm and dragged him to the window. Together they looked out over the scene below.

The sight was an extraordinary one. The remains of a lurid sunset still blazed across the heath and the wind was rising. At the moment when they first peered through the window together an immense dark object silhouetted against the sky was bearing down upon the buildings at an ever-increasing rate. As it came nearer they were just able to discern what it was. The decrepit char-a-banc which Penny had noticed in the Gypsy encampment the morning before charged upon the stables, bristling with an overload of wildly gesticulating figures.

They disappeared from the view of the watchers from the window beneath the outer wall, but the next moment a shattering crash echoed through the buildings as the iron gates were burst open. The char-a-banc swung into sight, churning off the near wheel of the Delage in its path and coming to a full stop in the gateway above which they stood. The noise was fiendish, the shrill Gypsy voices, their musical sibilance entirely vanished, mingled with the shrieking of brakes and the infuriated swearing of the members of Mrs Dick's peculiar household who came swarming out to attack the invaders.

Pandemonium broke loose. In her stable Bitter Aloes added to the increasing confusion by kicking at the woodwork in a frenzy. Innumerable figures tumbled out of the juggernaut and swarmed over the house and stables.

Mrs Dick's adherents defended themselves and their property from this unexpected attack with a savagery of their kind. The Professor, with his hands on the bars of the window and his eyes glued to the pane, whistled under his breath.

"Gee, this is the dirtiest fighting I've ever seen," he said.

Mr Campion did not reply at once. He was wrestling with the other window whose fittings he had tentatively loosened during the day.

"They got my signal," he said at last, between vigorous wrenches at the bars. "I put them on to this weeks ago. I never dreamed they'd do the thing so thoroughly. When they got the signal they were to attack. If there was no signal then they were to arrive at ten. Lugg took them the sign yesterday, so they've been waiting all day. They're old enemies of this lot. Gypsies and race gangs hate each other."

"I haven't heard any guns," said the Professor as he watched the battle with almost boyish enthusiasm.

"They don't use guns." Mr Campion had to raise his voice as the crashing of windows and splitting woodwork was added to the turmoil. "They've a prejudice against them. Makes it worse if they're caught. Their own methods are quite as effective and slightly more filthy. Who's winning?"

"Hard to tell," said the Professor. "They all look alike to

me. It's smashed up the attack on the Tower all right, I should think. I don't see Mrs Shannon anywhere."

He broke off abruptly as a pistol shot sounded above the general uproar.

"That's Sanderson, I bet," said Mr Campion. "That man'll get hanged before he's finished."

"Whoever it is," said the Professor, "they've got him." He paused. "Can you hear a car?"

"Can't hear anything through this din," Campion grunted as he detached a bar from the window. "Sounds like an early Christian idea of hell to me."

"Say, Campion," said the Professor, suddenly turning for a moment, "there's murder going on outside. Won't your Gypsy friends have some difficulty in getting away with it?"

"More disabling than killing." Mr Campion was edging himself through the window as he spoke. "You don't know Gypsies, Professor. There won't be a trace of them in the morning. They'll have split up and scattered to every corner of the country by dawn. Some of them just live for fighting. This is one of their gala nights. Look here," he added, as he prepared to lower himself out of the narrow aperture, "your best plan is to stay here. I'll unbolt the door downstairs and let you out. If anything happens to me, you're Orlando's friend, and any Gypsy will see you clear. Don't forget, *Orlando.* I'm going after Mrs Dick. I'll never forget what you've done for me tonight, Professor."

The old man returned to his window. "Boy, I wouldn't miss this for a fortune," he said. "It's an education."

"Going down," sang Mr Campion, and disappeared.

He dropped into the very centre of the char-a-banc, which was at the moment an oasis amid the tumult, and groped about him for a weapon. He kicked against something hard on the floor of the vehicle, and putting his hand down came across a bottle. He bound his handkerchief round his hand and seized the glass club by the neck. Then, still keeping low, he dropped gently out of the car and slipped back the bolt of the stairway to the lofts.

"All clear, Professor," he called softly up into the darkness. Then, stepping out gingerly once more, he was just about to work his way round to the house when he caught sight of a figure bearing down upon him, hand upraised. Campion put out his arm to ward off the blow and spoke instinctively.

"Jacob?" he said sharply.

The arm dropped to the man's side. "Orlando?"

"Himself," said Mr Campion, and added, drawing the Gypsy into the protecting shadow of the box: "Where's the donah?"

"Scarpered," said the Gypsy promptly. "Went off in a little red motor. The finger with the gun was going with her, but we got him."

"Scarpered?" said Mr Campion. "Alone?"

The man shrugged his shoulders. "I don't know. I think not; she went in a red motor that was standing by the side door when we came in. Been gone ten minutes. Took a coil of rope with her. Some of the boys started after her, I think, but she's away."

Mr Campion's scalp tingled. Mrs Dick had nerves of iron. She had nothing to lose, and once the genuine Chalice was in her possession she was safe. Moreover, the calmness with which she had attempted to dispose of him dispelled any doubts of personal squeamishness on her part. There was nothing she might not do.

He returned to the Gypsy. "I'm going after them," he said, "though Heaven knows how. I say, Jacob, there's an old finger upstairs, a great friend of Orlando's. See he gets out. Give Mrs Sarah my love. I'll see you all at Hull Fair, if not before. Round up this lot now and scarpa yourselves."

The Gypsy nodded and disappeared silently up the stairs

to carry out his instructions as far as the Professor was concerned.

Most of the fighting had by this time spread into the house whither the majority of the gang had retreated.

Mr Campion sped across the yard, which was now a mass of broken bottles, blood, and odd portions of garments, and made for the heath. It was still far from dark outside the walls. The wind was rushing great wisps of cloud across the pale sky and the stars seemed very near.

As he passed the groom's cottage a dark figure detached itself from the shadows and leapt at him. He swung his weapon which he still held and brought it down on something hard. His assailant went down. He was vaguely aware of the "Major's" red face gaping at him from the ground, but he hurried on, one thought only clear in his mind: Mrs Dick and a coil of rope.

He stepped hopefully into the garage and looked about. To his dismay it was empty, save for the recumbent and unconscious figure of Matt Sanderson. The Delage, now completely beyond repair, and the red Fraser Nash, in which Mrs Dick was speeding towards the Tower he had no doubt, were the only vehicles it had contained. His own car, besides being some distance off across the heath, was, according to the Professor, completely out of action, and the char-a-banc in which the Gypsies had arrived would take the concerted efforts of at least a dozen men to get out of the yard. There remained the Professor's bicycle, which was hardly fast enough even could it have been found.

The problem of transport seemed insoluble, and speed mattered more than anything in the world. Even telephoning was out of the question, as he knew from experience that to cut the wires was the first care of raiding Gypsy parties. It dawned upon him that the only chance he had was to make for the camp and borrow a horse from Mrs Sarah.

He set off across the heath towards the camp at a good steady pace, taking a diagonal course towards the northeast. Almost immediately he was conscious of footsteps behind him. He stopped and turned.

A man leading a horse was coming swiftly up. Mr Campion's lank form and spectacled face were recognizable in the faint light. "Orlando!" the man called softly.

"Who's that? Joey?" Campion recognized the voice as that belonging to Mrs Sarah's son Joey, the horse expert of the Benwell tribe. He came up.

"Jacob sent me after you. The old finger with him said you wanted to get off. I'll lend you this." The Gypsy indicated the horse with a jerk of his head. "Careful with her. She's all right for half an hour. She may be a bit wild after that. Lovely bit, though, ain't she?"

Mr Campion understood the insinuation perfectly. Joey, who had ever more an eye for business than for warfare, had taken the opportunity to raid Mrs Dick's stables, an act in which he had been detected by his kinsman, and straight away dispatched to Campion's assistance.

As he turned gratefully to take the bridle, forgetting for the moment the impoverished state of the lady's stables, a white stocking caught his eye. Instinctively he started back.

"Good Lord, you've got a nerve," he said. "This is Bitter Aloes. They keep her as a sort of executioner," he added grimly.

"She's all right," Joey insisted. "Run like a lamb for half an hour. You can trust me. I've fixed her with something."

Mr Campion glanced at the proud silky head with the ears now pricked forward, and the wild eyes comparatively mild. The mare was saddleless. It seemed madness to attempt such a ride.

The Gypsy handed him a broom-switch.

"Hurry," he whispered. "Turn her loose when you've done

with her. I'll come after her with something in me hand that she'll follow for miles. To Sanctuary you're goin', ain't you?"

Mr Campion looked over the heath. Sanctuary was five miles as the crow flew. Even now Mrs Dick might have reached her goal. He returned to the Gypsy.

"Thank you, Joey," he said quietly. "Sanctuary it is," and he vaulted lightly on to the gleaming back of Bitter Aloes.

CHAPTER TWENTY-FIVE

The Window

I**T WAS A LIGHT** summer's night with a strong wind blowing. Strips of indigo cloud scored the pale star-strewn sky, and the air was cool after the intense heat of the day.

The heath ticked and crackled in the darkness, and the broom bushes rustled together like the swish of many skirts.

It was not a night for staying indoors: everything seemed to be abroad and the wind carried sounds for great distances, far-off sheep cries, voices, and the barking of dogs.

Most of these things were lost upon Mr Campion as he thundered across the countryside. Whatever horse-witchery Joey had practised upon Bitter Aloes, her temper had certainly subsided, but she was still very nervy and inclined to be erratic, although for the moment her innate savagery was subdued. Campion, his long thin legs wrapped round her sleek sides, trusted devoutly that for the promised half-hour, at any rate it would remain so.

After the first breath-taking dash across the heath he forgot her vagaries and concentrated upon his goal. As he reached the road, a church clock from Heronhoe village struck eleven, and he abandoned his original intention of sticking to the road. Time was too precious. He turned the mare at the hedge which bordered one of the wide stretches of pasture-land which lay between him and the Tower. Bitter Aloes took the jump like a cat. As she rose beneath him the notion flashed into Campion's mind that she probably enjoyed the hazardous journey. Her curious twisted temperament was best pleased by danger.

He had no illusions about what he was doing. To ride a Gypsy-doctored horse over a tract of unfamiliar land in the half-darkness was more than ordinarily foolhardy. Trusting devoutly that they would not come up against any insurmountable object, and praying against wire—the recollection that this was a hunting district relieved him considerably on that score—he kept the mare's head in the direction of Sanctuary and urged her on to further efforts.

She had her moments of difficulty. A nesting partridge disturbed under her feet sent her rearing dangerously, and once when a sheep lumbered out of their path she plunged continuously for some seconds and all but unseated him.

Luck and his unerring sense of direction brought them safely over the meadows to the brow of Saddlehill, and as they galloped up the steep grassland Campion suddenly saw the end of his quest, the gaunt east wing of the Tower of Sanctuary standing up against the sky on the other side of the valley.

In the Tower, high in the topmost storey, was a lighted window. It stood out quite clearly, a little circular spot of red light in the blackness.

Although he had expected it, it startled him. It was higher than he had supposed the windows would come, and he identified it suddenly in his mind with the curious circular decoration over the centre window of the wing, an orifice which had looked like a plaque of deeply indented stone work from the ground.

As he stared at the Tower, something in the grounds attracted his attention, and he looked down to see a car's headlights turn in to the trees at the far end of the drive. Even as he looked they vanished. A panic seized him. He drove his heels gently into the mare's sides and she leapt forward quivering.

For a moment he thought he had lost control, but she quietened as the long gallop down the slope exerted her. He took her over a ditch into the lane at the foot of the hill, and they continued down the narrow road, her hoofs striking sparks from the ragged flints. The little white gate at the end of the home meadow she took almost in her stride and the steep incline hardly affected her pace: the effect of Joey's treatment was wearing off and she jerked her head angrily from time to time as though she were irritated by the reins.

Campion barely noticed her changing mood. He flung himself off her back at the end of the flower garden, and she kicked out at him as he disappeared through the gate and ran up the grass path towards the house.

There were beads of sweat on his forehead, and the expression on his pale face was no longer inane. A car had turned into the drive and had instantly switched off its lights; that was fifteen minutes ago at least, he reckoned. Even allowed for reckless driving, Mrs Dick could hardly have traversed the twelve miles of winding lane in less time than that would account for.

Therefore she was in the grounds now. He was prepared for anything. Mrs Dick's possibilities were numberless.

He glanced up at the Tower across the wide lawn. The single red eye, a significant and silent witness to the thousand rumours concerning the Gyrths' secret, glared down upon him. Behind that eye lay the Chalice, protected by something unknown, the intangible and perhaps terrible guardian upon which probably only three men living had ever looked. He had heard dozens of "genuine explanations"; men referred to it guardedly in famous clubs, well-known books of reminiscence hinted darkly at unprintable horrors. Val himself had seemed a little afraid to consider what it might be.

He wondered how many anxious eyes were fixed on the Tower that evening. Mrs Dick's band of experts had been put out of action, certainly. But there would surely be others waiting to bear the treasure to safety. The lady herself, he fancied, would keep out of it for fear of being recognized, but would general the attack from somewhere outside.

At present all was peaceful. There were only two other lights in the whole building, both in the west wing, in the drawing-room and in the library. The servants' quarters were dark; the staff had been sent to bed early, no doubt. Campion imagined Penny alone in the drawing-room, and Val seated with his father and the old Rector in the study. And somewhere in the darkness a group of watchers, utterly without fear or scruple, eyeing, even as he, the single glaring window in the Tower.

He advanced across the lawn, keeping carefully to the deep shadow.

The uncanny silence of the garden around him filled him with apprehension. He could have sworn that there was no one moving amid the belts of trees and shrubs which surrounded the lawn. Once again he paused and stood rigid. Somewhere there had been a movement. Instinctively he glanced up. The old house stood out black against the night sky. His eyes were drawn irresistibly to the circular window. Then he started. Just above it, standing out clearly over the battlements of the east wing, there was a figure.

He waited, silent, hoping against hope that it was Val or his father, but, even as he watched, something slender, snake-like, slid down across the circle of crimson light. As he strained his eyes to make it out, the truth came slowly home to him. It was a fine flexible rope, knotted at intervals.

Instantly the question which had been rankling at the back of his mind was made blindingly clear to him. The raiders were going to make sure of the exact whereabouts of their prize before they risked an open attack. The half-caste cat burglar's part in Sanderson's scheme became obvious. He was to have been the spy, possibly even their thief, if the window were negotiable. The simplicity of it appalled him. It would be so easy. Although the Tower was about a hundred and twenty feet high, a man with nerve could make a descent to the window once its whereabouts was made clear to him. It would be dangerous, but by no means impossible, to a man of Moggie's experience.

Then he remembered that Moggie was lying in the garage with Sanderson on Heronhoe Heath. Who, then, was the climber who was about to take his place? There was an answer to this question, but his mind shrank from considering it.

He raced for the house. His first impulse was to alarm the Colonel, but as he reached the base of the east wing the intruder's means of entry was instantly apparent. One of the narrow latticed windows stood open. He climbed through it without hesitation and crept across the flagged state dining-room within to the centre hall, where a huge wooden spiral staircase, one of the showpieces of the county, reared its way up into the darkness.

He crept up the steps, the wood creaking terrifyingly beneath his weight. It was a long climb in the darkness. The stairs wound up the whole height of the Tower. At last they began to narrow and presently he felt the cool night air upon his face.

Suddenly the faint light from the open doorway above his head warned him that he was reaching the roof. He paused to listen. There was no sound in the house. All was quiet and ghostly in the gloom. He moved silently up the last half-dozen stairs, and emerged at last from the little central turret on the flat stone roof of the Tower.

For a moment he looked about him, prepared for instant attack. As far as he could see the place was deserted. Keeping his back to the wall he worked his way round the turret. Then a chill feeling of horror crept over him. He was quite alone.

A movement almost like the passing of a shadow just in front of him made him start forward, and in doing so his thigh brushed against something stretched tightly from the central flagstaff and disappearing over the edge of the battlements. He touched it with his hand. It was a rope with knots in it. In that moment he realized that the one eventuality which he had never foreseen had taken place. Whoever was undertaking the theft of the Chalice was doing it alone.

Beads of sweat stood out on his forehead. There was only one person living who would have the nerve to make such an attempt, only one person who would consider the prize worth the risk. He moved to the edge of the Tower and drew out his torch, which he had been careful not to use until now.

"Hold on," he said firmly, "you'd better come back."

His voice sounded strained and theatrical to him after the silence, the words inadequate and ridiculous. He listened intently, but the reply was loud, almost as if the speaker had been standing beside him.

"I'll see you in hell first," said Mrs. Dick.

Following the rope, he bent over the parapet and switched his torch downwards. Although he had expected it, the sight sickened him. She lay against the side of the Tower like a fly on a wall, her steel hands gripping the rope which supported her as she picked her way down with easy precision. Not more than two feet below her the round window gleamed dully on to the cord as it squirmed and flopped against the stone work. In the daytime the height was sickening; at night it was impossible to see the ground, and Campion was glad of it.

He leant on the parapet looking down at her. He could

see her distinctly, still in the riding costume in which she had interviewed him only that afternoon. As he stared, a thought forced itself into his mind. Mrs Dick was the employee of the society; the responsibility lay upon her shoulders alone. Should she meet with her death the danger to the Chalice would end automatically.

The rope, which alone supported her from a hundred foot drop on to the flags beneath, lay under his hand. If the cord should slip its mooring round the flagstaff…

He leant on the parapet and kept his eyes fixed upon her. He could find plenty of moral justification in his own mind for this execution, and he did not flinch from the fact that it would be an execution. There were passages in Mrs Dick's past that no English jury would have excused in spite of their notorious leniency towards women. He gripped the stones, his knuckles showing white in the faint light.

"Come back," he said distinctly, turning the light full on her bent head. "Come back before you look in that room, or I swear I'll cut this rope."

As soon as he had spoken the meaning of his own words startled him. Once Mrs Dick, the agent for the most influential syndicate in the world, saw the prize she sought, no power on earth could save it from her. She must be prevented from reaching the window.

"I'll cut the rope," he repeated.

She looked up at him unflinchingly, and the merciless light revealed the twisted smile on her small, hideous mouth.

"You wouldn't dare," she said. "You haven't the courage. Get back; I'll deal with you later."

She descended another step deliberately.

"Come back!" Campion's voice was menacing. "Hold tight. I'm going to draw you up." He gripped the rope and took the strain, but she was a heavy woman, and he knew instinctively that in spite of the knots the task would be beyond him.

Mrs Dick, who had remained motionless on the rope, steadying herself for any such attempt, jeered at him openly.

"Mind your own business," she said. "If you must interfere, go downstairs and call a servant to help you."

Her voice sounded a little farther away, and he knew that she was climbing down. Again he bent over the parapet. He caught sight of her feet reflecting the red glare from the window.

"Come back!" he called hoarsely. "Come back, for God's sake!"

"Just a moment." The words came softly to him as she deliberately lowered herself another foot, and adjusting her position, peered into the window.

There was a pause which seemed like an age. The man bending forward with his torch directed upon the hunched figure on the rope received some of the tremor which shot through her body. The red light was on her face, and he saw her shoulders twitch as she hung there, apparently fascinated by what she saw. In that moment the world seemed to have paused. It was as if the Tower and garden had held their breath.

Then from somewhere beneath him he fancied he heard a faint, almost indetectable sound. It was a sound so intangible that it did not convey anything concrete to his mind, so soft that he questioned it immediately afterwards. The effect upon Mrs Dick, however, was instantaneous.

"No!" she said distinctly, "no!"

The last word was smothered by a shuddering intake of breath, and she swung round on the rope, hanging to the full length of her arms. Her face was turned up to the man on the Tower for an instant. He saw her lips drawn back over her teeth, her eyes wide and expressionless with fear, while a thin trickle of saliva escaped at one corner of her mouth. He bent forward.

"Hold on," he said, not realizing that he was whispering. "Hold on!"

But even as he looked, her limp fingers relinquished their grip, he heard the sickening hiss of the rope as it raced through her hands, and she receded with horrible slowness down, down, out of the range of his torch into the darkness below.

The body crunched as it hit the flags, and then—silence. The guardian of the Gyrth Chalice had protected its treasure.

Mr Campion, sick and trembling uncontrollably in the cold wind, reeled unsteadily to the turret and went quietly downstairs.

CHAPTER TWENTY-SIX

Mr Campion's Employer

The East Suffolk Courier and Hadleigh Argus for

July 7th

SAD FATALITY AT SANCTUARY

Coroner Comments on Curiosity

An inquest was held on Saturday last at the Three Drummers Inn, Sanctuary-by-Tower, before Doctor J. Cobden, Coroner for the district, on Daisy Adela Shannon (44) of Heronhoe Stables, Heronhoe, who fell from the tower in the east wing of the mansion of Colonel Sir Percival Gyrth, Bt, on the night of July 2nd while a birthday party was in progress.

The body was discovered by Mr Alfred Campion, a guest at the Tower. Mr Campion, 17 Battle Street, London, W1, said that on Thursday evening he was walking across the lawn at about 11.25 p.m. when he noticed someone moving on the top of the east wing tower. He thought that it was a member of the household, and hailed them. Receiving no reply he became alarmed, a state of mind which increased when he perceived that one of the dining-room windows stood open. He ran into the house and climbed the staircase to the top landing, coming out at last upon the roof. The jury subsequently viewed the staircase, which is one of the showpieces of Suffolk.

Mr Campion, continuing, said that when he reached the roof of the Tower he found himself alone. Running downstairs again he discovered the deceased lying on the flagstones at the foot of the Tower. He immediately summoned the household.

Corroborative evidence was given by Roger Arthur Branch, butler to Sir Percival, and by the Rev. P. R. Pembroke, of The Rectory, Sanctuary, who was visiting the Tower at the time of the accident.

Dr A. H. Moore, of Sanctuary Village, said that death was due to contusion of the brain following fracture of the skull. Death was instantaneous.

Evidence of identification was given by W. W. Croxon, Veterinary Surgeon, of The Kennels, Heronhoe.

P. C. Henry Proudfoot deposed that he was summoned to the Tower at 11.45 p.m. on the night in question. He climbed to the top of the Tower and there discovered a length of rope (produced) attached to a flagpole on the summit.

David Cossins, of 32 Bury Road, Hadleigh, dealer, identified the rope as having been sold to the deceased on the 18th or 19th June last. When asked if in his opinion this rope was sufficiently strong to bear the weight of a human body, witness opined that it undoubtedly was.

Sir Percival, asked by the Coroner if he could offer

any explanation for deceased's presence on his estate at so late an hour, replied that he was at a total loss to account for it. He was only casually acquainted with the deceased, and she was not a guest at his son's coming-of-age party, which was necessarily an intimate affair in view of the recent bereavement in the family.

By P.C. Proudfoot, recalled: A red two-seater Fraser Nash motor-car, later identified by registration marks as the property of deceased, was found drawn up against some bushes in the drive later in the evening. Lights were extinguished, and it was reasonable to suppose that this was done by deceased.

Questioned, Proudfoot suggested that the deceased had attempted to lower herself on to the centre window-sill of the fourth floor of the Tower, where, according to popular superstition, some festivities took place on the occasion of a birthday in the family. Proudfoot apologized to the Court for the intrusion of common superstition and gossip, but opined that the deceased had attempted her giddy descent in the execution of a wager with some third party who had not come forward. Deceased was a well-known sporting character of the district, and had been known to enter into undertakings of this sort in the past. Witness cited the occasion of the Horse v. Automobile race 1911, when deceased challenged Captain W. Probert, the well-known motorist, over a distance of twenty miles across country.

The Coroner told the jury that he was inclined to accept the Constable's very intelligently reasoned explanation as being as near the truth as they were likely to arrive. In her attempt to carry out this unparalleled piece of foolhardy daring in a woman of her age, the deceased had undoubtedly suffered from an attack of vertigo and so had fallen.

The Coroner added that it would be a lesson to all on the evils of undue curiosity and the undesirability of entering into foolish sporting contracts which might endanger life or limb. The Coroner said he could not express himself too strongly on the subject. He regretted, as must all those in Court, that such an unfortunate accident should have visited itself upon Colonel Sir Percival Gyrth and his family, who were already suffering from a very recent bereavement. He instructed the jury, therefore, to bring in a verdict of Accidental Death, the Foreman (Mr P. Peck, senr) remarking that they would like to second the Coroner's expressions of regret.

The funeral will take place at Heronhoe to-morrow, Tuesday. A short obituary notice appears in another column with a list of the deceased's sporting awards. It is understood that the deceased died intestate, and her property, which is in very bad repair, few of the windows being whole and many of the doors off their hinges, was in the hands of the Police when our Representative called yesterday.

"A very intelligently reasoned explanation indeed," remarked Mr Campion, putting down the paper. "Mark my words, Val. We shall have old Proudfoot a sergeant before we know where we are. And rightly so, as they say on the soap-box."

He lay back in his deck-chair and put his arms behind his head. They were all four of them, Penny, Beth, Val and himself, seated beneath the trees at the far corner of the lawn on a brilliant morning some days after the events so ably recorded by the *Argus*. The adventures of the preceding weeks had left their marks on the young people, but there was a distinct hint of relief in the manner which told plainly of a tension that had relaxed.

Val had assumed a new air of responsibility during the few days since his coming of age. He seemed, as Penny remarked, to have grown up. She and Beth were frankly happy; as they lay in the comfortable chairs they looked like a couple of schoolgirls with their bare arms and long thin legs spread out to the sunlight which dappled through the leaves.

Mr Campion alone bore concrete marks of battle. His face was still scored by the weals of Mrs Dick's whip, but apart from this slightly martial disfigurement, he looked even more amiably fatuous than ever.

"They're nearly as bright about the Gypsies," Penny observed as she took up the paper from the grass. "Apparently 'a raid was thought to have been made by van dwellers on a party of undesirables camping on Heronhoe Heath. The van dwellers have since disappeared, and some of the injured campers have been taken to the Police Infirmary.' I believe you managed that, Albert. Oh, to think that it's all all right!" She sighed luxuriously. "To look back upon it's like a welsh rarebit nightmare with you as the hero."

"With me as the rabbit," said Mr Campion feelingly. "The Professor was the hero. Lugg's painting an illuminated address that we're going to present to him. It begins 'Hon. Sir and Prof.' and goes on with all the long words he's ever heard from the Bench. All about Depravity, Degradation, and Unparalleled Viciousness. He's turning them into the negative, of course. It'll be a stupendous document when it's finished. Perhaps the Professor will let you two have a copy of it for a wedding present." He grinned at Val and Beth, who were quite blatantly holding hands between their deck-chairs. They smiled at each other and Mr Campion went on.

"Had it not been for the Professor, Mr 'Alfred Campion' would doubtless have figured in another role, and some crueller Coroner than old Doctor Cobden would be moralizing on the dangers of putting strange animals in other people's stables.

The Professor's a stout fellow, as we say in the Legion. How are the two papas to-day, by the way?"

"Splendid," said Penny. "I saw a sweet sight as I came past the library window. You know they retired to discuss deep archaeological secrets? Well, when I came past there were two arm-chairs drawn up by the open window, two little curls of cigar smoke, and there was Daddy deep in *The New Yorker*—a most indelicate young woman on the cover, my dears—and the Professor regaling himself with *Punch*. Too sweet."

"Hands across the sea, in fact," said Campion. "I shall hear the tinkle of little silver bells in a minute."

Beth laughed. "The way they forgave each other for the Gypsies and your Aunt Di's *faux pas* was rather cute," she said.

"I know," said Penny. "'My dear sir!' 'Nonsense! *My* dear sir!' 'Come and shoot partridges!' 'Rubbish. Come and pick my roses.' All boys together. What delightful neighbours we are, are we not? Do you know, this is the first time I've felt this summer was worth living? By the way, Albert, when did you arrange everything so neatly with your fat friend, Mrs Sarah? I was trying to work it out in bed last night."

"Irreverent hussy," said Mr Campion, shocked. "She'd put a spell on you for that. Then you'd know all about it. I called upon the lady in question, as a matter of fact, on the night before I came home to find Lugg so curiously indisposed. I'd previously seen her, of course, very early on in the proceedings. I guessed I might need a spot of assistance sooner or later, so I asked them to hang around. As Mr Sanderson was staying at Heronhoe, it occurred to me that the heath was very conveniently situated. I pointed this out to Mrs Sarah and she had no doubts in her mind as to where the fun would arise."

"Then you knew about Mrs Dick?" said Val. "From the beginning?"

"Well, yes and no," said Mr Campion. "I thought she

might be in it, but I did so hope she wouldn't be in it alone. Mrs Munsey almost convinced me, but just before I visited Mrs Dick, I inquired about her in all the likely quarters, and after that, well it seemed desperately likely. She was head over heels in debt, and on the verge of all sorts of unkind attention from the Jockey Club Stewards. I asked my own pet turf expert about her over the phone and the Exchange cut us off long before he got into his stride. My hat! She had a nerve, though."

Val looked at him in astonishment. "You talk as though you admired her," he said.

"She had a way of compelling admiration," said Mr Campion, stroking his face thoughtfully. "If you ask me, there weren't two hoots to choose between her and her horse. They were both vicious and both terrifying, both bad lots, but oh, boy! they both had Personality."

Val grimaced. "I never liked her," he said. "By the way, I never saw why she set Mrs Munsey on to Aunt Di. What was the point of it?"

Mr Campion considered. "That took me off my balance at the beginning," he admitted, "but the local witch herself put me on to the truth. You see, Val, your aunt, silly as she was, never let the Chalice out of her sight for a second except when it was in its niche, half-hidden behind iron bars. Arthur Earle, her artist friend, probably complained to Headquarters that his hostess was a nuisance in this respect, and Mrs Dick, knowing of Mrs Munsey's peculiarities, and your aunt's propensity for wandering about at night, hit on the idea of giving her Ladyship a shock that would keep her indisposed for a day or two, during which time the disappointed artist, deprived of his sitter, might easily get permission to continue his portrait of the Chalice. You see," he went on, "a man like Arthur would want to weigh it and examine it really thoroughly, which he could hardly do with your aunt about. Unfortunately for all concerned, Mrs Munsey was too much for your aunt and the whole scheme came unstuck."

Penny sighed. "It was bad luck on Aunt Di," she said. "Mr Pembroke's looking after the Munseys. Did you know? They'll have to go into a home, he says, poor things."

Val's mind still dwelt upon the mechanism of Mrs Dick's original scheme. "I suppose," he said bitterly, "they set out with the idea of bribing me to swap a copy for the cup? We owe a lot to you, Campion."

His friend did not appear to hear the last part of his remark.

"I think that was it," Campion agreed. "Later, the 'Major' and Sanderson came to spy out the nakedness of the land themselves. I believe that the 'Major' was the expert who decided that the Chalice in the Cup House was not the real one, once they got hold of it. I've never felt so sick in my life as I did when Stanislaus phoned me to tell me they'd got the copy. That was a darn clever raid of theirs. It was only sheer bad luck on Stanislaus' part that they were successful, though. If that bobby on the door had been an older hand it wouldn't have happened."

Penny grinned at him from where she lay basking like a kitten in the heat. "Thinking it over, Albert," she remarked, "it has occurred to me that you don't work up your publicity properly at all. Modesty is all very sweet and charming but it doesn't get you anywhere. According to your account of the whole thing to Daddy you haven't done anything at all worth talking about."

Mr Campion blinked at her from behind his spectacles.

"Beauty is truth, truth beauty, and these three
 Hover for ever round the gorbal tree—

"Ovid," he said. "Like Sir Isaac Newton and his fishing-rod, I cannot tell a lie."

"Still," said Penny, unimpressed, "you might have put it a bit better. For instance, about Val being kidnapped. When you're asked for an explanation you simply say you called for him at a garage, and brought him back and put him in a field because you were in a hurry to get back to London to see a bookmaker. You must learn to work up your stories more. A yarn like that gets you nowhere."

"But all quite true," said Mr Campion mildly. "And not really extraordinary. When Inspector Oates told me over the phone that Val had gone charging after the gentleman who had stolen his suitcase, it was perfectly obvious to me that if he had caught the thief he would have returned with him, and if he hadn't caught him, then the thieving gentleman's friends had caught Val. Therefore," he went on, beaming at them from behind his spectacles, "Val was the unwelcome guest of some-one who was probably Mr Matthew Sanderson or one of his associates. They didn't want to keep him about the place, you see. They thought they'd got their prize, and once they had disposed of it in the right quarter, they had nothing to fear. I guessed they'd plant him somewhere and say no more about it."

Beth's brown eyes opened wide. "But they might have killed him," she said.

"Hardly," said Campion judicially. "There is no one who is more anxious to avoid an unpleasant death in the house than your English crook. You see, in England, in nine cases out of ten, if there's a body there's a hanging. That rather cramps their style when disposing of people. Working all this out with lightning speed, what did Our Hero do? He got out his little motor-car and went-a-visiting." He paused.

"It may have dawned on you people that all my friends are not quite the article. So, sure enough, in one of their back-yards I found our juvenile lead lying happily on a lot of old motor tyres waiting to be dropped somewhere where he could be 'found wandering'. I relieved the gentleman in charge of his guest, admired his wife's new frock, kissed the baby and came home. It was so abominably easy that I hadn't the face to tell you all, even if I had had time, so I left him where I thought Beth might find him and went on to see our lady friend, who was beginning to worry me.

"You were at Ernie Walker's garage, as a matter of fact, Val. He specializes in that sort of thing. It was the second place I looked. No, Penny, I regret to say that in this case I do not find myself wearing my laurel wreath with that sense of righteous satisfaction which is my wont. The Professor and the Benwells get all the credit. The way they cleared up that bunch and scarpered fills me with a sense of my own clumsiness."

"Ah," said Beth, "that was the word. 'Scarpa'. Father was awfully interested in your Gypsy friend, who had some most extraordinary words. What does that one mean?"

"'Bunk' is the best English translation," said Mr Campion. "To bunk, that is—to clear off, scat, vamoose, beat it, make a getaway, hop it, or more simply, 'to go'. Jacob is a great lad, but Joey is the wizard. That horse was quite manageable when I rode her over, so bang goes your last illusion, Penny, of me as a second Dick Turpin. Joey must have had his eyes on Bitter Aloes for days, and as soon as the opportunity offered he left the fight and slipped into her box with some filthy concoction of his own. The crooks use a hypodermic, but I fancy he has other methods."

"I haven't got any illusions about you," said Penny. "I think you ought to go into a home. When I heard someone had fallen off the Tower, I took it for granted it was you. Yes, a good comfortable home with Lugg to dress you, and plenty of nice kind keepers who would laugh at your remarks. In the first place, I happen to know for a fact that that story about your coming into a fortune from your Uncle the Bishop is all rubbish. Lugg says he left you a hundred pounds and a couple of good books."

Mr Campion looked uncomfortable. "Curse Lugg," he said. "So much for my efforts to appear a gilded amateur. I'm sorry, Val, but this nosy little creature will have to be told. Yes, Angel-face, the poor vulgar gentleman is a Professional. I was employed, of course."

He lay back in his chair, the sunlight glinting on his spectacles. The three young people stared at him.

"Employed?" said Val. "Who employed you? It couldn't have been the Old Boy, because—I hate to be fearfully rude, but you must be—er well, awfully expensive."

"Incredibly," said Mr Campion placidly. "Only the highest in the land can possibly afford my services. But then, I need an immense income to support my army of spies, and my palatial office, to say nothing of my notorious helot, Lugg."

"He's lying," said Penny, yawning. "I wish you had been employed, though. You've done such a lot for us. I feel you ought to get something out of it. I'd offer you my hand if I thought I could bear you about the house. Ooh!" she added suddenly, "look!"

Her exclamation had been occasioned by the appearance of a magnificent limousine, whose long grey body gleamed in the sunlight as it whispered expensively up the drive to the front door. Val and Penny exchanged glances.

In the car, seated behind the chauffeur, was a single slim aristocratic figure, with the unmistakable poker back of the old regime.

"There he is," said Penny. "That's why if you stay to lunch, Beth, you'll have to have it with Albert and me in the morning room. That's why Branch is in his show swallowtails and we've got the flag flying. Here comes the honoured guest."

Beth leant forward in her chair. "Is that *him*?" she said. "No top hat? I haven't seen a good top hat since I came to England."

"Very remiss," said Mr Campion sternly. "Coming down

here representing the Crown without a top hat—why, the thing's absurd. Hang it, when a policeman brings a summons, which is a sort of invitation from the Crown, he wears a top hat."

"No?" said Beth.

"No," said Mr Campion. "Still, the principle's the same. I don't think it's cricket to come down on a special formal occasion in an ordinary trilby that any man might wear. Look here, Val, you'd better wear yours at lunch just to show him. We keep the old flag flying, dammit."

Beth was puzzled. "Why don't you get lunch with this Lord whatever he is?"

"Because it's an ancient ceremony," said Penny. "Not the lunch—unless cook's muffed it—but the whole business. We shall be expected to be all voile and violets at tea-time."

"Leaving the Honourable Gentleman out of the question," said Val, "and returning to your last sensational announcement, Campion, in which you stated that you were not enjoying our shooting and hunting, as it were, for private but for professional reasons, may I ask, if this is so, who put you on to it, and where is your hope of reward?"

"Oh, I shall get my fourpence, don't you worry, young sir," said Mr Campion. "The gent who put me up to this is a real toff." He paused. Coming across the lawn towards them, sedate, and about as graceful as a circus elephant, was Mr. Lugg. As he came nearer they saw that his immense white face wore an almost reverent expression.

"'Ere," he said huskily as he approached his master, "see 'oo's come? Orders are for you to nip into the 'ouse and report in the library. Lumme," he added, "you in flannels, too. I believe there's an 'ole comin' in the sole of them shoes."

Mr Campion rose to his feet. "Don't worry, Lugg," he said. "I shouldn't think he'd go into that."

In the general astonishment it was Penny whose curiosity found voice.

"You?" she said. "He wants to see you? Whatever for?"

Mr Campion turned a mildly reproachful eye in their direction. "I thought you'd have got it a long while before now," he said. "He is my employer. If all goes well I shall be able to treat you to a fish-and-chip supper to-night."

CHAPTER TWENTY-SEVEN

There Were Giants in those Days

AT HALF-PAST THREE in the afternoon, with the strong sunlight tracing the diamond pattern of the window panes on the polished floor of the Colonel's library, lending that great austere room some of the indolent warmth of the garden, five men surrounded the heavy table desk on which the yellow length of an historic document was spread.

The great house was pleasantly silent. There were birds singing in the creeper and the droning of a bumble bee against the panes, but the thick walls successfully shut out any sounds of domestic bustle. The air was redolent with the faint mustiness of old leather-bound books, mingling delightfully with the scent of the flowers from the bed outside the windows.

The distinguished stranger, a tall, grey-headed man with cold blue eyes and a curious dry little voice, coughed formally.

"There's really no need for me to read all this through, Colonel," he said. "After all, we've read it through together several times before. It makes one feel old. Every reading means another decade gone."

He sighed and shot a faint, unexpectedly shy smile at Campion and the Professor, who were standing side by side. The old American was alert and deeply interested, but his companion stood fingering his tie awkwardly, an almost imbecile smile on his mild, affable face. Val stood at his father's elbow, his young face deadly serious, a distinct hint of nervousness in his manner. The memory of his first excursion to the secret room on the night of Mrs Shannon's death was still clear in his mind. Sir Percival himself was more human than Campion or the Professor had ever seen him before. In sharing the secret of the Room with his son he seemed to have halved a burden that had been a little over-heavy for him alone.

"I think this one clause will be sufficient," the visitor continued, placing a forefinger on a rubric at the foot of the sheet. He cleared his throat again and began to read huskily and without expression.

"'And the said representative of Her Gracious Majesty or Her Heirs shall go up into the chamber accompanied by the master and his eldest son, providing he be of sufficient age, and they shall show him and prove to his satisfaction that the treasure which they hold in the stead of the Crown be whole and free from blemish, that it may be known to Us that they have kept their loyal and sacred trust. This shall be done by the light of day that neither use of candle or lamp shall be needed to show the true state of the said vessel.

"'Further, We also command that in times of trouble, or such days as the House of Gyrth may be in danger, that the master allow two witnesses to go with them, strong men and true, sworn to keep faith and all secrecy as to the Treasure and the manner of its keeping.

"'Given under Our Hand and Seal, this day…' and so on. I think that covers the matter, Colonel."

His quiet voice died away, and rolling up the parchment he returned it to his host who locked it in a dispatch-box on the table.

The visitor turned to Campion and the Professor.

"Strong men and true," he said, smiling at them. "Of course, I understand, strictly speaking, my dear Albert, that 'such days as the House of Gyrth may be in danger' are past. But I certainly agree with the Colonel that in the circumstances we might stretch a point in this—er—archaic formula. It seems the only courtesy, Professor, that we can extend to you for your tremendous assistance in this unfortunate and distressing affair."

The Professor made a deprecatory gesture. "There's nothing I would consider a greater honour," he said.

Mr Campion opened his mouth to speak, but thought better of it, and was silent.

The Colonel took a small iron instrument which looked like a tiny crowbar from his desk and led the way out of the room. They followed him through the hall and down the long stone corridor into the seldom used banqueting room in the east wing. They passed no one in their journey. Branch had gathered his myrmidons in their own quarters at the back of the west wing, while Penny and Beth remained discreetly in the drawing room.

In the cool shadow of the great apartment the Colonel paused and turned to them, a slightly embarrassed expression in his very blue eyes. The visitor relieved him of an awkward duty.

"The Colonel and I," he began, prefacing his remark with his now familiar cough, "feel that we should adhere to tradition in this matter. The entrance to the—er—chamber is, and always has been, a closely guarded secret, known only to my predecessors and the Colonel's. I feel sure that I shall offend neither of you if I ask you to lend me your handkerchiefs and allow me to blindfold you just until we approach the treasure."

The Professor took out a voluminous silk bandana which proved more suitable than Mr Campion's white cambric. The blindfolding was accomplished with great solemnity.

On any other occasion such an incident might have been absurd, but there was a deadly earnestness in the precaution which no one in the group could ignore after the terrifying events of the preceding weeks. Val's hand shook as he tied the knot behind Campion's head and some of his nervousness was conveyed to the other man. After all, they were about to share a secret of no ordinary magnitude. Campion had not forgotten the expression upon Mrs Shannon's face when she had looked up for a moment after peering into the window of the grim treasure house.

The Professor, too, was unusually apprehensive. It was evident that in spite of his vast store of archaic knowledge he had no inkling of what he was to expect.

The visitor's voice came to them in the darkness. "Val, if you'll take Campion's arm I'll look after Professor Cairey. Colonel, will you go first?"

Val linked his arm through Campion's, and he felt himself being led forward, the last of a little procession.

"Look out," Val's voice sounded unsteadily in his ear. "The stairs begin here."

They ascended, and once more the wood creaked beneath his feet. They went up in silence for what seemed a long time. There were so many turns that he lost his sense of direction almost immediately. He had suffered many odd experiences in his life, but this strange halting procession was more unnerving than anything he had ever known. Curiosity is the most natural of human emotions, but there came a point in the journey when he almost wished that the mystery might remain unsolved, for him at any rate, for ever. He could hear the

Professor breathing hard in front of him, and he knew that it was not the steepness of the stairs which inconvenienced the old man.

Val's pressure on his arm increased. "Wait," he said so softly that he was scarcely audible. Then followed a period of silence, and they went on again. The stairs had ended and they were crossing a stone floor. Then again there was a halt. The air still smelt fresh and the song of the birds sounded very near.

"Step," whispered Val, as the procession restarted. "Keep your head down. I shall have to come behind you."

Mr Campion felt himself clambering up a narrow stone spiral staircase, and here the air was scarcer and there was a faint, almost intangible smell of spices. He heard the grating of iron on stone and stepped forward on to a level floor. Val was close behind him, and once again there was the grating of the iron, and then complete silence. He felt his scalp tingling. He sensed that he was in a very small space, and with them he was certain, in the instinctive fashion that one is conscious of such things, there was something else, something incredibly old, something terrible.

"Take off the bandages."

He was never sure whether it was the Colonel or the visitor who had spoken. The voice was unrecognizable. He felt Val's icy fingers pulling at the knot behind his head. Then the cambric slipped from his eyes.

The first thing of which he was conscious as he blinked was the extraordinary crimson light in the room, and he turned instinctively to its source, the circular window with the heavy stone framework which had been sealed at some time with blood-red glass. The sunlight outside was very strong so that the tiny cell seemed full of particles of glittering red dust.

Campion turned from the window and started violently. The Gyrths' secret lay revealed.

Set immediately below the window so that the light fell directly upon it was a little stone altar, and kneeling before it, directly in front of the huddled group, was a figure in full Tourney armour.

As Campion stared, a pulse in his throat throbbing violently, the light seemed to concentrate on the figure.

It was that of a giant, and at first he thought it was but an immense suit of black armour only, fashioned for a man of legendary stature, but as his eye travelled slowly down the great gyves to the wrists, he caught sight of the human hands, gnarled, yellow, and shapeless like knotted willow roots. Between them, resting on the slab, was the Gyrth Chalice, whose history was lost behind the veils of legend.

It was a little shallow bowl of red gold, washed from the English mountain streams before the Romans came. A little shallow bowl whose beaten sides showed the marks of a long-dead goldsmith's hammer, and in whose red heart a cluster of uncut rubies lay like blood, still guarded by the first Messire Gyrth who earned for Sanctuary its name.

Campion raised his eyes slowly to the head of the figure and was relieved to find that the visor was down. The head was thrown back, the mute iron face raised to the circular window through which Mrs Dick had peered.

There was utter silence in the little cell with its ancient frescoes and dust-strewn floor of coloured flags. The door by which they had entered was hidden in the stonework. Turning again, Campion saw the great sword of the warrior hanging on the wall behind the kneeling figure, the huge hilt forming a cross behind its head.

The Professor was gazing at the Chalice with tears in his eyes, a spontaneous tribute to its beauty which he did not attempt to hide.

As Campion stared at the figure he was obsessed by the uncanny feeling that it might move at any moment, that the

mummified hands might snatch the sword from the wall and
the great figure tower above the impious strangers who had
disturbed his vigil. It was with relief that he heard the Colonel's
quiet voice.

"If you are ready, gentlemen—"

No other word was spoken. Val retied the handkerchief
and once again there was the grating of metal and the procession started on its return journey. The Professor stumbled
once or twice on the stairs, and Campion felt that his own
knees were a little unsteady. It was not that the sight had been
particularly horrible, although there had been a suggestion
about the hands that was not pleasant; nor did the idea of the
lonely watcher keeping eternal vigil over the treasured relic he
had won fill him with repugnance. But there had been something more than mortal about this ageless giant, something
uncanny which filled him with almost superstitious awe, and
he was glad that Penny did not know, that she could live and
laugh in a house that hid this strange piece of history within its
walls, unconscious of its existence.

They were still silent when once more they stood in the
daylight in the old banqueting hall. The Colonel glanced at his
watch.

"We meet the ladies for tea on the lawn in fifteen minutes,"
he said. "Mrs Cairey promised me she'd come, Professor."

The old man dusted his hands abstractedly. There were
plaster and cobwebs on all their clothes. Campion carried the
Professor off to his room, leaving his host to attend to the other
visitor.

No word of comment had been made, nor did anyone feel
that any such remark was possible.

In Mr Campion's pleasant Georgian room the tension
relaxed.

"Lands sakes," said the Professor, subsiding into a little tub
chair by the window. "Lands sakes."

Mr. Campion glanced over the lawn. The white table surrounded by garden chairs was set under the trees. Branch was already half-way towards it with a tea-wagon on which glittered the best silver, and a service which had been old when Penny's grandmother was a girl. Mrs Cairey, Beth and Penny, looking cool and charming, their flowered chiffon frocks sweeping the lawn, were admiring the flowerbeds in the far distance. It was a graceful, twentieth-century picture, peaceful and ineffably soothing, incredibly removed from the world they had just left. The tinkle of china came pleasantly to them as Branch began to arrange the table.

They were interrupted by the unceremonious entrance of Lugg with a tray bearing glasses, a siphon and a decanter.

"Branch sent me up with this lot," he remarked. "I should 'ave it. A b and s will do yer good any time o' day."

Even the Professor, who restricted himself to one whisky-and-soda a day out of deference to his wife's principles, accepted the proffered drink gratefully. Lugg hung about, apparently seeking an opening for conversation.

"They ain't 'alf doing 'Is Nibs proud downstairs," he said. "I've bin 'elping that girl I took a fancy to to clean the silver all the afternoon. Old Branch didn't take 'is eyes off me the 'ole time. If 'e counted them spoons once 'e counted 'em a dozen times. I couldn't 'elp pinchin' this." He laid a delicate pair of Georgian sugar-tongs on the dressing-table with a certain pride.

His master looked at him in disgust. "Don't lay your filthy bone at my feet," he said. "What do you expect me to do with it?"

"Put it back for me," said Mr Lugg unabashed. "It won't look so bad if you get noticed. I've got me record to think of. There's nothing in writin' against you."

"Go away," said Campion. "I'm going to sell you to a designer of children's cuddle-toys. You can pack my things after tea, by the way. We go back to Town to-morrow morning."

"Then you've finished?" said the Professor, looking up.

Campion nodded. "It's over," he said. "They'll stick to their rules, you know. Their employee is dead; that finishes it. I was talking to old poker-back downstairs. He's convinced we shall hear no more from them. The Maharajah has had his turn. They're connoisseurs more than criminals, you see. This is so definitely not one of their successes that I should think they'll turn their attention to Continental museums again for a bit."

"I see." The Professor was silent for some moments. Then he frowned. "I wonder—" he began, and hesitated.

Campion seemed to understand the unspoken thought, for he turned to Lugg.

"You can go back to Audrey," he said. "Any more thieving, and I'll tell her about the picture of Greta Garbo you keep under your pillow."

As the door was closed behind the disconsolate and still inquisitive Lugg, the Professor remained silent, and Campion went on.

"I couldn't understand why my precious boss downstairs hadn't told me about the second Chalice at the beginning," he said. "I see it now. He's a man of very conservative ideas, and after the awe-inspiring oath of secrecy I suppose he thought he had no alternative but to let me find it out for myself. That complicated things at the start, but I'm not sure it didn't make it easier for us in the long run."

The Professor nodded absently. His mind was still dwelling upon the experience of the afternoon.

"What a lovely, lovely thing," he said. "I may sound a bit inhuman, but when I looked at that Chalice to-day, it occurred to me that probably in the last fifteen hundred years it cost the lives of Heaven knows how many thieves and envious people, by looking at it. Campion, do you know, I thought it was worth it."

Mr Campion did not answer. The thought in his mind was one that had rankled ever since he had stood with the others in that little painted cell, looking in at the Chalice and its guardian. What had Mrs Dick seen when she had looked in the window that had differed from their own experience? She had been no easily frightened woman, nor was hers an imaginative nature. He spoke aloud, almost without realizing it.

"What exactly did she see when she looked through the window? Why did she say 'no'? Who did she say it to? Just what was it that made her let go?"

He paused. Outside on the lawn the chatter of feminine voices was coming nearer. Mr Campion was still puzzled.

"I don't understand it," he said.

The Professor glanced up at him. "Oh, that?" he said. "That's quite obvious. The light was shining directly upon the figure. The head was raised to the window, if you remember."

"Yes, but—" said Mr Campion, and was silent.

"Yes," said the Professor thoughtfully, "I think it's perfectly clear. On the night of the birthday, when she looked in, the visor was up. She saw his face…I'm afraid it may be a very shocking sight."

"But she spoke," said Mr Campion. "She spoke as if she was replying to someone. And I heard something, I swear it."

The Professor leant forward in his chair and spoke with unusual emphasis. "My very dear boy," he said, "I'll say this. It doesn't do to dwell on these things."

The gentle clangour of the gong in the hall below broke in upon the silence.